TU

AND THE COLLECTORS

BY

TOM SCHAEFER

© 2014 TOM SCHAEFER

Dedication

Special Thanks to
Lea Ann Lewis – my great friend and companion!
Stephenie Schaefer - awesome daughter!
Isabella George – excellent editor!
Ralph Ring
Nikola Tesla

"Without life's challenges, creativity suffers"

I have personally been a science fiction fan since the earliest time I can remember, growing up reading and watching scifi on television and in movies. Inspired not only by scifi, but by the Apollo moon landings, and men like Carl Sagan, I have had a dream for a long time to go to the stars.

Tu and The Collectors is a story I have been thinking about for some time. It's a journey into the world of "what if".

While there are a multitude of stories about mankind reaching space, I think maybe sometime in the near future, space will reach mankind.

Tu and The Collectors is a story that supposes, a "what if" - A what-if in which the future of extra-terrestrial contact, their intentions, and that the future of mankind could actually take a turn for the better, not for the worse.

The story supposes no utopian dream, only possibility, challenges and a trip to the stars.

Thank you for taking this journey with me!

Table of Contents

Preface..5
Global Acquisitions Inc..7
We Have A Winner...18
Non-Disclosure..32
The First Revelation...39
The Annunaki 47
The History Of Tu...50
Earth Rebooted..57
Operation Exodus...59
The Big Question..61
Space DJ...70
We're All In...76
Departure...80
Good Bye 85
The Liberation Of Replication..92
Life On Cloud Nine...98
Welcome To The Party...114
The Zui..119
John Foster of The Five...133
The Failure Of Self Guidance..137
The Governance of Tu 141
Tu Council Of Governors..146
Personal Citizenship On Tu...149
On The Formation of Localities..154
The Prime Defenders..157
On Crime and Punishment...159
Intellectual Evolution 161
Continental Structures...164
Minor Continents...166
Minora..167
Ellis Island...168
Southern Territory..169
New Didiza...171

Gargantua..172
Arrival..174
The Best Laid Plans...189
My Pilot...194
Stand Down..202
Cover Story...204
Evil Seed..212
Walk In The Park..228
Dark Star...243
The Message 252
Green Light...269
The Reveal...276
The Dawn of A New Age.......................................285
RSVP Received...292
Operation Exodus Begins......................................297
The Villa..302
Arrival II..313
On Tour..330
The First 90 Days After..335
The Next Step 337
The Outing..342
The Loss...352
Colonize Me..359
Immensity..363

Preface

Ever since ancient times, and more recently, events like the UFO crash at Roswell some 67 years ago (at this writing), humanity has been faced with a huge dilemma.

We can all admit that we are not alone, that extra-terrestrials do indeed exist, or buy into an idea that such things are preposterous, and could never happen.

This book proposes another twist on all of the lore, and creates new lore. A new story, a new mythology closer to home, in a present tense future, not some distant dream hundreds or thousands of years into the future, but happening right now.

The story and lore presented here is really a desire to express an even greater thought about the future of mankind.

Are we going to painfully plod on, living the same kind of existence in the future, trapped on this planet, with no hope of ever reaching the stars, or is there a possibility for a much brighter future?

In the past couple of years real scientists have discovered several hundred real Earth like planets, called "exoplanets".

Mankind's biggest problem is the lack of viable space transportation to go to these planets to explore, and colonize.

But what if the transportation problem is solved. Then comes habitability, and sustainability. What if mankind gets some much needed help from some old friends from the stars?

Consider this quote from Carl Sagan:

"Since, in the long run, every planetary civilization will be endangered by impacts from space.

Every surviving civilization is obliged to become spacefaring--not because of exploratory or romantic zeal, but for the most practical reason imaginable: staying alive...

If our long-term survival is at stake, we have a basic responsibility to our species to venture to other worlds."

The significance of a finding that there are other beings who share this universe with us would be absolutely phenomenal, it would be an epochal event in human history."

– Carl Sagan

Global Acquisitions Inc.

The warehouse district on the south side of downtown Nashville serves as the perfect place for Michael Stetson to run his collection business.

Michael wasn't your usual kind of collector, he collected *everything*. However, Michael wasn't really collecting for himself.

He was a professional collector for a large, secretive company called Global Acquisitions. Global Acquisitions hired him to procure whatever it was they were after.

He really didn't see himself as a 'collector', more of a 'procurement guy'. It was a good job, and Michael had been at it for almost 20 years.

Michael wasn't their only 'collector'. Global Acquisitions had collectors in every major city in the US, as well as in other countries. Global Acquisitions had been in business for over 50 years.

Collectors were recruited, and *chosen*. There were never any job openings advertised.

A collector could recommend a friend, but they had to go through a rigorous series of background checks. They came from all walks of life.

The unusual thing was that Global Acquisitions never did business with the government, at least *not directly*.

One of Global Acquisitions' primary goals was to remain obscure and low key. Nothing they were doing was illegal, it's just that the nature of their business and their success depended upon a low profile.

No one Michael Stetson ever purchased from would know the final destinations of whatever was purchased.

Sometimes it was animals, livestock, commodities, food, appliances, large scale manufacturing equipment, and even aerospace and aircraft related.

Global Acquisitions never imported or exported under their own name, and used other front companies to manage imports and exports.

It really didn't matter to Michael, he was their man to go and get whatever they wanted. The end result was that it all wound up in the warehouse in Nashville.

Nashville provided a reasonable central location for the warehouse, such that anything coming into or being shipped out, was all heading into or out of the center of the country.

With several major interstate highways running through the heart of the city, north, south east and west, it provided an ideal location.

Michaels' shipments went to an even larger distribution center that Global Acquisitions ran themselves. He'd been there too many times to count. But it was never Michael's job to worry about that, his mission was procurement and that's what he did.

There were other collectors covering Georgia, Kentucky, Missouri, Illinois and Indiana – all using nondescript warehouses in inconspicuous corners of whatever city or town they operated in. *Low-key, low-profile was the company's policy.*

The secrecy levels with Global Acquisitions may have seemed a bit extreme to some, but corporate espionage doesn't happen to small companies buying a lathe or a press.

It is when you buy large scale manufacturing equipment, people begin asking questions about where it will wind up and how it will be used. Michael always created cover stories for whatever Global Acquisitions bought whenever inquiring minds wanted to know.

Michael's superiors always had an outstanding order for cases of vodka, bourbon, expensive Scotch, and all manner of expensive wine. But Michael never bought it under Global's name, he always paid cash and so there was never an issue about who or where it was going.

Today was a nice bright Saturday afternoon and Michael was just finishing up a liquor store run at the large liquor warehouse in downtown Nashville.

This would be a great time to hop next door at a newly opened sports bar. The atmosphere was always festive, the bar tenders were cute twenty-somethings who only knew him as Michael.

Among Michael's collections, something he found along the way was his prized 2003 Jaguar XJ/R. The R series was a special version of the XJ. The pretty green R in the fender logo designated it to be the Sport Sedan. 600Hp, turbo charged. All black. Some called it a *sleeper*. Stoplight drag racers routinely lose to an XJ/R.

It looks like a classy black car used by limo drivers, or that accountant you know, but this car is as fast or faster than a Corvette. Yet, when you pull up to a nice restaurant or hotel, or a business meeting, you're all *class*.

With his sunglasses and full length black leather jacket, Michael looked like a hit-man – or a record producer in his Jag. A handsome black man, tall and lean, he liked to work out a couple of times a week.

Michael hated the term *"African American"*. For him it was bullshit. He may be black, but born and raised in America. He'd been to Africa *but not as an American*. One of his missions for Global Acquisitions was the procurement of two large northern white rhinos from Kenya.

White rhinos were on the verge of extinction, and Global Acquisitions had a special buyer who wanted to make sure this species did not go extinct. The whole mission was akin to a spy novel, but such was the nature of many of Michael's procurement missions. Bribes, payoffs, clandestine meetings, it was all routine for a collector.

As he drove to the bar, there was old man Clive, in his usual place on the corner selling homeless newspapers. Clive was born and raised in Jamaica, but had lived in the US for over 30 years, and loved Nashville.

He could be seen down on Music Row, his green-yellow-red brim on, playing blues on his harmonica on the street for tips. An old man now, with a scruffy grey beard, Clive smiled and waved at everyone as they passed by, including Michael.

Michael never had a problem stopping and passing a few dollars to him.

Clive - "Hey Michael, good to see ya. I hear things gonna be changin' soon friend! My friends are comin' just you wait and see. I don't know if I should tell you this or not, but I seen another UFO last night and it was amazing!"

Michael smiled, handed him a small roll of bills and drove on. "You never know man ... Take care brother!"

Michael parked the Jag right on the street in front of the sports bar. It was a great place to sit, look at his iPad and catch up on some emails.

Michael's phone was ringing on vibrate with an unknown id. Michael let it go to voicemail. He knew who it was.

That meant '*check your email*'.

A new collection order had just come into his InBox. It was a personnel related item and read:

> "Michael
> New work order from the website.
> Personnel, standard 10 day shipment.
> Interview Shelbyville, TN, Monday, noon.
> Your security contact there is Morgan, and he's in your address book.
> Rendezvous Parkway Cafeteria.
> Personnel names and contact protocols to follow via text message.

*The voicemail has a passphrase for Morgan.
P.S.
Please be sure the liquor order is fulfilled in the next outbound.*

*Thanks
Adam"*

Michael chuckled to himself. Aside from everything else on his collection order, he knew the liquor had top priority.

Michael headed back to the warehouse and dropped off the liquor. He had several college age men working at the warehouse, and the company kept a number of apartments setup for employees right down town.

Another text message was waiting unread and it was from Shandra.

It was Saturday and that meant it was probably going to be an evening with Shandra if she was in town.

Shandra didn't work for Global Acquisitions but for one of its other front companies, a security company. She was a beautiful chocolate brown, with long black hair. She met Michael at a local gym in New York City a few years back.

Their love affair was secret, and not really something that should have happened, but such is life.

Technically Global Acquisitions employees were discouraged from dating others in the organization, or from any of its other companies.

It's generally not uncommon in the course of human events

that when attraction happens, people break this rule routinely, and try to get away with it as long as possible.

Their chemistry was always hot when they were together and it was something neither could seem to stop.

The thought of Shandra coming by put a smile on Michael's face.

Saturday evening rolled around quickly and Michael decided to stay in one of the Global Acquisition apartments downtown in what had been called The Gulch.

It was one of their better apartments, several floors up with a view, and Michael always had it reserved for himself even though it was technically leased by Global Acquisitions.

A familiar knock on the door and it was Shandra.

Michael, opened the door smiling - "You got here quickly I see!"

Shandra - "Hazards of the business I suppose."

They paused in the foyer for a passionate kiss.

Michael - "Well then ... welcome to Nashville! I imagine you're a little hungry?"

Shandra - "Starving!"

Michael - "What – long drive and no truck stops along the way?"

Shandra - *"Something like that"*

Michael – "Great, I picked up some nice salmon and a nice red, and I put a salad together."

Dinner was always a festive occasion at Michaels' apartment downtown Nashville followed by hot sex and little regret.

Saturday evening was followed by a leisure Sunday of lounging around and just enjoying each other's company.

Shandra smiled – "We just never seem to get out much when I come to Nashville!"

Michael laughing – "Seems to be a pattern with us!"

Shandra – "Well one of these days I want to see what the fuss is with music city! You've never really shown me much about this town."

Michael – "You're never here long enough for me to give you the tour. Although there's a lot of country shit here, I'm more into the blues, and there's a great blues club right across the block from here.

Plus they have great music and food. We'll have to go there next time you're in town."

They knew work came first, it was something they both signed on to and the company always came first, and they knew that whatever they were enjoying for the time being could be interrupted since both were always on call.

Monday rolled around quickly. Shandra was out the door early but left a small note with a smiley face hand written on top of Michael's kitchen counter.

Under the note were two manila folders with the profile information about the people Michael was supposed to check out.

The morning was flying by quickly and he quickly scanned through their profiles.

Michael soon found himself in his black Jag on the road to Shelbyville, a small town just a short drive from Nashville.

It was a hot, sunny August day for a drive.

Tennessee is one of those beautiful seasonal states, with a pretty spring, hot summers with plenty of green foliage everywhere, and gorgeous fall colors. Winters are mild and everything is brown.

Summer is just hot and humid.

The scenery driving through middle Tennessee was relaxing, with beautiful rolling hills, postcard views of farms with cattle and horses.

Shandra was still on his mind during the drive. He really looked forward to his time with her and it was difficult to get her out of his mind. Her sensual nature and high intellect were extremely attractive.

Michaels' latest order was to interview two new people - Bob Willets and Amy Noble. They had been selected to become collectors.

They had been chosen by his superiors, so it was Michael's job to check them out, and if he felt they were as qualified as his superiors did, offer them the job. This was really more of a formality, if he was getting orders to go meet them, they had pretty much been selected and the only thing left was to offer them the job.

Global Acquisitions screening and selection process was not typical, in fact far from it. Many of the people they selected did not fit any particular pattern. Some were old, some young, and included all nationalities and personality types.

Bob Willets and Amy Noble would be in Shelbyville TN on Monday for the annual *Tennessee Walking Horse 'Celebration'*.

The Celebration event would actually start a couple of days before, and run all week. Bob and Amy would only be able to afford coming down to Shelbyville one evening, and Monday was the day.

They had reserved tickets for the entire event, plus parking, *courtesy of Global Acquisitions.*

Tickets like these would normally cost $100 each, and parking alone was almost $100. So the whole deal was worth around $300. All they had to do was show up.

In fact, Bob and Amy had no idea they were about to be interviewed for the job. This was a critical part of the process. A critical part of the process was observing their behavior in unusual circumstances.

Shelbyville is a quaint small town set in rural Tennessee.

Shelbyville has small town charm, mixed with the evils of the Walking Horse industry.

Tennessee Walking Horses are known for their gait, especially for the way they raise their front feet high in the air while walking.

The Celebration is the annual showcase event for the Tennessee Walking Horse association at the end of August annually.

The entire town becomes a focal point for Walking Horse enthusiasts, horse owners, trainers and the entire industry converges on Shelbyville for *The Celebration*. The event is held at its own private stadium in Shelbyville.

The problem with the Walking Horse culture, is that this high-stepping gait behavior is trained into these horses with extremely cruel methods known as "soring" - literally training by pain. The practice, although illegal, has recently fallen out of favor. As more and more states started cracking down on the practice the "sport" is slowly dying off.

This has left the countryside full of Walking Horse trainers, horses, farms, stables and the surrounding culture of "fans", who are generally wealthy people who have no concern about the welfare of the horses, but for their profitability.

Part of the reason Michael was heading to Shelbyville was to help another collector who was on a mission to Shelbyville to scout out some undamaged Walking Horses for Global Acquisitions.

We Have A Winner

Outside of Nashville in a small suburban apartment, Amy Noble was opening a plain envelope which contained the free tickets to *The Celebration*.

Her boyfriend, Bob Willets had been under-employed for several weeks. Bob's only income was that of working as a barista at a local coffee shop and selling a few website deals from time to time to bring in some extra income.

After almost 2 years of frustration of trying to find meaningful work in electronic engineering, Bob needed a real break.

Bob had served in the Navy as a submarine sailor in his early twenties, working in electronics and encryption technologies. After leaving the Navy Bob had earned a degree in electronic engineering, but because of all the offshoring of jobs from the US to countries like India and China, jobs were tight.

They were always teetering on the edge of economic disaster and had narrowly escaped being evicted only a couple of months ago had it not been for a loan from one of Amy's friends to get them through.

Bob also liked to tinker with *magnet motor generator projects* he would find on the internet.

There was a grass roots community of electronics hobbyists on the internet growing daily who were experimenting with magnets, and motor generator projects.

There was a new wave of experimentation happening where new ideas about maximizing the efficiencies of motors and generators had become part of a larger quest for *"over unity"*.

Over unity is the concept that the output power exceeds the power in. It sounded like something for nothing. How could you get more power out than you put in?

Many considered this snake oil, but there was a growing consensus that the energy produced *would not come from the machine itself*, but that the motor/generator would actually tap into an energy field, essentially opening a channel or gateway of energy through the device, so that indeed more power would be coming out of the device than it took to run it.

The quest then, was to build a motor generator that would produce as those in the community often referred to it, *"energy from the vacuum"*.

The challenge was huge, many had tried and failed, but there was always this hope that maybe it could be achieved.

Bob kept himself read up on subjects about alternative energy, **Nikola Tesla** and other inventors of alternative energy. He had a few projects on a small table in their apartment.

One project was a *crystal battery*, made from common household chemicals. These crystal batteries would last for months, providing a very low voltage from common household chemicals.

They could be bundled together to create a real 12 volt battery, that Bob had hoped to use as a source of power in his own version of the magnet motor generator.

Bob's own magnet motor generator was based upon designs by a man named **John Bedini**.

The machine Bob built could self charge itself for an extended amount of time, and had his machine run for almost a week generating about 400 watts of power before it ran down.

The machine was actually pretty simple. A hand crafted motor with magnets would spin, using a small battery, just enough power to spin the rotor.

The circuit that controlled it would trickle some of the energy right back into the battery running the rotor, giving back some of the unused energy it was consuming, *charging while running*.

The entire system would also generate enough charge to recharge a larger battery hooked up to a 400 watt inverter like you plug into your car's cigarette lighter socket – one that converts car voltage to household alternating current voltage.

The trick was to tune the little system so that the net gain was a charger system that would recharge its own batteries and be self contained.

A portable power supply that could recharge itself and give you portable power for a week or two if the main power grid was down.

And if it fully ran down, you could hook up a small solar panel to run it, and recharge its internal battery.

Bob's goal was a system that could supply power by day, and recharge itself at night with the built in motor/generator circuit.

Money was tight and he couldn't afford to really spend as much time and energy as he wanted to on his projects. He had made progress, but his prototype was still a good ways away from being finished.

A good number of parts and components came from old electronics he would disassemble and then reuse the parts.

Fortunately, tools and test equipment were dirt cheap and he had accumulated a nice little cache of tools and components to pursue his passion for his experiments.

Who knows, one of them may lead to bigger things, maybe even a job, or something he could sell as an inventor.

Amy's work as part time assistant for an animal rescue shelter that took in dogs and cats filled a need in Amy to be around animals. She was known among her friends and family as '*animal girl*'. Amy had spent years in school, off and on in hopes of becoming a veterinarian.

It was with utter amazement that Amy had received free tickets to the annual "*Celebration*" in Shelbyville. She had been planning all week for this little adventure.

As they headed out the door, Amy said "Bob, I can't believe it, I'm so excited, this is gonna be fun!"

Bob was a bit more cynical though. "Yeah, I'm just worried it's burning up gas we can't really afford".

Bob - "Looks like we're taking the bicycles along — I forgot to take them off the back of the car when we got back from riding yesterday."

Amy - "Who knows, maybe there will be a place we can ride when we get down to Shelbyville."

They loved to ride their bikes. Nashville has numerous paved bike trails throughout the city that takes riders, walkers, and joggers on miles of paved nature trails throughout the entire metro area.

Their little Toyota Corolla was running well, but it was old. It was only a matter of time before it would be on its last legs and need to be replaced.

Their jaunt to *The Celebration* would provide a nice tourist getaway to a world far removed from an exhausting never ending job search and a life of just getting by from week to week.

Along with the tickets was a coupon for a free dinner at the Parkway Cafeteria. It did seem a bit strange but the offer was *only good for lunch from 11am – 1pm on Monday of The Celebration*.

Amy - "We're going to have fun, plus we get a free buffet or something at this little cafeteria".

After a quiet drive, Bob and Amy soon found themselves on the road to Shelbyville and around noon they settled in at the Parkway Cafeteria in Shelbyville.

Parkway Cafeteria in Shelbyville is nothing pretentious. The scene is not unlike something from a classic television show or movie about small towns.

Parked outside was the usual assortment of vehicles, a local police car, farm trucks and ordinary cars, and Michael's Jaguar.

Michael's Jaguar would normally look out of place but because of the number of wealthy people in town for The Celebration, it looked like another big spender was in town.

The aging sign in front of the Parkway Cafeteria is not a retro design based upon some new trend, it is rather, the original sign. *It's been there a while.* A small mom and pop operation, featuring "good ol' home cookin' " and hospitality, something very rare in 21st century America.

One needed to remind themselves - it's not health food, it's comfort food. The clientèle is the locals, the farmers, the ranchers, stable owners.

Something larger though was about to happen that would change Bob and Amy's lives forever.

They had come for a free dinner and a Walking Horse Show, unknown to them that something larger was about to unfold.

Michael Stetson had situated himself in the corner and after an hour on the road, he was happy to be dining on the cafeterias' catfish, mashed potatoes and some green beans. The food was as if it had come from a time machine in 1960's.

Michael waited for one of the cooks to come back out to refill the steam trays with fresh catfish and got him to tell him how they prepared it. They had a lively conversation and Michael headed back to his table with a fresh load of country fried catfish.

Michael had Bob and Amy's profile folders on the table with their pictures out so he could spot them when they came in.

He watched as Bob and Amy got themselves situated at a table.

As they dined, Michael watched them and waited for the right moment to come over and introduce himself. Glancing at his phone, he went over their names and some profile information before getting up and walking over to their table.

Michael introduced himself - "*Bob Willets?*"

Bob was a bit startled to have a stranger introduce himself, even more so in this small country town.

Bob - "Ub, yes?"

Michael - "Hello, my name is Michael Stetson, and as much as I know I'm intruding a bit on your dinner, it's very important that I speak to you," and turning to Amy, "and your girlfriend here, uh, Amy Noble I believe?"

At this point, Bob and Amy were feeling a bit invaded.

Michael could have just told them at the outset who he was, but he liked to maintain an air of mystery and enjoyed holding out until the last moment the real details.

Bob - "Um, excuse me but what's this all about?"

Bending over slightly and speaking in a low voice, Michael asked "Well, I just need a few minutes of your time. May I sit down?"

Michael really didn't wait for Bob or Amy to respond and sat down.

There were a few other people in the cafeteria, including a cop seated by the window and this was not a good place to draw too much attention out of the ordinary.

Bob responded nervously - "OK but we really do need to be leaving shortly, we're heading down to *The Celebration* in just a few minutes."

Michael - "Actually – I'm here about that. Amy? You got an envelope with tickets for *The Celebration*?"

Amy - "Oh right! Yes!"

Michael - "Exactly! Well I need to speak with you folks for a few minutes about that.

First, I'm Michael Stetson. I run a website called **Free People Of The Cosmos** – we're the ones who sponsored the tickets!

Bob, do you remember it, and the website"?

Bob- "Yeah, very cool site, I really like it. Lots of UFO reports and stuff ..."

Michael - "Well, I run the site. Glad you like it."

Pausing a moment, Michael asked - "Bob, you filled out a questionnaire on the site, a **"Transport Request"** on the website – do you remember that? Where you could request a ride on a UFO?"

Bob - "Well yeah, I thought it was kinda cool. But – *really* – is that what this is about?"

Michael - "Well, yes but it's a lot more than that actually ..."

Bob - "You're kidding – *this is some kind of joke* – right?"

Michael - "Not really. The site is designed to appeal to a certain personality type, namely people like yourself with a sci-fi mindset, who can grasp the concepts of space, space travel, extraterrestrials, ufos - the whole genre.

And you filled out the profile, mentioned Amy and you uploaded your resume, and mentioned Amy was into horses – right?"

Bob - "Ub, right -"

Amy was looking at Bob with a frown. Bob knew that look and he started to get that feeling that maybe Amy was going to be upset. Michael picked up on that as well.

Michael - "It's all good – everyone relax - we use it as a tool, a way of finding people with a specific *personality type*.

You're the kind of people who would find a lot of what I am about to explain to you - *not really that unusual.*

The company I work for wants to talk to you about your skills," and turning to Amy "as well as yours Amy, and they want to hire you both for a project.

It's a long term project, and they felt based upon your qualifications that you were their ideal candidates. The urgent nature of this project is such that you are needed immediately, and *it pays very well*."

Amy - "so are the tickets still good?"

Michael - "Oh yes, definitely – but let me explain a bit more. Honestly, we used the 'contest' as a means of getting you here so I could talk to you, and what I need to explain to you won't take that long and you can still get to *The Celebration* on time."

Now he had their attention. The thought of a good money project, and turning the corner on long term unemployment was giving Bob a sense of hope.

Michael - "Truthfully, Bob, they've been looking at your work on the net, your Youtube videos, and your work tells us a lot about who and what you're capable of.

We like what you're doing with the magnet motor stuff. We'd actually like to talk about taking it to the next level."

Bob - "Seriously?"

Michael - "Absolutely. We've also done some basic background checks, and we had wanted to meet with you at your home, but felt it important to get you folks way from distractions in Nashville, and since we learned from the profile you submitted that *The Celebration* would be interesting to Amy, they set this meeting up here to meet you right away."

At this point both Bob and Amy have very puzzled looks on their faces.

Bob asked *"What company did you say you were with?"*

Michael loved this moment – it was his crescendo moment.

Michael - "Oh right, here's my card. Sorry. I work for a company called **Global Acquisitions.**

There is another individual from the company, actually my boss – he's a huge fan of horses, and so he's here for *The Celebration* as well, looking to buy some horses. That's why they wanted you here, and so the free tickets for the Celebration was a great incentive – right?"

Amy laughed - "It worked for *me!*"

Bob - "So, this isn't really about the '**Transport Request**' then?"

Michael, glanced out the window, and then checked his watch, deliberately evading the question.

Michael - "We rented a small farm just outside of town, it has stables and the people I work for rented it for the week to have place they could stable their horses. It's got plenty of room and so I'm staying there tonight.

I'd like you to come to out there to show you the project details.

I think in light of your magnet motor projects, you will definitely want in on this. What I have to show you won't take long, and you should have plenty of time to see the horses. And you'll get to meet one of the other key people from the company as well."

Bob was still reeling and caught a bit off guard by Michael's reference to his magnet motor projects. He didn't even have a working prototype, and nothing really to show anyone.

Michael turned towards the window again, waving at Bill Morgan, and motioned with his hand to come over to the table with Bob and Amy.

Bill Morgan had been with the Shelbyville police for almost 10 years. Bill was a portly man in his 50's who definitely hadn't missed any meals.

As he walked over to Bob and Amy's table, he laughingly said to the waitress, "I ain't done yet! Still gotta get me something from the dessert rack!"

Amy looked at Michael and said "Is he the other person you mentioned from your company?"

Michael - "No – the person we will meet is already at the farm."

Michael lowered his voice to almost a whisper, glanced at Bill and then looked back at Bob.

"Bill's a local, and he works for us indirectly. We have known him for a few years and works as a security guard for us on his off time."

Minnie was short cute 30-something with a charming smile and blonde hair. "Bill Morgan I'm sure there's a piece of apple pie there with your name on it!" she quipped.

Bill wandered over to Bob and Amy's table.

Michael - "Bill, this is Bob and Amy, they're coming by the farm later on, and I was wondering if you can meet them back here in a few hours and show them how to get there?

I have to meet with a couple of people about some horses before I get there - and I was wondering if you didn't mind showing them how to get there – could they meet you here around 6, and follow you? "

Bill - "Sure no problem, be happy to show them."

Morgan made his way back to his table by the window.

Bob was a bit worried and at the same time a heightened expectation was beginning to rise up inside.

Maybe this was a break, a badly needed break.

The circumstances were a bit unusual but then whoever was behind all this seemed to need them urgently.

Bob - "Why us, and what's with all the cloak and dagger, and the urgency?"

At this point, Michael was getting up and heading for the door.

Handing a small slip of paper to Bob, "The farm is not far.

Bill will pick you up back here around 6pm? That will give you plenty of time to check out the Celebration and then we can meet?"

Bob and Amy were completely floored at this point and not quite sure what to make of it.

Turning quietly to Amy, Bob was excited but apprehensive. "Well, my curiosity has the best of me. We need to check this out."

Amy - "What about The Celebration?"

Bob - "Well, we have a few hours, let's go check it out and then we'll go meet with Michael."

Michael - "6pm then, we'll see you there."

They all headed out the door.

Non-Disclosure

Bob and Amy spent a few hours at the Celebration grounds checking out the stables, and looking at the horses.

Veteran trainers would design elaborate and expensive temporary customizations of their stables on the grounds of The Celebration. They would bring in beautiful flowers and plants, erect special lounges with flat screen TVs and all manner of comforts, with beautiful fountains – all for a one week show. All of which would have to be dismantled at the end of the event. Many had special lighting, and lighted signs declaring the horse and their riders.

The time passed quickly and the whole mystery of Michael was really on Bob's mind. The whole idea was really exciting him, that this could well be the break he needed.

After wandering The Celebration grounds for a few hours, they headed back over to the Parkway and met up with Bill Morgan who was in his patrol car waiting for them.

Bill rolled down his window and motioned them to follow.

They followed him a few minutes drive to the farm where Michael was staying, and once they had parked, Bill motioned a thumbs up.

Rolling down his window, Bill smiled and said "Nice meetin' you folks!" As he drove off, they waved goodbye. Everyone was so friendly it was a bit unnerving.

Michael stood in the door of the main house and motioned

Bob and Amy to come in.

Michael - "Glad you could make it."

As they entered into a main living room, everything looked like a typical business trip. Michael had a mini office setup on the table with a laptop, printer and a large computer monitor.

Michael - "Bob, Amy, welcome!"

Shandra was there, dressed casually and seated on a chair near the room's television.

She was focused on a laptop on a tv tray in front of her. As they entered she hastily closed the lid on her laptop and got up to meet them.

Michael - "This is my associate, Shandra, she is part of our, uh, *Human Resources* team."

Shandra got up, smiled politely and shook their hands.

Amy's feminine instincts sensed that Shandra *was more than HR for Michael. Her woman's intuition was telling her there may be a little bit more going on than just business. For Amy, Michael and Shandra looked a bit more like a couple than they probably realized.*

Shandra directed Bob and Amy to sit down at a couple of chairs in from of the table with Michael's computer and monitor.

Michael - "Ok ... Sorry but I need to cut to the chase, in the interests of time.

I have to tell you that because of our lawyers, I need you to sign a simple non-disclosure about this meeting, that what we discuss here will be completely confidential, and should any part of this meeting be discussed to anyone else that you would be removed from consideration and even liable for a law suit.

So, take a quick look and sign it, if not, I have to send you right back out the door."

Bob was hastily signing without really reading it and Amy was quick to remind him to read it.

Amy - *"Bob, don't you think you should read it?"*

Bob - "I'm good, I've seen and signed dozens of non-competes and NDA's. I have a good feeling honey, let's just get these signed so we can see what this is all about."

Amy was looking at the letterhead and the logo on the papers ... the logo was the same logo as on the *Free People Of The Cosmos* website.

Amy - "So this *'Free People of The Cosmos'* thing is real?"

Michael - "Like I said at the restaurant, every bit of it, and more. The website is actually owned by Global Acquisitions."

Amy signed a bit reluctantly and handed her papers to Michael, who turned and took both of their agreements and fed them into a waiting scanner, which was emailing the scans to Michael's superiors.

"Now all we need to do is wait about a moment or two for a phone call.

Can I get either of you something to drink? I've just picked up some very good Glen Livet, or how about a beer or wine, or water?"

Bob and Amy initially declined the drinks. Michael poured himself a shot of Glen Livet.

Shandra - "Bob, Amy, it's early evening, you're sure you won't have a glass of wine or a cocktail? Please don't worry, it's fine ..."

Amy was feeling a bit anxious - "Actually, yes, a glass of wine would be great."

Shandra quipped, "Didn't you recently take a wine tasting class?"

Amy - "Yes, I did, it's always been an interest of mine."

As nervous as she was in the moment, it was a bit unnerving that Shandra knew Amy had taken a wine tasting class. She wondered if Bob had mentioned this – how did Shandra know this?

Shandra - "Well I think you'll like this, it's a very good German Riesling".

Shandra poured Amy a glass of *Egon Muller-Scharzhof Scharzhofberger Riesling* from Eiswein, Mosel, Germany.

Amy could see the label and recognized it among the top wines in the world, but wasn't entirely sure. She took a sip and savored it.

Amy - "Wow. Very good. Can I see the bottle?"

Shandra handed her the bottle.

Amy - "I'll have to look this one up when we get home, *it's very good!*"

Not to mention the wine was over a thousand dollars a bottle.

It had occurred to Bob that it was a bit unusual for someone conducting a job interview to be drinking, and drinking very expensive liquor.

As he watched the interchange between Shandra and Amy, it seemed that there wouldn't be any harm in having "just one". After all, he did not want to appear prudish and spoil a potential job opportunity.

Bob - "Well, ok, you did say *Glen Livet*?"

As Michael smiled and poured Bob a small glass. He quipped - "It's one of my favorites."

Michaels' phone was alerting him of a new text message, affirming him that the papers had indeed been received and to proceed with the meeting.

Michael - "Ah we're good to go. I have a movie to show you, to give you the bigger picture. All of this will give you enough information to make another, larger critical decision once our meeting has concluded, which is to meet again in reference to starting the project.

The reality of who I am is that I am referred to by my superiors as a *"Collector"*.

The very word sent a chill down Amy's spine, having had to deal with bill collectors on hers and Bob's behalf for the past several months. She was looking visibly uncomfortable.

Michael - "Amy, relax, I'm not a bill collector, rather I collect things for Global Acquisitions.

And I don't collect things in any sense you may already be familiar with though, but as you begin to understand my role, it will all make perfect sense.

Just so you know, I sometimes have 2 to three meetings a week like the one we're having now.

I'm really not a recruiter or consultant, my role is more that of *procurement,* so you're not speaking with a recruiter – I'm the guy who you would be working for.

So - it is my role to 'collect' – this includes new people who have been selected for the project, as well as whatever else is necessary for the project, or whatever my superiors want me to collect.

I travel quite a bit, and I have to delegate a lot of tasks to many different people. Shandra handles a lot of our personnel related matters. We're a very quiet, low-key company. We don't really work a regular schedule.

If you start the project, you will be connected with myself and a project leader and go from there.

OK, so now I need to explain *the project*.

By now you're wondering what all the skulduggery and secrecy is all about. And I'm sure you're wondering "Why us?".

One of the reasons you were selected for this project is more about *who you are and how you think – it's about your capabilities* more than it is about your credentials.

Your backgrounds are important, but we have a greater sense that we can take you further than you can by yourselves.

It is your life experience and personality type we are looking for, and you will be utilizing it extensively in your roles in the project. Everything you've both done not just in your respective careers, but your hobbies, passions and life story will be a part of this project's success. "

Bob's immediate reaction was that this would somehow enable him to finish his power generator project. That was only partially true. Michael had bigger plans in mind.

The First Revelation

Michael continued - "First, I am going to ask you to *suspend your disbelief.*

What I am about to share with you may sound a bit overwhelming and even a bit *much*, but as we go through this presentation you will find all of this very legit, and believe me, you're quite capable of handling it.

We know quite a bit about you both. We monitored your Facebook, emails and websites and even interviewed your friends and neighbors.

None of your friends or neighbors knows the real reasons we were asking around about you, but believe me *we're very selective, and thorough.*

That brings us to this meeting.

And probably a good reason to have offered you a drink, to give you a little something to brace yourselves.

What I am about to show you, will seem like *science fiction*, but I assure you, it is not. I also have with me the proof you will need to believe that what I am about to share with you is indeed quite believable.

Bob, laughing "What do you mean science fiction, like what, *next you're going to tell us you're aliens?"*

Michael - "Not exactly Bob. I'm as human as you are, born in Milwaukee, in 1958, and I can give you my full bio as well, and if you want to check me out you can, but let's save that for later.

Let's watch a little movie I put together."

Turning on the monitor and laptop, Michael began his presentation. At this point Bob and Amy are spellbound.

"As you are both aware - because we know you are aware - that this country and the planet are in dire straights. If things continue on their present course, the planet is, in a nutshell, *doomed*.

From our rather conclusive research, we, and by that I mean the company I work for, *Global Acquisitions* – we see that the planet does not have that many years left – *if things continue along their present course.*

The ruling classes, the elites, along with the corporate raping of planetary resources, and a collapsing monetary system, are all working against the common man, *the 99%* as it were.

They are using a system based upon *false scarcity* to control the human race.

It is not just causing human misery but it is actually causing a crisis in the very ecosystem of the planet.

There are those in very high places who are quite aware of all of this, who have the power to change it but do not, and the status quo is maintained, at the expense of man and the planet itself. All of it in the name of power, money and greed.

There is also another group of *individuals*, as it were, who are also in a place of power, with the ability to do something about it, working quietly and in secret, to the benefit of mankind and the planet, and they are my superiors."

Michael paused a moment. He wanted his next statement to have full impact.

Michale - The fact is Bob, Amy, *my superiors are those you have come to understand as extraterrestrials."*

Bob - "You mean ufos, all of that? *You're shitting me right?"*

Michael - "Yes Bob, all of it. My 'superiors' as it were, are not from Earth, although they are very similar to humans in many ways, and even look like us, and speak like we do, they are definitely not Earth-humans. Extremely advanced. They call themselves **The Zui**." *(pronounced Zee)*

A constant source of frustration within the UFO communities was **credibility**. Like the infamous television show, *X-Files*, many in the community shared the main character's motto, *"I want to believe"*.

Because of the lack of credible evidence, no matter what you saw and heard about the subject, there was always a hint of doubt.

That "desire to believe", that we could have "space brothers" or that there is extraterrestrial, intelligent life beyond our own planet was always overshadowed by doubt, no matter how good the story.

A common term within the community was the search for *"smoking gun evidence"*.

Bob - "No shit ... I knew it ... I knew all that shit had to be real, I just didn't -"

Michael - "Keep your seat belt on Bob, there's more. Like I said, my superiors and their people have been watching this planet for some time. Some of them have even come to live among us, as a mission to understand us.

A large part of their research was to learn enough about us to make **a very large decision**.

They are the '*who*' behind Global Acquisitions.

To get the bigger picture, there is an alliance of races who refer to themselves as ***The Free People of The Cosmos*** which includes a huge number of inhabited planets in our galaxy, and in neighboring galaxies.

Many of these races have been around many many times longer than humanity, and their technologies are extremely advanced. I'm sure you are aware of this through some of the UFO lore, it's just never really been corroborated or proven here on Earth.

Like I said earlier, a very large effort has been undertaken to convince humanity that ETs are just science-fiction.

The reality is, these advanced races, their ability to travel throughout the universe is a settled science. They can move from world to world in an instant.

They don't use faster than light travel, they just go through *the singularity*. Keep in mind stuff that Nikola Tesla said about *vibrations* – well he was right."

Michael knew he was preaching to the choir at this point.

Bob interrupted - "I remember that quote!"

"If you want to find the secrets of the universe, think in terms of energy, frequency and vibration." --Nikola Tesla

Bob - "And you're talking about stuff like quantum entanglement – right?"

Michael - "Right - quantum entanglement is just one part of it."

Quantum entanglement is defined as "the unusual behavior of elementary particles where they become linked so that when something happens to one, something happens to the other; no matter how far apart they are.

This bizarre behavior of particles that become inextricably linked together is what Einstein supposedly called "*spooky action at a distance.*"

Michael continued - "The Zui have explained that this is part of what they use in their technology so they can move between planets almost instantaneously.

It's basic math to them. Earth is among many habitable planets in our own galaxy - with sentient intelligent life - that they visit and work with routinely.

But let's stay on point. These advanced races have been watching Earth for some time, and some of them have relayed technology from time to time into the hands of mankind throughout Earth's history.

Their original strategy was to have mankind focus on spiritual development, with scientific development as a second focus, so that we would be a balanced race.

Much of the technology was given to mankind in an innocent manner with the assumption the knowledge would be put to the betterment of mankind.

The idea was to give a little bit more, here and there, and let mankind advance both spiritually and technologically.

Instead, the religion and the science were corrupted at the highest levels. Mankind left on its own has a tendency towards corruption, without some kind of higher guidance.

Now we're living with monetary, social and religious systems that are literally *killing the planet.*

As mankind developed and evolved into a primarily warlike species with little regard for human life, the governing body in this local part of our galaxy made a very large decision to do one of two things.

1) adopt a policy of non-intervention, to let us stay on the course of our own imminent destruction, or

2) intervene and basically rescue us from ourselves.

Fortunately, they chose the latter course of action, **to intervene.**

One of the mistakes these higher races realized they had made was that of staying too far removed from the human race.

Mankind has been an orphaned species for several thousand years.

Without the higher guidance of the other advanced races in our own galaxy, mankind has evolved into a highly intelligent species that has learned more about how to self destruct than we have about how to mature in love, hope, peace and useful technologies that would make this planet a beautiful world.

Not to mention technologies that we have already that would enable us to travel as the ETs do.

At certain points in human history they gave some technology, but the true story was always hidden. The ETs had the mistaken belief that we would somehow "*get it*" and evolve up.

Instead of science, we got religion. They felt that we should develop spiritually first, *then get science*. The idea was to hide the science inside of religion, but that failed.

They sent us teachers, who mankind killed or elevated into god-like or demigod status, and the truths they attempted to bring were always overshadowed and twisted by the ruling elites so that the rulers of this planet still maintained control.

The unfortunate side effect of all of this was a huge retardation in the development of mankind as a species.

The inmates are running the asylum as it were.

Every attempt to bring a message of hope, peace and love

was being thwarted by both the evil that man has learned over the centuries, and man-made religions that use fear and intimidation to hold people in a kind of hypnosis, getting them to believe fairy tales instead of science.

Waiting for things to get better became more and more painful to watch.

Mankind has also been disconnected from nature, and this has had disastrous consequences.

So, there is a recovery plan in place.

The plan is long range, all because of several other serious changes and events that have taken place, they have had to accelerate the plan.

There is a galactic federation of advanced species that has directed the Zui to make things right. It's a sort of penance they have to do to make things right.

But there's more to the story.

The Annunaki

Archeologists, scientists and historians here on Earth are only now starting to take the ancient stories from the Sumerian tablets seriously that describe a race of aliens referred to as *The Anunnaki*."

Amy - "Yes – I saw this on one of those *ancient alien* shows on cable."

Michael - "Right – well then you know that the Annunaki was supposedly an alien race who dominated planet earth thousands of years ago. If you know anything about the Annunaki, according to some scholars, they had little interest in humanity other than using us as slaves.

The Sumerian tablets that archaeologists have dug up in the middle east, like in Iraq - state that these Annunaki are the aliens who seeded planet Earth, by creating humans through genetic engineering.

Some say they used ape DNA and this is the missing link. We're still not sure how much is religious legend or fact.

Some scientists speculated, based upon loose evidence in ancient texts, like where the Bible mentions the "*Nephilum*" - that these Annunaki were those *Nephilum,* giants several times larger than humans.

Some believed that they mined gold for use back on their home world, as a chemical to purify their atmosphere.

They supposedly came from a planet in our solar system they called Nibiru that is on an elliptical orbit that takes

3000 years to orbit around our sun, but no one knows for sure if the story is true or not. We have some circumstantial evidence but nothing conclusive.

The whole reason I mentioned all of that was because the very people I work for are descendants from the original humans that the Annunaki seeded here on Earth.

What happened is that as time went on, there were obviously humans coming and going to the Annunaki home world. Their treatment was that of slaves, and this did not seem ethical to some of the Annunaki. They felt that humans, as sentient beings should be treated with equal status, respect, with rights and responsibilities.

However, Annunaki who thought this way were not the majority, and so humanity had to suffer as slaves under the Annunaki. That did not stop this sympathetic minority from helping some of the humans escape from the Annunaki home world, Nibiru.

Many humans were secretly helped in their escape from Nibiru – at great risk to their sympathizers through a kind of *"underground railroad"*.

One such escape ship was damaged in space and drifting when it was found and rescued by another highly advanced race, the race I told you about - the Zui.

The Zui are even more advanced technologically than the Annunaki – but we'll get into that later.

They were exploring the same region of space and found the Annunaki escape ship drifting with almost 2000 humans on board.

The Zui transplanted these humans to a planet they were already in the process of terraforming, a planet called "*Tu*".

So, I said all that to say this - my superiors are from a planet called **Tu.**

Amy " – wow!"

I'm getting a little ahead of myself - let's watch this next little movie that outlines the history of the planet Tu because there's even more you need to know.

Some of what you will see next is a repeat of that story, about the Zui, but it's worth watching.

Michael turned off the lights in the room and started the movie. Michael had one of his coworkers prepare the movie so that Michael and other collectors could show the story more effectively than just telling the story.

Michael had even hired a well known voice-over artist to narrate the movie.

The History Of Tu

The planet Tu is located in a solar system 2500 light years away from Earth. Its solar system has several planets, and Tu is one of those planets positioned in what our own scientists refer to as a *"goldilocks zone"*.

That means it's close enough to its star to keep it warm and support life, but not too close to burn it. *"Just right, not too hot, not too cold"*.

Tu is about 5 times the size of Earth, has two moons, one of which has atmosphere and is actually habitable. It's what scientists refer to as a "super Earth".

But it wasn't always this way.

The actual planet is about 6 billion years old, and was originally a very hot and lifeless planet, orbiting too closely to its star. That made the surface temperature several hundred degrees too hot for human life.

Like Venus, trapped in the atmosphere around Tu was a massive amount of moisture, as well as water trapped within the planet's crust.

It had many of the right elements for life, it was just sitting in the wrong orbit, too hot for life as we know it.

Unlike Earth though, the planet Tu was not a planet that had been sitting for millions of years with a slowly evolving biological timeline. Evolution as we know it was not really doing much.

There is a highly developed, highly advanced race called the Zui whose home world lies in a star system in the Andromeda galaxy.

These 'Zui' are so advanced as to be able to perform massive terraforming and literal reconstruction of an entire planet.

The Zui took Tu and re-architected it, rebuilt it. What scientists call 'terraforming'. The planet Tu was deliberately planned and rebuilt according to the way the Zui wanted it.

Sometime in what would be around the year 1173 on Earth, the Zui, using their massive terraforming ships began a 700 year process of terraforming Tu.

Now, remember what I said about Tu being 5 times the size of Earth – well mathematically, if it had more mass than Earth its gravity would be much greater.

The Zui, using their terraforming ships, altered the molecular structure of the inner and outer core of the planet, to lighter mass elements, effectively changing its mass so that its gravity would be similar to Earth's.

Remember, the Zui are very similar to humans, just several million years older as a race, but their habitability requirements are remarkably similar, for natural resources such as air, water and food.

While some have speculated that it was the Annunaki who spawned the human race, we now suspect that the Annunaki may have acquired humans through trade proxies from the Zui. We may actually have been spawned by the Zui.

Once they had the mass of Tu setup to what they wanted, they would then alter its orbit, and its rotational spin, so that it would have a 24 hour day, and set its orbit around its star-sun to be that of 385 days. *Sound familiar?*

This would allow the planet to cool down. The water in the atmosphere would condense from the atmosphere, and fall to the land, filling the dry hot planet with water, creating oceans, lakes and rivers. As the planet cooled, rain and weather cycles would begin to make the planet habitable, and then the Zui would begin to introduce plant life, and then animals and sea creatures.

The Zui would normally allot about 700 Earth years to foster the environment on the planet to make it a habitable world. It was not just science, it was truly art and science *in concert*.

For them, *it was their art, their masterpiece.*

A small dwarf planet was moved into orbit around Tu like a moon, that would serve as an orbiting observatory and science lab for Zui to operate from.

Inside of about 5 Earth years, the Zui converted the small dwarf planet into a beautiful colony for their scientists to live and work in as they did their work of preparing the planet Tu for habitability.

Populating the planet Tu with all kinds of plants, animals, microorganisms. Zui geneticists were adept at creating animal life that was living art.

The Zui also imported life of all kinds, using an ecological pattern developed over thousands of years. They knew the art of terraforming and building ecologically sound planets that supported sentient life like their own.

Their original plan was that one day they would colonize Tu with their own people onto a beautiful and pristine planet. Tu was but one of many that the Zui would terraform and make ready for their people.

Their plan for Tu was that it would not be ready to be inhabited until shortly after what would be the early 1900's Earth time.

However, sometime around the 689th year of Tu's terraforming, a Zui scout ship, on a routine scouting mission, in another star system several thousand light years from Tu, intercepted a large spaceship that was damaged and drifting in space.

They soon found out that it was full of humans who had escaped from the Annunaki home world, Nibiru, many light years away.

This escape ship the Zui found, had been drifting in space for several months. The humans on board were barely hanging on, with barely enough power and habitability to keep the humans on board alive. They were hanging on by a thread.

The Zui scout ship contacted their home world, and a large Zui *ark ship* was dispatched to the scene.

The Zui then transplanted the humans from that escape ship onto Tu, even though the Zui had not intended for any humans or sentient life to live there until a few more years had passed.

The opportunity presented itself and they made the decision to seed Tu with the Annunaki humans ahead of schedule.

Timing and circumstance created the first inhabitants on Tu.

Studying the history of the humans from Nibiru, the whole subject of Earth was once again brought to the forefront of the Zui and the galactic alliance, The Free People of The Cosmos.

They were reminded about their own contact with Earth over thousands of years, which had largely been non-interventionist.

So it was shortly after establishing the first human colony on Tu, around the the late 1930's on Earth, the Zui began covertly visiting Earth once again.

They had come in times past, when mankind was still ignorant, and often mankind treated them as gods, and some of the Zui mistakenly let them. This was a huge temptation that even the Zui were not totally immune from.

Coming back to Earth covertly in the early part of the 20th century, the Zui witnessed the massive changes that had occurred, nuclear weapons, the global wars, the lack of real spiritual transformation they thought they had provided many years prior.

They saw mankind as becoming too consumptive, too industrial, with too little compassion, and twisted leadership in very corner of the planet.

Science and industry were tipping the balance in the wrong direction.

They saw that it was time to begin working on a plan to save Earth.

The freed humans from Nibiru implored the Zui to help them save Earth.

The galactic alliance, The Free People Of The Cosmos agreed – it was time for the Zui to intervene and fix the problem.

Earth was somewhat mythical to the humans from Nibiru, since none of them had ever been there, but they saw it as a part of their history, that the humans on Earth were also their brothers and sisters, and should be saved as much as any human on Nibiru.

During the 1920's through the 1950's, the Zui transplanted a group of 1000 humans from Earth into yet another colony on Tu, hidden away from the humans from Nibiru.

Several years later, the Zui introduced the two separate colonies to each other and began some serious building on Tu, to make it into a full blown working planet, with farms, villages, towns, cities, high speed underground transport systems (like rail) and all manner of technology.

The Zui, the Annunaki humans, and the Earth-humans all began work on a larger colony.

Thus began the work of turning Tu into a fully functioning planet, with cities, towns, villages, and farms.

All in all, the people of the planet refer to themselves as *"The Tu"*.

There is a representative government in place, but overall, the planet-wide government is run by the Zui.

The Zui take a rather libertarian attitude towards how they rule. If it doesn't make sense on a higher plane, they don't support it.

The Zui maintain a rather secretive presence and are rarely seen on Tu, but they are there and provide guidance to run the planet. They only intervene when absolutely necessary.

Since the original 1000 were colonized, there has been a slow trickle over the years of humans from Earth, and the Annunaki escape ships.

The population there is now around 1,800,000 humans on a planet 5 times the size of Earth.

The past 65 years has transformed Tu into one of the best planets in the universe for mankind to live on.

Earth Rebooted

The video ended and Shandra turned on the room lights.

Michael - "The cities and towns are small, beautiful and inviting to live in. Imagine if the past 65 years had been done right on Earth, all the senseless wars, all the bad decisions, the pollution, waste – all of that is non-existent on Tu.

Between the Zui, and the Tui, the planet has become a beautiful world to live on. It's not perfect, but you will find it much better than Earth.

Now I know the questions about all of this are probably flooding your mind, and if you continue with us past this meeting, you will learn all you need to know about the Tu, their planet, and the current mission, and the Zui.

Bob - *"Current mission?"*

Michael - "**Operation Exodus**. The current mission is to collect, specific humans, animals and resources from planet Earth, and relocate them to Tu. That's all I do.

The Zui feel time is short, and much work to do.

I am here to collect *you*, and take you to Tu, and train you as collectors.

You and your skills are desperately needed. The human population size there is nothing like planet Earth.

Originally the Zui wanted to keep the population sizes

small, but in light of how things are decaying on Earth, they have decided to prepare for an extremely large mass migration, or mass exodus of mankind from Earth to Tu.

The plan involves several stages, among the first is quietly migrating scientists, teachers, educators, computer people like yourselves and other educated classes of people to Tu.

When they feel the time is right, the Zui will begin an open migration.

Operation Exodus

The Zui are helping the Tu to build large arks which they will bring to Earth for this migration. But this will be precipitated first by what they call, **The Reveal, or Revelation.**

They are well aware of how humans on Earth have been conditioned to ignore and disbelieve the very evidence that proves the existence of ufos, extraterrestrials and aliens.

Even earlier accounts of the plan were so badly distorted as to become a fairy tales that have evolved over time into religious texts and stories.

I'm sure you've read the Book Of Revelation in the Bible – it's the one book in the Bible everyone reads because it's so so full of spooky shit.

But it's so far from reality that even though the plan is there, it has been so twisted you can't understand it as well as the fact that there's a lot missing.

The Zui are extremely saddened by *how things got so out of whack.*

It is their own belief that mankind's evolution without proper guidance has been a major disaster.

The conditioning on Earth has been quite extensive.

In fact, so extensive and thorough as to have people disbelieve it even when there is overwhelming evidence right in front of them.

So they know they cannot safely evacuate the planet of a sizable portion of the population without causing collateral social and economic upheaval to a planet that is sitting dangerously close to a complete collapse as it is already.

The Zui are planning to reveal themselves to Earth, but only when they feel there is no more time or reason to keep themselves hidden and for the time being they and those of us allied with them are working quietly behind the scenes.

Like I said, you were both selected because your skills and life experience will be used on Tu, as well as educate and train humans on Tu.

Your first job will be as collectors, like myself.

The Big Question

Which leads me to **the next big question.**

If you want to continue, past this point, you will only have 10 days to put your affairs in order, and to let your friends and family know only a cover story that you are being hired for '*a project that is out of the country by wealthy individuals who need you right away.* '

At this point I have to ask you if you are willing to essentially disappear from planet Earth, unable to return for at least 3 years?

The room was quiet for a moment as Bob and Amy tried to get a grasp of everything they had just been told. Bob was still feeling a bit skeptical.

Bob - "Well, I guess – this is awesome and exciting, *but hell yeah I want to go* - but I have so many questions – I mean, how do we know this is not all bullshit? And -"

Michael - "Hang on Bob. Just so you know Bob – and Amy, it is because of this Earth-like similarity, we can disguise your absence.

You will be able to communicate from time to time to friends and family as if you were here on Earth, except you won't actually be on Earth at all.

The Tu use a mothership to relay communications and maintain your identities from a ship located close enough to Earth, and you will continue to exist in the internet here on

Earth, from there."

Bob "OK so – fascinating as it all sounds, like some kind of *Stargate* episode, where's the proof of any of this?"

Michael - "Well Bob, I need to know if you and Amy are in?"

Bob - "Well, hell yeah, *I'm all in* – Amy?"

Amy "Are you kidding? Of course I'm in, what do we need to do next?"

Michael - "Have you ever heard of those planetarium shows with all the lasers?"

Bob - "Well yeah, but I went to one, it was kinda cool but kinda lame too."

Michael - "Well, on Tu, they have something much better, and I want to show you something similar, I think it will help you and Amy make your mind up about all this – it's a great piece of *technology*."

Bob - "Well *sure* ..."

Michael - "Before I show you, I need the two of you to stand over there, I need a little room for this demo ..."

Michael was pointing to a spot on the floor that was somewhat away from everything else.

Michael dialed a number, and when the other voice answered, Michael said, "Ready for *the demo*" and hung up.

Michael - "OK, hang on to your hats."

A few seconds later, a very high pitched whine almost imperceptible to human hearing filled the room, and then the room was flooded with a bright light.

Bob and Amy suddenly found themselves being teleported up to a Tu ark ship.

In just a few moments, they found themselves standing in a nicely furnished lobby aboard *The Cloud Nine*.

They were both stunned. Afraid to move and disoriented.

A few moments later, they were greeted by a man in coveralls that resembled a kind of military uniform.

"Hello – welcome to the Cloud Nine! I'm Ted and I'll be giving you a quick tour before the show begins."

Bob and Amy were frozen.

Bob - "*Did we just get transported?*"

Ted - "Exactly. You've been beamed up! Just like on TV. You're now on a Tu *ark ship* about 480 kilometers up from Earth.

Oh, and you can step down from *the transport bay.*"

Bob and Amy stepped down a couple of carpeted steps onto a beautifully tiled floor, as if they were in a beautiful office building.

Uh, currently we're near the hangar deck, what you might consider the bottom belly of the ship.

There's an observation gallery just ahead, which I'm sure you will find amazing.

Bob - "So this ship has its own gravity, and *transporters*?-"

Ted laughing - "I love you new recruits. Yep, everything you ever saw in sci-fi land is a reality here. We have an amazing power plant, and the ability to replicate whatever we need for food and water."

Ted loved to show off to new recruits and visitors. He knew their minds were already blown by the transporter, and they would be his captive audience for his tour.

Ted - "But we don't really eat and drink like you would on a planet, we use something a bit different that replenishes the body at a cellular level while you're on the ship, reducing the need to eat or drink. It also heals the body and kills unfriendly bacteria and viruses in the body.

The longer we are on the ship, the healthier we get. And uh, actually it's affecting you right now, and you'll return home in a little while a bit healthier than before you got here."

Opening a door to the observation gallery, they found themselves standing in front of a huge window that gave them a beautiful view of the planet Earth from about 480 kilometers up.

Bob and Amy were stunned and spellbound, dazed.

After a few moments, Ted had to break them away from the gallery window.

Ted - "Well, we gotta keep the tour moving. Follow me. "

Ted led them up a small flight of stairs and opened a door into a large room.

"This is the cargo and hangar bay."

The cargo bay had several wheeled vehicles, including several collectible cars – an old Corvette, an old Mercedes Benz, a 1995 Jaguar convertible, several Hummers, Land Rovers and some animal capture trucks.

The cars would be put into a museum on Tu. Tu had a working automobile museum in the main arrival colony. There were very few roads on Tu outside of any of the colonies, since they really were not needed. Mass transit and widespread use of *anti-gravitic* vehicles meant roads were largely unnecessary.

The animal capture trucks were used by collectors on missions to collect whatever Earth species was directed by the Tu to pick up.

Along one side of the cargo bay were two levels of cages with animals in them. In one cage, a rather large lion growled and in several other cages there were wild wolves.

There were several huge but empty cages, used for very large animals like elephants and giraffes.

"We're relocating another entire pack of wolves to Tu. Tu's also got a very large population of bison, elk, deer, and we're needing more wolves as part of an eco-balancing program."

Bob - "*So how is all of this financed?*"

Ted - "We do a lot of precious metals trading, in gold and platinum and so we are extremely well financed, we can get everything we need."

Various crates were stacked and strapped down, and there was a garage-door sized door that had a sign on it labeled 'Passenger Storage Area'.

"These ships are like Noah's Ark. We are gathering people, animals, supplies, and stuff from every continent every time we come back to Earth. We have dozens of ships like this one making constant trips back and forth.

I'm sure Michael mentioned one of the reasons he was in Shelbyville for *The Celebration* is to get some thoroughbreds. He'll be bringing back some really nice horses.

Let's wander up to the control deck and you can see the control room and flight center."

Ascending yet another small flight of stairs they found themselves in the main control room. Unlike what they saw in familiar science fiction movies, the control room was largely uncluttered and devoid of monitors and technology.

It was more like a large lounge, with very streamlined control consoles and controls, with beautiful lounges, couches and stylish chairs. Plants and artwork were tastefully adorned throughout the control room.

There was an artful, architectural feel. Beautiful blonde wood adorned the doorways and consoles and cabinets.

It had more the feel of a large living room. Hints of Asian and Northern European design were everywhere.

There were shelves with vases and sculptures. Large 10 ft tall windows provided a spectacular view of space, and of the Earth below.

Bob - "Wow this is nothing like I imagined an alien spacecraft to look like!"

Ted - "Well, that's because it's not entirely alien. It's been designed by humans who have had the past 80 - 100 years to build these ships.

They've taken what they were taught and learned from the Tu, who learned from their friends in the Annunaki, and the Zui-human hybrids and built these ships. So these ships are a combination of Earth, Annunaki and Zui technologies.

The technology is way out beyond anything we ever thought possible, and at the same time so freaking simple it is astounding.

The cool thing about these ships is that they can set down, on land and water, and even go under water. I'm sure you've heard about sightings of ufos coming up out of the water?"

Bob "Well yeah. *USOs*. And there's a lot of activity off the coast of California as well, they say there's underground bases there under the channel?"

Ted - "Yeah well we can't talk about any of that right now, but yes there are various underground bases, but those locations are only on a need to know basis, they just don't tell everyone that info if you get what I mean."

Bob - "So Ted, what is your role in all of this?"

Ted - "I was a high school science teacher until I was contacted by someone like Michael back in the early 1960's. The whole thing was really just starting and had only been in operation a few years when I came into it."

Amy - "But – you don't look that old?"

Ted looked like a man in his 30's, and very athletic.

Ted - "I told you these ships have a cellular level regeneration system built in. Your body is being energized right now by that system.

Years of exposure and constant repair to the body extends the human life span and literally reverses the aging process.

I'm actually over 80 years old, pushing 85. So my long term work in this program has actually been very beneficial to me."

The whole idea left Bob wandering off in his mind. But Bob was one to gather information, and it was all coming at him fast, but he wanted more.

Bob – "Wow ... One other thing, I'm curious, what about us being detected up here in orbit?"

Ted - "Not to worry, the Tu use a shielding system as well as phase shifting technology, so we're just another ufo that NASA won't admit to being out here.

But listen, uh, you folks are also here to see *a special*

concert and it's just about to begin in our amusement deck. Follow me.

Space DJ

Ted led them down to the amusement deck. The amusement deck was a large auditorium sized room, with seating that could easily handle 3000.

Ted paused in a hallway leading into the main amusement deck auditorium.

Ted - "Did Michael tell you about the *Planetarium Experience* with *Miresa*?"

Amy - "No, he didn't say anything about that? Well he mentioned something about a 'demo' - but I think he was being deliberately vague."

They all laughed.

The word *"planetarium experience"* immediately conjured up images of planetarium light shows done with music. The concept was great, the execution was generally boring.

Bob - "Tell me this isn't going to be one of those lame laser light shows?"

Ted - "You won't be disappointed Bob. Before I take you into the amusement deck - you folks are in for a treat. We've got about 500 other new recruits on board this evening and you're all going to experience something definitely out of this world.

Bob - "So what's it all about?"

Ted - "Michael queued you folks in about the Zui - right?

Bob - "Right?"

Ted - "Well as much as we've been learning from the Zui, they've been learning from us. One Zui in particular is a musical genius named *Miresa*.

Miresa has developed a special fascination with the music from David Gilmour, aka *Pink Floyd*.

He can't get enough of it, and has idolized their music to that of a super fan. He was quoted as saying that David Gilmour's music is what gave evidence to the Zui that the human race was worth saving – if you can believe that! He's literally elevated Pink Floyd to an almost religious experience."

They all laughed.

Ted - "Well, the Zui have something special that they do, - *because they can*.

As you are now aware, their technologies, their spacecraft – all of it enables them to travel to any point in their star charts they want to in near instantaneousness. They tap into *the singularity* and arrive in less time than it takes to talk about it.

This opened up a lot of possibilities for them. As a side benefit, they have taken theatre to a new level. They perform music concerts with real live backgrounds of stars, nebulas, gas clouds, and planetary explorations.

On Earth, we rely on special effects wizards to produce wonderful movies on a screen. All of it based upon unreality.

What you are about to witness, first hand is a special performance by Miresa as he mixes Pink Floyd *with the visual experience of what you see out of the ship's largest gallery window in the amusement deck.*

Miresa will literally be positioning the ship like a night club DJ as a visual presentation to match the music.

His "playlist" is really charted positioning throughout the galaxy. We will literally be bouncing all over the galaxy as he repositions the ship for various segments of the music.

The show usually lasts an hour or two, and then we'll be right back here to put you down back home.

So kids, strap your seat belts, the show is about to begin!"

Ted led them through a set of double doors and they entered the auditorium.

Ted - "Enjoy, I'll see you folks when the show is over"

There was complete silence as Bob and Amy hastily found a seat.

Slowly the lights came up on the area just in front of the gallery window. The window was opaque, black and the room was still.

Off to the left side of the window was a podium. Standing at the podium was Miresa, of the Zui. Miresa was about 6 feet tall, very thin, almost frail.

He was pale in complexion, with long white hair, and beautiful blue eyes. He was wearing a beautifully crafted multicolored robe, which had a sort of middle-eastern style to it. He was also wearing one of those headset microphones like concert performers wear.

Miresa - "Welcome Earth brothers and sisters. I am Miresa, and I will be your host for an evening of musical interpretation, in *The Planetarium Experience.*"

An immediate enthusiastic applause rose up from the crowd. There was a huge anticipation in the air, as well as the smell of cannabis, although no one in the audience really knew what was about to happen next.

Someone was handing Bob a small pipe with cannabis and Bob indulged for the moment.

Bob - "Thanks!" Bob handed it to Amy and she took a hit.

Miresa implored his audience - "*Are you ready?*"

They were indeed ready!

As he said that, the lights went down, and the opaqueness of the gallery window faded away and a beautiful view of Earth showcased itself.

Another applause rose up from the crowd. None of the people in attendance had ever been to space, or experienced what was about to happen. The view of the Earth was a crowd pleaser in and of itself.

As the applause died down fading into the surround sound in the auditorium was the familiar sound of the heartbeat from Pink Floyd's *Dark Side of the Moon*.

Miresa guided the ship into Earths' atmosphere, and then diving directly into the Pacific Ocean. The ship was underwater! As the musical scenes changed, as simple as a fade out in a slide show, the ship was back in space!

Bob nudged Amy to look at several people, several rows down and to their right. *It was none other than the rock band U2.*

Bob - "Is that who I think it is?"

Amy - "Oh no way, oh my god!"

Over the course of an hour, as the music played, and the scenes changed in the music, Miresa took the ship on a fantastic ride through his own orchestration, a "playlist" of planets, stars, constellations, and all manner of space phenomena. It was truly breathtaking.

Everyone was spellbound by the mix of music and a magical space ride.

Bob and Amy were no less transformed, spellbound and speechless.

As the music ended, Miresa had returned the ship to the exact starting point in orbit around Earth.

Bob and Amy had just experienced galactic tourism first hand with an alien who enjoyed listening to 70's rock music.

Bob turned to Amy - "*Now that is a real Planetarium Experience!*"

Amy - "I am blown away – I do not have words!"

People were exiting the auditorium, all were visibly moved and excited about the performance, as the realization began to sink in for all of them that they had just bounced around the Milky Way like a ping pong ball, enjoying music and space travel.

Ted came into the auditorium to find Bob and Amy still somewhat in shock, dazed and yet blissful from the performance.

Ted - "So what do you think?"

Bob - "Are you shitting me? That *rocked!*"

Amy - "Oh my God, so utterly cool! That was *amazing!*"

Ted - "Well, that's just scratching the surface – there's more stuff like that you have yet to see.

But now. I have to be '*Captain Killjoy*' and return you to the place we picked you up. So, follow me, and we'll get you back on the ground in no time."

Ted led them back to the transporter lobby.

Hundreds of new recruits were all "high" on this new experience, but it was time for all to return to Earth.

Soon it was Bob and Amy's turn to step up onto the transporter pad. Another bright flash of light and within moments they were back at the farm with Michael.

We're All In

Bob and Amy were speechless.

Laughing, Michael had a huge grin on his face. "So did you enjoy the show?"

Bob - "That was *off the hook*!"

Michael - "OK, like I said, you are sworn to secrecy. Let me say this, to help alleviate any desire you have to tell anyone about this.

After you are safely relocated to Tu, you will enter a training period, and you will be able to recommend friends and family that we should pick up as well.

So there is no need to let anyone know the truth about where you are going, in time you will be part of relocating them as well.

Like I said, you are only allowed to tell them that you have been hired by a wealthy businessman in a foreign country who is paying all expenses to relocate you immediately, in 10 days.

Got it?"

Bob and Amy nodded their heads 'yes'.

Michael - "Good. You will have 10 days from today to prepare to leave. "

Shandra handed Michael a large bulging manila envelope,

which he then handed to Amy.

"This is your welcome packet of sorts and in it is a list of items you will be permitted to bring.

We have plenty of computers, but if you want to bring your own computer, make sure it's a laptop, with portable hard drives and you have everything it needs.

If you want to bring a camera, and whatever small electronics you want, really don't even need that - no need to bring any clothing other than what you are wearing – like I say, you will be able to get whatever you need there. Your food, clothing and housing are all provided.

We will contact you in 7 days to coordinate the time and location for pickup. In 10 days you will leave Earth.

So really you have very little time to wrap things up. I know this is all a bit overwhelming, so I need you to focus in and get done what needs to be done.

You may bring your pets, like a dog or cats but no fish. Please realize you and your pets will be quarantined for a time after your arrival to detox.

Any questions?"

Bob and Amy were numb – this was all too overwhelming.

Michael - "Good - In this packet is also a list of things we need you to go out and purchase prior to pickup.

Here is a debit card you can use to make the purchases on the list. You should have no problems, the card has a rather large amount of money on it, so there isn't anything on the list you cannot afford.

If you need to pay rent or some bills, go ahead, but remember *only what you need.*

Don't be tempted to pay bills for other people like friends and family, we're trying to keep things on the down low if you understand what I mean. If you have any issues with it, call me, I am now your personal banker.

 Just keep in mind, *I don't always know the specific reason why I am asked to collect some items, I only know they are needed.*

As far as real medical issues are concerned, do not worry, we have excellent medical facilities on our ships and on Tu.

Tu has an **arrival colony**, and you have to live there a short time for training, to acclimate and detoxify, and then you can migrate to any number of other communities on the planet.

The arrival colony's training center will give you all the information about your new planet, and how its communities and social structures are setup.

Tu is not a recreation of Earth, it's probably *what Earth could have been*, had Earth not been enslaved so many thousands of years ago.

It's getting late, and we need to wrap this up for tonight. I'm sure it's all been a little overwhelming, but as you begin to digest it all over the coming days, you will be anxious to leave.

So without further ado – hit the road! Everything you need to do is on checklists in the packet.

I'll be in touch, and you can email or call me with any questions."

Bob and Amy said goodbye to Michael and Shandra and began heading back to Nashville.

Bob pulled into a gas station and stopped the car.

The meeting with Michael and the Planetarium Experience had left Bob disoriented, and somewhat bewildered. He needed a moment to regroup.

Bob - "HOLY SHIT! I mean, *WHAT THE FUCK*?"

Bob just sat there staring out the windshield of the car, and began to chuckle, which soon became full blown laughter.

"So much for The Celebration!"

They laughed.

Amy - "Let's head home and start packing! I can't even think about the horses now."

Bob - "We have a lot to do to before we leave."

Departure

10 days is really a week and 3 days. Bob and Amy were busy. About three days into the mad rush to get things packed, it became quite apparent that they had to do something with all of the stuff they no longer needed.

Bob - "Geez what do we do with all this personal crap we have accumulated?"

Amy - "Well, unlike SOME of us, I actually read the stuff in that packet of materials Michael gave us. There's a number there of a special moving company that comes and collects furniture and household items.

All we need to do is call them, they come and get everything out of the apartment a couple of days before we leave. They wind up donating it to Goodwill or other charities.

Michael said in the packet to pick up one of those inflatable beds, as well as a ton of boxes from the moving store down the street and just box up everything that has value, and dumpster the rest.

Let me read you this from the packet – which is funny because it has all the logos and information disguised as this company in Singapore we are relocating to ... "*your relocation package includes a furnished apartment with all of the household items you will need for life, such as cooking, cleaning, etc. Do not pack more than a day or two of clothing as all clothing is provided as needed.*

Please keep to a minimum any non essential items, only small sentimental items will be permitted, no paintings or portraits or large art pieces. Special arrangements can be made for their care."

Bob - "There isn't much they haven't thought of. I got an email from Michael about a couple of documentary videos he wanted us to watch on the computer, prior to departure, one on Netflix and a couple from some other sites."

Amy - "Yes, and we are supposed to go pick up several DVD boxed sets of some educational stuff, one on chemistry, another on architecture, and some latest releases in movies. I have to get some stuff overnighted from Amazon, and we need to make a couple of Costco runs".

Bob - "I am going to photograph and scan a lot of stuff that I want to remember, stuff we're going to have to cut loose and say good bye to. I already ordered the cameras and laptops Michael had on the list a couple of days ago, and that stuff should be here today. He said even though there were plenty of computers where we are going he had his reasons for ordering them anyway.

We have to un-box all of it and make it ready to go. He even included a list of accessories for all of it.

Amy - "Yeah he even has special luggage on the list – "*all natural materials, no plastic*" - weird. If he didn't have the supplier on this list I have no idea where we would be able to buy it. And he said to pick up a can of anchovies – weird, but I did and we are to have it with us, like in my purse – very weird.

As they were speaking there was a knock at the door.

"Amy - "Who is it?"

From outside the door *"UPS, delivery"*

Opening the door, the UPS guy had several large boxes of computer equipment and assorted unmarked packages.

Amy - "Thanks!"

Closing the door, their living room now had a huge pile of boxes and stuff scattered about.

Bob - "It's a full time job just getting all this stuff figured out. Thank god they gave us 10 days."

Bob spent a day setting up their tablets and laptops, and cameras. The next several days were spent unpacking and repacking for departure. There was also the added task of informing friends and relatives about their move to "Singapore" and the pretense could be exhausting at times.

Bob - "I get why Michael mentioned keeping the communication about all this to a minimum, it's exhausting trying to explain the cover story to people, and none of it is even true!"

Amy - "I know, I'm really having some issues with leaving family behind."

Bob - "You have to keep in mind the greater good. We're going to prepare the way for them, so keep that in mind. I really want to tell my brother so badly, but I know we can't".

The days passed quickly and right on schedule, Michael was

calling exactly on the seventh day.

Michael - "Hey Bob, so everything packed and ready?"

Bob - "Yes, actually going very smooth. Only a few small items left for pick up tomorrow and we're set."

Michael - "Good. How is Amy holding up?"

Bob - "She's stressed and the family separation thing has been getting to her. She's been a bit moody about it. The furniture household effects truck came today and it was a little hard on her, the house is pretty much empty now."

Michael - "You want me to give her a pep talk?"

Bob - "No, I think she'll be fine. I keep reminding her of the greater good, and that her family will be along later. We've got our lease terminated at the apartment complex and it looks like we're *moving to Singapore*."

Michael - "Good job Bob. I need to give you specific instructions now, that I cannot email. There is a small convenience store located a couple of miles from you, just up the road. Load up everything you have for departure in a rental van Friday morning and meet me at that store at noon. We will proceed from there to the departure location."

Bob - "Got it"

Michael - "If I am not there, and you are met by anyone else, offer them the can of anchovies. If they look puzzled, they are not legit. If they say something like "Oh awesome for putting on pizza," they are legit. Crazy, but we had to come up with something unusual for verifying."

Bob - "Got it ... love all this cloak and dagger stuff"

Michael - "This is the real deal Bob, always keep that in mind. Make sure you've got a rental van lined up for Friday, and I'll see you there."

Good Bye

Friday morning Bob and Amy had the van all loaded and ready by 11. They were filled with anticipation about their departure.

Arriving at the convenience store, they saw Michael in his car already waiting, and noticing their arrival, he got out to meet them.

Bob rolled down his window as Michael walked up.

Michael - "All set?"

Bob - "Ready for lift off captain!"

Michael "Follow me, we have about a 20 minute drive."

They proceeded to head towards downtown Nashville. It was an unusually bright and sunny day, minimal traffic.

Amy sighing - "I know I'm gonna miss some of this, but definitely not most of it. Especially the drivers here. All we gotta do now is make it to the departure location! This is so exciting."

As they approached Michael's warehouse, the doors opened and a couple of men motioned them to pull inside the warehouse and waved at Michael.

Michael parked in a parking space inside the warehouse but motioned Bob.

Michael - "Bob, let Amy out of the van, and then pull your van right over there and center it right over that big white X painted on the floor."

Bob - "Got it"

Amy hopped out of the van and Bob centered the van right over the big X on the floor and got out.

Michael - "OK so first they pick up the van, unload it and send it back, so while they're handling that come on into the little office here.

By the way, those guys working in the warehouse are all 6-month interns from Tu. They come here to learn about Earth as part of their training."

They all proceeded to walk down a small hallway and as they closed the door behind them a bright flash of light bled through the doorway.

Michael - "OK looks like the van has been picked up. They'll have it back to us shortly. You folks hungry, thirsty? "

Bob – "No, I'm good – way too excited actually."

Michael - "Amy?"

Amy - "I'm good – can't wait actually."

Michael - "I'm excited for the two of you. You need to focus as much as you can on the initial training phase when you get to Tu. Absorb and learn everything you can as quickly as possible."

Few moments later another bright flash illuminated the interior of the warehouse.

Michael - "Looks like your van is back. One of the guys will return it to the rental company. We try to keep suspicious activity to a minimum. The van goes back on time and clean."

Bob - "Those guys are quick"

Michael - "Max is one of my best. All the crews are all so used to this it doesn't take much time, and they are like Indy pit crews to see how fast they can get a van unloaded. There is a day coming very soon when it will be super critical to unload in record time.

We have an even bigger warehouse at another part of town, in a more inconspicuous location for larger loads.

The Tu are already talking about an accelerated roundtrip schedule. As it is, they get a couple of days off between runs, but as things get more critical, the shifts will run longer and non-stop.

We also make trade runs between Earth and Tu.

Well, it's time. I'm heading up with you to introduce you and get you situated. You'll be riding on the *Cloud Nine* – same ship you toured.

Stand here in this open area with me and let's get out of here ...

Oh wait ..."

Michael stepped out of the office a few feet and shouted "Hey Max, we're heading up"

Max - "Roger that Michael, travel well!"

Stepping back into the office, Michael stood next to Bob and Amy and dialed up to the Cloud Nine - "We're ready, 3 for transport"

Within a few moments, another bright flash and they found themselves once more in the transport lobby aboard *Cloud Nine*.

As the door to the transport room opened, they were greeted once more by Ted.

Ted - "Welcome back"

Michael stepped off the transport - "Hey Ted. How soon before we wink out?"

Ted - "About 3 hours, we have another pickup over London, and then one over Sydney."

Michael - "Great. Can you get these folks settled in guest berthing? I have to meet with Adam in control beforehand."

Ted - "Sure, no sweat, Bob, Amy, follow me"

Michael - "See you folks shortly after you've settled in. Ted will show you around a bit more than what you saw in the first tour, and acquaint you with some of the amenities."

Bob - "Thanks Michael! Thanks for everything."

Amy - "Yes, thank you so much Michael – it's all a bit overwhelming but I'm so ready for this!"

Ted - "Well, c'mon kids. Follow me and let's get you settled in. First I want to take you back down to cargo, and show you where we stashed your cargo, so if you need get to anything it's all easily available during the trip. "

They found themselves back down in the cargo bay. Crew members were stacking forklifts of crates and containers of various items that had been collected and transported up from all over the planet.

Ted led them to their storage locker.

"Here's your stuff and it's not locked, just come and go as you need".

Leading them out of the storage area, back through the cargo bay they took another passageway down a short hall and it opened up into a large nicely furnished lounge-like cafeteria.

"By the way, I forgot to mention, the gallery – it has two levels, the level I showed you on the first tour is the upper level, but there's a gym below that level, and all the treadmills face out and so you get a nice space view when you're on a treadmill or elliptical.

Let's head up into the galley/lounge area.

This is where we all come to relax, hang out, have a few drinks, enjoy a movie from time to time.

The replication room is just over there, and it's all kiosk

driven, just follow the instructions on the screens and you can have it make any kind of meal you want, including the plates, silverware and the napkins.

There's some pre-set menu selections which are all gourmet – we've had numerous gourmet chefs set up some great meals, so it's all 5-star coming out of these machines. "

Bob - *"Replication?"*

Ted - "Ah yes, just like sci-fi but very real"

Ted - "It's a lot like those 3D printers, but way more advanced. It has access to a giant library simply called *the replicator library*.

The replicator library has been accumulating data over almost 50 years of food, clothing and all manner of human engineering. You can replicate a tomato or cabbage from 1962 if you want, or a leisure suit from 1973.

Not only are there are numerous contributions from gourmet chefs, old recipes from all over the planet. It's truly amazing.

We've got bacon and eggs in there from old country diners. You can also add your own recipes to the library and it will be available throughout all of our ships and throughout Tu immediately.

Like I say, for the past 50 years, Collectors have been adding to the replication library, so there's a huge amount of stuff you can replicate.

The replication library is also tied into the main ship's

library, which is in turn networked to the planet's library, both on Earth and on Tu.

There's even contests where you can compete with things you make, from food, clothing, engineering. You make it, upload it, other people can replicate it, examine it, improve on it. It's quite amazing actually."

The Liberation Of Replication

When you think about building a better world, there are obvious ideas that come to mind.

You think about building human dwellings not based upon cost, but about total integration with the environment.

You start to think about economic systems that work better than what is currently in place on planet Earth.

As you will hear many conservationists say, "... *humans are the only species on the planet that have to pay to live there ...*"

Replication technology *is one of the single-most transformative principles about Tu.*

It is the replication technology that makes a huge part of the freedom on Tu possible.

Replicators convert energy into matter. Much like a 3D printer, a replicator can be used to create material objects of all kinds.

But unlike a 3D printer, *a replicator uses* **energy** *to assemble molecules into desired material objects.*

Couple the replicator with a giant computer database of objects, such as food, clothing, tools, computers, electronic devices, and you can re-create these objects at will with a replicator.

If every home, school, library, hospital, workplace has a replicator, then there is no human need that cannot be met, *instantaneously*.

People can get what they need any time a need arises. For example, you need shoes, or clothing, you replicate from the library what you need.

You need hand tools, or electronic test equipment, or *even replacement human organs*, it can all be replicated.

The ability to replicate means that no one needs money for anything.

On Tu, with the abundance of replication, there is no economy necessary for provision, mankind is free to spend time doing other things. Things like bettering oneself, to evolve up. Go back to school. Learn something new.

The only thing required then was **energy** to power a replication machine, and the Zui had that problem solved.

If you can have anything you want for food, clothing, personal electronics, home furnishings, and the necessities for daily living – **the entire structure of life changes.**

Now you do not have to take a job to survive. You can meet your basic human needs without working.

Now you have time to find out what your true talents and abilities are, and pursue that, and in that, you find your place in humanity.

Since you can have anything you want, *you actually learn to want less*, and find out you really don't need or want that much. It is a process of maturation of wants and desires.

Replicators also means there is very little crime based upon greed or lack. It also means *no poverty*.

On Earth, scarcity, and *false scarcity* are among the biggest contributors to crime and war.

Newcomers to Tu are given restricted basic access to replication machines so that they can get basics, such as food, clothing and personal electronics and basic necessities, as well as home furnishings, hand tools and computers.

For many newcomers, they have to learn *'replicator discipline'*. Just because you can have all you want, how much do you really need?

As newcomers begin to understand the new world where consumption and the personal accumulation of material things *is not* the emphasis for daily life, their privileges can be increased.

The replicator library is well stocked, but it can not contain everything. There were always things that needed to be added. Old books, antiques, art and artifacts.

The scanning facilities at Ellis Island, New Didiza and Minora South, as well as at the Aquatica storage facility were often a first stop for returning collection teams.

The Ellis Island arrival colony has the second largest object scanning facility on Tu, and can scan everything from microscopic to objects up to 120m in length and 30m in height.

The largest scanning and replication facility was at the Zui compound at South Minora.

It was there the Zui would build by replication many of their larger pieces of technology, such as jump ships, and large scale power systems.

This gave the Tu the ability to construct arrival colony homes in massive quantities, turning out and installing several new homes at a time, wherever needed.

Buildings were simple to "install". All you had to do was setup a building order through the replication library.

The replication library would then contact the colony's building team, and they would setup a building replication at whatever site you needed it.

You could pick from several pre-designed buildings, such as machine shops, general purpose buildings, small tool sheds, medical facilities, and just empty buildings of all sizes.

Once you selected a building, it would be replicated at the larger replication facility, and then transported directly to a mounting pad at the site. Robot pad builders would clear a space and setup a mounting pad for the home.

The same process was used for all of the colony homes and structures.

Plumbing and sewage systems were a bit more complex.

Using robotic transport enabled tractors, the Zui could run large scale plumbing and sewage systems in a few days for several thousand homes.

 The robotic tractors would follow a GPS course. As they went along the course, they would use a combination of replication and transporter technology – literally creating pipe as they traveled. New pipe would *"grow"* as they traveled.

And since they used transport technology, it meant the pipe would be created, on the fly, *right into the ground*. No digging, no ditches. No need to rip out trees.

They could run thousands of feet of pipe this way, setting up water and sewage systems for large scale colonies inside of a few days, without having to rip up the ground with construction equipment.

Once the water and sewer systems were in place, they could transport home after home into place, and then it was only a simple thing to make sure the connections were good.

Android building teams would then go through each newly installed home to turn on the self contained power system and make sure everything was in place and connected.

Replication in the fields of science and education provided the ability to replicate artifacts from archaeological digs.

This meant a student, or scientist on any corner of the planet could replicate an artifact to examine it. This transformed education in archaeology. (Such replications were always logged, and the originals were safeguarded.)

If a rare artifact could be replicated, by anyone, it was no longer rare. However, this also meant that if you wanted to decorate your apartment or home with artifacts, you could do so.

Previously rare paintings and artwork could be reproduced exactly as they were, so you could literally hang the Mona Lisa, or something from any of the great artists such as Van Gogh on your living room wall if you wanted to.

Because of this, it gave new meaning to concepts such as *"priceless"* or *"irreplaceable"*. Replication also meant *"the best backup system ever"*.

If something unique and "one of a kind" needed to be doubly safeguarded, then a backup of it into the replication library was one means of securing it.

Replicated backups of an item could then be stored in different locations – so even if the replication library was destroyed, physical duplicates would exist.

This also meant there was direct application for the medical sciences. Human organs could be replicated.

Human beings could be replicated, but there were strict controls in place to prohibit the replication of human beings.

The Zui had specific moral issues with the replication of persons. They believed in the randomness of procreation, of family lineages, and natural genetic processes. They only allowed organ replication where necessary.

When a civilization extends beyond a single planet, then its history is capable of being preserved in multiple locations. The idea that a planet failure would wipe out that civilization no longer applied.

And so this was part of the growth of the human race, to extend outward to other planets, and ensure its long term survival.

Life On Cloud Nine

Ted - "Each table has a pop-up computer terminal you can use to access the library, or get on the Earth internet when we're close enough to Earth. So you don't need to lug around a laptop, these terminals are everywhere, but there's shipboard wifi, so if you'd rather use your own laptop you can.

A lot of people really enjoy sitting in here or the gallery and just space gazing."

Leading them out and down another hallway, they entered the berthing spaces.

"OK, we have you in guest berthing, and let me see, your room is A121."

They walked a bit further and Ted approached the door and entered a code on the keypad on the door.

Ted - "Your code is 8080, just punch it in here and wa-lah, the door opens like a good old door."

With a bit of a chuckle Ted anticipated Bob and quipped "And no, we don't have sliding doors like *Star Trek!*"

They entered what would be their new home for the next couple of days.

Ted - "The trip only takes about 3 days, and is pretty uneventful. You can take that time to do some preliminary reading and watching some videos to help prep you for Tu.

Oh, and watch the ship's safety video, it will give you a lot of critical info about the ship, and emergency procedures."

Bob - "I thought that travel between the two planets was almost instantaneous?"

Ted - "It is, but we have a couple of trading stops to make, and pick up people on a couple of other planets who are also heading to Tu, so there's some down time at each of those locations en route."

Sitting on the bed were 2 smartphone-like devices.

Ted - "You each get one of these, we call them 'ship phones', there's one for each of you with your own code, and you can use it to get ahold of me if you need anything during the trip.

Just push to talk old school. They have a little directory in them of everyone on board, you just pick a name and it connects like a phone. I don't see your names yet in the directory but that will update shortly before we leave.

And it looks like this room has a replicator, nice. Not all the cabins have one. Just follow the instructions, it's all voice and touch screen activated. Like I was telling you earlier, it makes food, shoes, clothing, whatever you need."

Ted pointed to a square panel on one of the walls.

Ted - "Behind this panel is the recycle chute, just put any waste here - anything to be disposed of, food, dirty dishes, dirty clothing, etc.

It all goes in the waste chute, and the ship recycles it all using a reverse replication technology which breaks down the trash into reusable materials, or into pure energy for the ships' use. If you create something with the replicator you don't need, just put it into the chute and it gets recycled.

I suggest you go through the clothing setup – have it make you some coveralls which are very comfortable.

Put the search term in 'Ted's coveralls' - I have it setup for a quick search to the coveralls we wear, and it's got both male and female setups. You just describe your measurements and it does the rest.

And there's a catalog built in with some of the clothing that people are wearing on Tu. Go ahead, experiment and create a few items – but really your apartment in the arrival colony will have a replicator as well, so you can make whatever you need whenever you need it, so there's no need to create a pile of stuff here, when you can make what you need there.

Like I mentioned before, you really won't be hungry or thirsty during the ride, but if you feel you need a real meal, you can use your in-room replicator or the ones I showed you in the galley.

As you can see your cabin has a double bed, and a bathroom shower combo. There should be all the amenities and fully stockpiled. We do have a full library server on board, so there's plenty to keep you entertained or educational stuff as well. Again, it's all touch screen and voice activated.

Also, you should set your alarm clock to Earth time. We all have our own preferred clocks going, and you will see dual clocks in key places around the ship, the E means Earth Time, GMT, and the T time is of course Tu time at the arrival colony.

Once you set your phone with your personal time zone, the phone will link to the ship-wide calendar and it lets everyone know your sleep and awake schedule.

If there's meetings you need to attend, the app will show you the conflicts so you can adjust accordingly.

A common phrase is *"what time of day is it for you?"* especially on these pickup runs.

Bob - "I think it's still mid-afternoon or early evening for us"

Ted – "By the way, everyone on Tu goes by a central clock, like GMT and there are time zones like on Earth, and the AM / PM nomenclature. But you can learn more about that using the library terminals in your cabin and in the galley or lounge.

Most relocated humans, who are really new to the planet generally have a dual clock and calendar running on their computers an phones to keep a kind of mental link with their former planet. We have an Earth clock server setup to keep computers people bring from Earth from getting too messed up.

Every home and building is wired for Tu's own version of the internet. When your Earth-made laptops connect to the net on Tu, they think they are connecting to the same time servers they did on Earth. Everything is wireless on the planet, and you generally get good signal even in extremely remote areas.

The libraries on Tu get regular news updates, and you can tap into them for summaries and updates of what is happening on Earth. However, realize these updates only occur a couple of times a week or so.

Each ship arriving from Earth carries updates from Earth automatically, and they update Tu automatically when they land. There is a whole army of technicians and media people who manage the news gathering process from Earth because of the amount of information gathered.

The Tu have ships deployed for a week around Earth, gathering news from Earth's own media and Earth's internet and then they build out summaries they bring back to Tu.

They don't censor anything, so you will have to adjust your thinking a bit. There was a planet wide consensus many years ago and the people of Tu decided to leave things open and uncensored as much as possible."

Ted's ship phone was beeping.

"As you begin to become more acclimated to Tu, you will find yourself less interested in what is happening on Earth. Tu becomes a whole new world of discovery and learning.

However, there is a huge amount of interest from scientists and social studies experts on Tu who are monitoring Earth on a daily basis. "

Ted's attention was now on his ship phone.

"This is Ted"

Michael - "Ted, would you please send Bob and Amy up to the conference room just off of control. I wanted to chat with them a bit and introduce them to Adam".

Ted - "Got it, will send them right up"

Michael – 'Thanks Ted"

Ted - "Well, so much for all this, Michael needs you folks up in the control room and is going to introduce you to your new project lead, so let's head on up."

They proceeded to make their way back up towards the ship's control room and met Michael there, along with Adam Orus, their new project leader. They were just outside of what looked like a small conference room.

Michael - "Hello Bob, Amy, come on in and make yourselves comfortable. I'd like to introduce you to your project leader. This is Adam Orus, and Adam, this is Bob and Amy."

Michael turned to a beautiful young woman with very long, blond, straight hair seated a few feet away at a table. She was wearing a full length *saree,* with a beautiful yellow safron blouse.

Michael - "And this is *Melissa*, Adams' assistant."

Melissa - "Welcome, Bob, Amy. So good to see you both. I've heard so much about the both of you."

Michael deliberately turned back to the group, so that Melissa could not see his face.

Michael mouthed the word "ROBOT".

Melissa - "*Android* Michael, I am an Android. You forget I have excellent vision and caught you in the reflection of that glass of water."

They laughed.

Michael - "She knew I was gonna do that, it's a running joke between us. Can't keep to many secrets around here. I also like to show off her abilities. She's invaluable to us and has saved my life a few times. "

Michael joked - "But she *is* heartless, cruel and downright mean sometimes. "

Melissa laughed - "You can count on me Michael"

They chuckled again.

Androids were not all the same size and shape, but you could generally spot an android by their perfect physique that was seriously hard to match in a human.

Their bodies, while similar to humans, were composed of biologically advanced "components" that gave them long life spans and they never aged. The Zui considered them a life form, and gave them the same respect as any other humanoid species.

Michael - "All in good humor. Anyway, just for the record and a little history, Adam has been a part of the entire Tu project since 1947.

He was one of the initial people instrumental in setting the entire project up. Adam served in World War II as an enlisted gunner on a B-17 doing bombing runs over Germany, and after the war was one of the first people contacted by the Tu."

Adam barely looked older than 40, and it was obvious that Adam had been life extended by the same cell rejuvenation process that Ted had.

"Since that time, Adam has been instrumental in the on-going terra-forming of Tu, and the setting up of colonial cities."

Adam, I'll let you take it from here."

Adam - "Thanks Michael. And thanks for making me feel old!" he said laughing. "Wait, I am old! HA!

Well, it's certainly nice to finally meet you folks and I trust from everything Michael has told me about you that you are both going to be huge assets to the project.

Your initial phase is your basic training after relocation. This training phase is about 30 days. This gives you a basic time frame to get accustomed to the planet, and to begin to learn about Tu, the people, the governing systems, and culture.

We've found that it generally takes a couple of months to start getting comfortable with life there. It's a major adjustment, not just in a slightly higher gravity, a slightly different time cycle for day and night, but culturally as well.

The enormity of the planet itself takes getting used to.

Even the small, practical things you deal with day to day

will take some adjustment. You're going to learn what it is like to live without money, and what it is like to pursue your passions, at the same time giving back into a community lifestyle.

I can't begin to describe the personal satisfaction you will begin to experience. In fact it may take a few months for everything to sink in.

This whole adventure is downright amazing every day, and I think you will find your lives completely enriched on Tu, and what you give back to the community as a whole will give you something so wonderful on the inside that you will really not want to go back to life on Earth, *at least how it is now*.

So, your initial entrance into life on Tu is to be situated in **Arrival Colony One**, on *Ellis Island*.

In fact many of the cities there are nostalgic. There's a New Miami, and a New Dodge City among them. However, as you'll soon find out, the cities on Tu are constructed from the ground up completely different.

There's a high speed tube transport between cities, and local transportation is really walking, biking or they have these small electric scooters and trams you can use for local travel.

Like I mentioned, you will not be allowed to leave Arrival Colony One for the first 30 days. This is for your own good, and like I mentioned before it's going to be an intense learning phase where you do nothing but learn.

You will also be undergoing a detoxification process, and it's completely painless, and is life extending. Your bodies will undergo some changes, and healing, and you will begin to feel better than you ever have, and your thinking will clarify as you detox from Earth.

Keep in mind that Tu has had a human colony now for almost 100 years. There are humans, from Earth who have been living life and raising families there for several decades.

They along with native Tu, Zui-hybrids, The Zui – they are the ones building these ships, and an even larger class of ship affectionately called "*arks*".

The ark ships will hopefully be ready in the next couple of years as the mass migration is ramped up.

We have a couple of them in service already doing some major moves, and we're very happy with how they're handling.

Just so you know, while people on Tu try to keep the differentiation of natives versus new arrivals to a minimum, although it is a fact of life that people do have certain attitudes towards newcomers.

People are really judged about their attitudes towards change, as you begin to learn a more natural way of living, in tune with nature and the cosmos.

The more the Tu learn about Earth, the less they like it. The longer you stay on Tu, the less you will want to come back to Earth. The Tu are eager for Earthers to transition as quickly as possible.

The thinking is so much more on an elevated plane on Tu, and newcomers that hold on to some of the bad habits from Earth tend to be the ones who get into the most trouble.

You will find most of the Tu want to show and tell as much as possible. If you do your best to want to fit in, you will be received with open arms. We've rarely had anyone not fit in. The keyword is *harmony*.

So, you won't hear from me a whole lot during your training phase. But after that, we will be working together and I think the project is going to be rewarding for you both. Just be patient and roll with the punches and you'll see what I'm trying to tell you now.

I'm not at liberty to discuss all of the details of the project until after your training and orientation phase is over, at which time we'll get together and get you started.

Enjoy the trip, it takes a couple of days for us to get to Tu from Earth as we have a couple of stops to make along the way, and that will give you some time to watch a few informational videos and begin to learn about your new home and Tu.

Any questions?"

Bob and Amy both were spell bound.

Adam "Oh – and use the tablet computers you procured before leaving as your project manager.

Keep your notes and questions there, and Melissa can help you as well.

Our email system is coordinated to work with pretty much wherever we're at, and has a sophisticated forwarding system so no matter where I'm at you can generally get a reply back from me inside of a couple of days. She can help you with a lot of mundane stuff as well. And what she can't help you with I'll be happy to help with.

OK – so, that's plenty for now. Enjoy the ride and when we arrive at Tu, Michael here will get you situated with the arrival colony.

By the way, there is a profiler application we need to install that you can use to fill out your food preferences with, and some other stuff, and it will be used to outfit your arrival apartment with food and necessities so you basically arrive and you're moved in within a day you're all set to go into training.

I need to make you folks aware of one other thing. You're on my team, and my team is under special direction of *John Foster*, who you will learn more about later. That means you'll have a bit more access than your typical emigre.

You're job titles will be "Collectors". That gives you some priority access for certain things on the replicators.

Your titles will change yet again after training as we get into the project. Unfortunately, the quarters we provide you in arrival colony will be a bit spartan in nature due to the huge numbers of people expected to be coming in.

Once the main migration phase is started, which we have aptly named *Operation Exodus*, the process for relocation for large groups will be much different, and unfortunately not as personal as what you folks are getting.

It will probably be more chaotic by comparison. The standard arks have less in travel amenities like this ship, and are more utilitarian, to get the job done, not designed for extensive time in space like this one is. The transit time is less than an hour and so the standard arks don't need to have anything other than basics and a medical facility.

Your actual apartment in the city you wind up in is no different than what the majority of the population has.

Governing rules on Tu dictate that there is no ruling class, so housing is built according to need, and most people find the standard 2 bedroom condos there are quite nice. There are also larger units for larger families.

Anyway, enough for now, I imagine we're not to far off from departure.

Again, nice to meet you both. Enjoy the ride!"

Bob - "Thanks so much Adam, I am so excited and grateful to be a part of this whole thing"

Amy -"Thanks Adam and ditto what Bob said!"

With that they headed back to their cabin.

Cloud Nine was positioned over Sydney for the final pickup before departure. As Bob and Amy made their way past the door of the cargo hold, the familiar flash of transporter light illuminated the passageway.

Looking through the windows into the cargo area a crew was hastily unloading a small moving van just like they did with Bob and Amy's van, except that this one had an advertising wrap on it for a Sydney based rental company.

Bob and Amy stopped to watch. One of the crew was standing off the side with a stop watch timing their unload time.

Bob - *"Amazing"*

Amy - "I know"

Within a few moments the van was unloaded and each crew member was jumping off to the side and shouting "Clear!"

As soon as the entire unload team was clear, there was another flash of transport light and the van was gone.

In a few moments, another flash and two people appeared, new recruits like Bob and Amy. There was Ted, welcoming them aboard just as he had with them.

Overhead a soothing female voice was coming out of a loudspeaker of some kind that sounded like it was coming from everywhere, announcing *"Departure in 10 minutes"*

Ted and the two new people from Sydney were coming into the passageway.

Ted - "Hey Bob, Amy, this is *Robin and David Sutter from Sydney.*"

Bob - "Hi nice to meet you!"

Ted - "Well, listen, we're getting ready to *wink out* and on our way in just a few minutes"

Amy - "*Wink out?*"

Ted - "That's what it looks like when we go — we're literally gone in a wink."

Bob - "Do we need to be strapped in or something?"

Ted - "Nope, you won't even feel any kind of acceleration — we just *GO* - it feels no different from standing here.

So enjoy the ride, you may want to watch out the gallery windows though, it is quite fascinating, although once we go, you won't see much until we arrive at wherever we're going."

Bob - "Can you elaborate a bit more about some of the stops we'll be making?"

Ted - "Sorry, can't. Everything for you new recruits is all on a need to know basis. Once you get through your orientation and training you'll get more information about what's happening."

The loudspeaker was alive again with "*Departure in 2 minutes.*"

Ted- "There's the 2 minute warning. Better hurry down to the gallery!"

With that Bob, Amy, Robin and David were all on their way to the gallery to watch the departure from Earth.

Not too long after they were all situated in front of the gallery window, from the ships PA system came the announcement *"Departure"*

They were all standing there, waiting, and suddenly, the view of Earth was reduced to a speck in an instant, and the surrounding space became a white fog.

Amy - "Well that was quick! Can we get a slow motion replay? Ha!"

Bob - *"I don't think we're in Kansas anymore ... amazing"*

Amy whispered quietly in Bob's ear - "I think it's time for some champagne from the replicator thingee in our room!"

Bob - "Ah got it!"

With that they were officially underway to Tu.

This would be the first quiet, romantic time they would have since meeting Michael and having 10 days of crazy time to pack and depart Earth.

Welcome To The Party

It had only taken a few moments for the Cloud Nine to arrive and settle in to an orbit at their first stop, a trading planet called Mayorga several hundred light years from Earth.

There were about 500 relocation guests aboard Cloud Nine, hailing from all over planet Earth.

Bob and Amy's ship phones were buzzing with voice mails with welcome announcements and an invitation to a party in the main lounge in 18 hours, which put the party at about the halfway point in the schedule to Tu.

Time for some much needed shuteye, but with all the excitement, it was hard to sleep. Catnaps were more the order of the day.

They felt less of a need for sleep because of the ships radiant bio-energy field which caused the body to heal and realign itself. Over several months time of exposure to this field, the body would revert to an age of around 30 years old.

Bob and Amy spent the day watching videos in their cabin and enjoying the personal time together, something they hadn't had for several days.

Bob was soaking up information about the planet's geography, the tube transports and colony architecture.

A trip to the gym was more invigorating and seemed to accelerate the bio-energetic healing. They both felt better after one day on board than they had in years.

Finally it was time for the ship's party.

Amy had already availed herself of the replicator to create a beautiful body hugging mini skirt that flattered her athletic shape. Bob had on a nice designer shirt and jeans with a fedora. They were ready to party.

Bob and Amy entered the lounge. Just to the right was a beautiful bar. Behind it stood a beautiful young woman, another android named *Kira* who looked like Melissa's twin sister.

She was wearing a beautiful sheer, nearly see through full length gown that definitely did not hide her beauty.

Amy gouged Bob in the ribs because it was apparent he was a bit *distracted*.

Among the various liquors arranged on shelves behind the bar were also various types of cannabis, as well as various types of glass pipes. A full humidor of cigars and tobacco pipes was available as well.

"Hello, my name is Kira. Welcome to the party. Would you like something to drink or smoke?"

This was going to take getting used to.

There was the pungent aroma of cannabis in the air. There was a nice jazz band playing and the lighting was low like a very nice restaurant.

Bob and Amy made their way into the lounge and scoped the party out a bit.

Beautiful androids were milling about the crowd introducing themselves to the guests.

Ted was talking and joking with that couple from Sydney, and there was Michael talking again with Adam near the stage where the band was playing.

A male android waiter named Paul walked up with a tray of wine in one hand and tray of hors d'oeuvres and offered it to Amy.

Amy - "Oh – thank you".

The male androids were just as much a picture of perfection as the females were. Paul was very attractive. Medium build, tanned skin, with straight long brown hair, braided, almost to his waist, and blue eyes. He could have been Irish, or Scots Irish.

Amy was visibly charmed by Paul and a little intimidated.
Paul - "*At your service, if there's anything you need*"

Bob almost thought that Paul was hitting on Amy. Bob picked up an hors d'oeuvre. "*Thank you*"

Amy grabbed Bob's arm and they moved away from Paul. Paul continued on with his hors d'oeuvres.

Bob was speaking quietly in Amy's ear "*You do know it's 8 am back in Nashville!*"

Amy - "I know, I'm still whacked out on the time of day, but I can't sleep!"

Bob was looking around the room, and found himself a bit transfixed on the female androids - "There's certainly a lot of eye candy here. I think it's really an alien plot! They're going to seduce us with hot androids."

Amy ribbed Bob - "Um, *yeah*!"

They laughed.

Michael spotted them and motioned them to come over and join them.

As they walked towards Michael, Michael motioned the band to stop playing, stepped up onto the small stage and raised his voice - "Can I have everyone's attention please!"

Pausing a moment he announced - "Welcome everyone!" Everyone in the room began to applaud.

Pausing again for a moment to wait for everyone to quiet down, Michael continued:

"We really didn't plan on this party, it was kind of impromptu, and spur of the moment. I know you're all tired, probably feeling a bit dazed and confused about everything, and a bit messed up on what time of day it is. That will pass. You will get your rest, and the best part is that you won't even be hung over!

But for now, *we party*!

Just tell our hosts what you want and it's yours."

Adam - "Exactly. This is a monumental occasion, because even though we have done hundreds of these relocations, over the years, this one is *special!*

This is the largest group we have assembled for a single project. Our teams are usually small, but this one is probably one of the largest I can remember in years. And although I can't get into the details, it is one of our most critical projects.

Take a few minutes to introduce yourselves to the others here, as you will be working with them in the coming months. That's all I have for now - enjoy!

Oh – one other thing – there is a video about the Zui and the governing structures of Tu that we'd like you all to review before we get there, it takes about 20 minutes to watch and will provide you a mental framework with how things are run, please review it in your quarters before we arrive."

With that the lights went back down low, the music was back up and the party resumed.

Bob and Amy made the rounds and met as many people as they could.

After a couple of hours at the party though, the distortion of what time of day it was began to catch up with both of them and it was time to call it a night. With that they said good night to all and headed back to their cabin.

Bob - "I want to check out that video that Adam mentioned about the Zui and the government on Tu."

Amy - "Sounds good, let's make some popcorn."

The Zui

The top governing body on Tu is a 5 member team called simply, **The Top 5**.

The Top 5 are the highest ranking members of the Tu Council Of Governors. The Top 5 are the final deciders, they are the final arbiters of Tu's main issues.

Four of the members are Zui, and called '**The Four**', and only one is an Earth human named **John Foster**.

Two members of The Four are Zui ambassadors direct from the Zui home world, ***Didiza***, in the Andromeda galaxy. Their names are translated loosely as **Old Father** and **Old Mother.**

The other two members are Zui-human hybrids. Their names are loosely translated as Zui Brother, and Zui Sister, as a title, like you might refer to someone in a religious order - *not as relation.*

They are routinely called '***Brother***' *and* '***Sister***' and are mated for life.

Old Father and Old Mother - their names were really rather misleading in English, because when you saw them, they didn't look any older than about 30. However, their true age was somewhere around 2000 years old.

Brother and Sister didn't look any older either, and were probably close to 80 Earth years based upon the time that had passed since Tu was colonized. Another key characteristic was that both males and females had extremely long hair.

They abhorred the cutting of their hair. They admonished humans for cutting their hair as well, because they knew that it kills creativity in humans and limits psychic capabilities and psychic senses, like a kind of antenna system.

(Some asian religions, American Indians and other cultures including some sects of Christianity such as the Nazarenes teach the abstinence of cutting one's hair.)

They really were not concerned with their age or names, but knew that humans needed these kinds of associations for reference points.

Their points of reference were often linked to the terraforming of planets, and how old their own civilization was.

Didiza was thought to be several million years older than Earth, but it was still difficult to get a straight answer from the Zui.

The Zui found pure science uninteresting by itself. For them, it was always about context. They had a tendency to mix motive, reason, science and philosophy.

As advanced as the Zui were, their humility and personalities were always gracious. For them, it did not matter how primitive a culture was, there was always something there for them to learn.

They could be just as comfortable around a camp fire of

primitive peoples dancing a tribal dance, or in a sophisticated night club. For them it was always about learning.

A common thread throughout Zui culture were things that touched on inspiration and creativity.

"Where there is little challenge, there is little creativity"

This is what captivated Miresa, his love of Pink Floyd. He loved the culture and loved exploring their concepts, and it challenged his thinking.

Zui Embassies

There are two Zui embassies on Tu, one at Minora South and the other at New Didiza. Both are beautiful places.

At the New Didiza compound, the architecture blends beautifully with the mountain back drop, and is situated within a short walking distance to a beautiful lake.

Some say it is reminiscent of Tibetan city of Lhasa, but less primitive, with a mix of European minimalism and modernism. Often a Zui transport ship can be seen coming and going, or in a hovering state right over the embassy.

These embassies are their home away from home.

No territorial charters or colonization, towns, cities or encampments are allowed within 2000 km of their embassies. You will see a Zui Exclusion zone around each embassy.

Visiting their compounds is by appointment only.

The psychic and extrasensory abilities of the Zui are amazing and scary to say the least. There is no lying to them as they can read mind and thought.

The Zui had literally evolved over millions of years into not just extremely intelligent beings, but also *extremely sensitive beings*.

The Zui actually suffered pain around 'lower sentients', from *'lower worlds'* as they referred to them.

The emotional and psychic sensitivity of the Zui made it difficult to be around the raw emotional makeup of humans. It was literally painful for them to be around humans.

They had difficulty getting a full grasp of warlike races like Annunaki and the humans.

It wasn't so much about understanding them, it was trying to relate to the negative energies, like hate, sadness, and man's inhumanity to man.

The emotions of both Annunaki and humans were so extreme, and capable of huge amounts of negative energy which literally caused pain to the Zui.

Emotions of anger, deep sadness, loss, and conversely even extreme happiness could upset the Zui and throw them off balance.

Some of the earliest contacts with the Zui caused the Zui so much pain they would suffer nose-bleeds, or bleeding from their ears and eyes.

The Zui would report being extremely exhausted around

humans as well as the Annunaki.

There was a mutual problem for humans as well. The open, exposed aura of the Zui was not hidden. It affected anyone coming to their home world in such a way as to transform them at a deep inner core.

From a human perspective, the Zui were also difficult to be around. Part of being human is precisely the fact that our minds cannot be read amongst other humans.

As such, being around beings as the Zui who can read your mind is not a comfortable experience. It is one thing to communicate telepathically, it is another to have your mind read like an open book.

A very small fraternity of people on Tu had actually visited the Zui home world.

When the Zui first made overt contact with Earth back in the 1940's they brought 1000 scientists and engineers directly from Earth to Tu. Of those first 1000, 50 were taken directly to the Zui home world, Didiza.

Neither humans or the Zui anticipated how emotionally devastating coming to Didiza could be to humans. The psychic energy on is more than most humans can handle.

Whatever internal baggage you have on you when you go to Didiza, the energy of the Zui will expose it. You will be forced to deal with your own imbalance, your internal demons, deep down in your own psyche.

And since a large part of being human is the personal shaping of our own perceptions, often deluding ourselves with false perceptions and outlooks, the shattering of these assumptions, false beliefs, can be devastating.

A visit to Didiza can literally be a bad trip for some people in the same sense taking LSD would for someone not able to comprehend the exposure of their own psychological make up.

Most of the first contactees visiting Didiza suffered emotional and nervous breakdowns and had to be put into special medical facilities back on Tu at the Zui embassy on Tu to recover.

Those affected the most deeply were those who had a less than spiritual outlook on life, science purists, those with a "type A" personality, these more logical types suffered the most, as well as those with low psychic vibrations.

This mutual hypersensitivity to each other gave cause for the Zui perform selective interbreeding with humans to create a race that could act as a bridge for contact and communication. The resulting race became known as *The Zui-human Hybrids*.

Some 50 Zui-human hybrids were born and raised at the Zui embassy at New Didiza.

Two of those hybrids were members of the Top 5. (As previously mentioned their names were loosely translated as Zui Brother, and Zui Sister. They were routinely called *'Brother' and 'Sister'* and were mated for life.)

Their names implied a childlike innocence, but then this reflected the Zui philosophy to always strive for ultra simplicity.

These hybrids formed yet another colony on Tu, and it is located on the southwest coast of New Didiza. *(See the chapter "Continental Structures)*

Additionally, because of the mutual hypersensitivity of humans and Zui, any future visits by humans to Didiza required that visitors spend several days with Zui in one of the Zui embassies on Tu, where their minds could be quieted, and get used to being around the Zui, before going to a planet where the collective energy from the Zui race was generally overwhelming.

The Zui have a human-like form, human-like bodies, but they are so far advanced on the evolutionary scale, their external form is the only similarity. Like humans, they have 2 sexes, male and female.

The Zui said little vocally and communicated primarily through telepathy. They saw themselves evolving towards energy. They molded themselves in every aspect towards that end.

The Zui wore little clothing, and there was an ever present but subtle aura of energy around them, making them seem almost transparent.

Their bodies have a natural fitness in the same way animals on Earth have natural fitness. Humans as a whole require considerable training to become totally fit with a muscular physique, whereas the Zui had a natural fitness without much effort.

They have a blood system like humans but their internal organs are much more highly evolved. The Zui have highly developed self healing capabilities such that they do not suffer death "from natural causes" the way humans do, although they could be killed like humans, such as a stabbing, shooting, weapon or poison of some kind.

They could regrow any part of their body, and legend has it that they could *even regrow their heads.*

They reproduced sexually or the females can reproduce asexually, at will whenever they feel it is time to do so.

A Zui baby grows ten times as fast a human baby, and can live several thousand years. Physical death for the Zui means *transcendence to an energy being.* This was not a faith exercise but could be witnessed and seen with the naked eye at the time of death.

The Zui believed in personal responsibility and self governance. They felt it was an extremely crucial point of personal development for all sentient beings to be personally responsible and self sufficient.

They did not like the idea of leading or herding populations. Their role was primarily that of guidance. It was a simple philosophy of self sufficiency and liberty.

It starts with yourself, your family, your community or village, your town, city, and planet. It affected everything about how they approached life, from their architecture and how their space-craft were built.

Although they are a peaceful race, they have extremely advanced weapons technology to defend when necessary. The use of force for them is *always last resort.*

They have used certain mind control techniques where an attacker turns on themselves and winds up using their own negative energy against themselves.

This made them a formidable foe with other races who did not have this ability, and those that attempted to attack the Zui thinking they were easy prey for their kind nature found out the Zui were not to be trifled with.

The Zui had mastery of full planetary manipulation, terraforming, and harnessing the energy from stars.

They could terraform large planets, with enormously sized terraforming spacecraft, some as large as small planets or moons.

The arrival of one of their large terraforming ships could cause massive gravitational and tidal influences on a planet if they weren't careful.

They would use this capability to alter the orbits of planets they wanted to make habitable, like Tu.

They prided themselves on their craft of taking desolate worlds and building them into habitable worlds, and placing not just their own species on those planets, but it was their mission to take distressed worlds, and desolate planets and fix them.

They had the ability to use stars as energy sources for traveling, and could use the energy from some stars as portals or gateways to other parts of their galaxy or the universe.

They had rarely met other species as advanced as

themselves.

The Zui saw it as their mission to bring their knowledge and wisdom to the *'lower worlds'*.

Many times it was painful, but they felt it was necessary for the advancement of all intelligent species in the universe.

Their missions would benefit the lower worlds, which they believed would in turn give themselves a huge "*karmic boost*", "*paying it forward*".

The Zui philosophy was a delicate balance of sharing and withholding of their advanced knowledge. It wasn't just knowledge, but wisdom. Any sharing must be done according to a very long range plan.

It was a matter of the maturity of the races they were helping along.

This was a highly advanced philosophy. The Zui elders were consumed with philosophy about how to advance inferior species.

There were protocols, methods and procedures which must be followed. There were huge debates about non-interference, at the expense of advancement.

There were huge debates among the Zui elders about natural development and allowing the course of events on a planet to remain off limits unless absolutely necessary.

Monitoring a species or race for hundreds, even thousands of years was common without any involvement.

The process of proper planetary development was something the Zui knew could take hundreds if not thousands of years.

Many of the Zui planets under construction formed the basis of scientific and sociological experiments. All were at various stages of development, some guided, others unguided.

Sometimes the Zui would send one of their own to a planet and try to impart some wisdom.

A Zui ambassador had to learn how not to be affected by 'lower species' so that they could function around them.

The Zui ambassadors on Tu had been through such conditioning, but on Tu, their presence was not masked, theirs was an overt presence on Tu.

Earth and Tu represented one of each kind of experiment. Earth, a covert experiment with minimal guidance, and Tu with open guidance. They had learned almost too late, that mankind, without guidance was doomed.

They knew full well what small incremental changes would have on societies.

On planets where they only had covert involvement in, they would introduce small incremental changes.

This might be by helping a scientist or inventor with a breakthrough discovery. It might be by giving a people the idea they should create a language, an an alphabet.

Each of these incremental steps would be allowed to mature

over time. Sometimes this maturation process would take centuries.

The Seeds of Failure

Ancient Earth-men attempting to understand the grandness of creation, as explained to them by higher beings who, *in a moment of their own mis-guidance, gave mankind a religious interpretation instead of a scientific interpretation.*

Those who had led mankind astray now had to work to redeem mankind.

Earth religions proliferated over thousands of years, with huge gaps in logic. It was this absence of logic, science and guidance that was painfully apparent to the Zui.

In centuries past, the Zui had sent several of their own ambassadors on veiled missions to Earth, such as Aristotle, Pythagoras, Confucius, Gandhi, Buddha, Jesus, Helen Keller, Martin Luther King Jr, Nelson Mandela and others.

They would sometimes pose as shamans in primitive cultures to give themselves a first hand view of a culture and impart wisdom.

The Zui had reached a conclusion that where Earth was concerned, they with all of their veiled influences, they had simply not imparted the correct wisdom. They had simply failed to reach humanity with the proper guidance.

Earth was seen as essentially mentally, spiritually and technologically retarded.

Tu is mankind's place of redemption *as a species*.

The Zui felt their role as fatherly caretakers of mankind was something they owed humankind as a kind of **penance** for the lack of mentoring and guidance the human race had endured on Earth.

Tu is redemption for the Zui as well.

In their own culture, the Zui were also on a quest to find who they called *"The Prime Creator"*. There were stories in Zui lore that related to *The Unseen Ones*, and *The Prime Creator*, but this contact had been lost several millennia ago, and it was their quest, like a knight's quest for the '*holy grail*'.

It wasn't really a religious quest, but a desire to get to the core of the origins of the universe.

The Unseen Ones were a group of sentients several orders of magnitude more advanced than the Zui, and lived in a multidimensional reality that allowed them universal travel, and could appear in various forms, like humans or other races.

The Unseen Ones were the higher guidance of the Zui. They only interacted at a psychic level with the oldest elders of the Zui, so no Zui had ever been in physical contact with them.

Lore had it that *The Unseen Ones* were in direct contact with The Prime Creator. The Unseen Ones could never reveal the location of The Prime Creator, only eluding to his location in metaphors and poetic hints.

They felt that the only real way to fully interact with The Prime Creator was as an energy being, which you would transcend into at the death of the physical body.

Stories passed down through millennia from The Unseen Ones told of how they interacted with the Prime Creator.

Their story of the history of the creation of the universe was tied to The Prime Creator.

The Zui believed The Prime Creator was essentially an immensely powerful energy being who had such intense psychic and mental powers that he could spawn and create at will, and created not just the universe we live in, but other universes as well.

They told of a story that sounded amazingly similar to what many Earth religions refer to as *"creation theory"* and even what Earth scientists refer to as *'the big bang'*.

The biggest unanswered question to the big bang theory or story, was, *who or what started the big bang?*

John Foster of The Five

John Foster was a science and philosophy major on Earth, completing degrees at 3 different universities. He and his wife Anna were among those first 50 to visit the Zui home world of Didiza.

John Foster came back rejuvenated. He was the only human who was able to do so.

The Zui saw that there was something different in this one human.

Because of the way he was able to embrace their home world, John Foster was the only human member of the top of the government on Tu, thus the name "Top-5".

He was specifically chosen by the Zui and Zui-human hybrids to serve as their liaison.

He was able to embrace the moment, the massive love energy and positiveness of the planet Didiza and the Zui in a way none of the other contactees were able to.

Traveling to the Zui home world transformed Foster to a such a degree he could rarely talk about the experience without it bringing tears to his eyes.

For him it was so overwhelmingly positive and mind blowing it was hard for a human mind to comprehend.

Such was not the case for the others. All the rest had come back with massive emotional and mental scars.

While most recovered within a few months upon returning to Tu, some of them took years to recover.

The Zui liked John Foster. *They loved John Foster.* It was symbiotic, he loved them as well, with a deep familial love.

He was the only human thus far that was able to visit Didiza and come back better than before he left. Scientists on Tu were often looking to John as a model for future visits and were constantly analyzing him.

The communication between the Zui and humanity on Tu used a very simple hierarchy.

The Zui-human hybrids – *Brother and Sister* served as liaison to the Zui between John Foster.

If Foster had something he needed to bring to the Zui, he would go to Brother first. If things needed to be taken to a higher authority, then Brother would take it to Old Father.

The Four made themselves scarce, rarely seen, and preferred to keep a distance, and only interacted with John Foster, and from time to time they might interact with senior delegates along with John Foster, from the various territories on the planet, but this was kept to a minimum.

If *The Four* wanted something changed about the way things were done on the planet, it was generally for a good reason.

Old Father would relay the thoughts and intentions of the Zui to Foster through Brother.

Brother would summon Foster to come out to one of the Zui

compounds to meet.

They would have tea, and quiet conversation. He could tolerate Foster better than Old Father, which was the Zui intention to begin with.

They would discuss the planet's situation, and Brother would inform John of any new developments that were happening with the Zui that would affect the planet.

John Foster knew that whatever direction he was being given by the Zui was generally good for the planet and for mankind on the planet.

Sometimes their dictates did not seem to make sense, but time had shown Foster that they were usually right.

Anna Foster

John Foster's wife Anna suffered deep trauma from the trip to Didiza.

Anna was a highly intelligent astrophysicist, an extremely logical scientist. Her super scientific nature contrasted John's boy-like innocence.

He was a bit of a *"Peter Panner"* as some would say. She drew from this. It helped to offset her super-serious scientific nature.

He was the only man she ever met who could make her laugh. Probably because he loved her tough nature and the quest for pure scientific truth.

The visit to Didiza devastated Anna Foster, and it initially left her in a sort of waking depression. For her, pure science was the essence of everything she believed.

Anna regarded spiritual concepts, psychic energy – it was all pseudoscience, *"just so much horseshit"*. The visit caused an internal crash of her inner psyche.

While it may have seemed strange to stay at the Zui embassy compound, the Zui-hybrids were actually better equipped to deal with the trauma that humans had suffered by their visit to Didiza. With the help of the Zui-human hybrids, she was able to gradually recover her sense of self.

She was having to re-learn what life was really all about. *"Damn the science-fiction, damn the pseudo-science".*

She was learning that science doesn't always explain some of the bigger mysteries of life.

John would endure emotionally painful visits to see her from time to time. Their relationship as husband and wife had suffered as a result of the visit to Didiza.

Although John still loved her, he often wondered if they would ever have what they had before the trip to Didiza.

He hoped that she would one day be able to come back to arrival colony to live with her.

The Failure Of Self Guidance

Tu was meant to be a guided planet, not a self guided planet.

Earth had already proven that humanity was not mature enough to handle self guidance.

Without a sane, wise, *higher authority*, real or imagined, mankind successfully proved self guidance would fail.

As the concept of an imaginary "higher authority" in a "*God*" or *gods* has begun to disappear from Earth, there has been a rise of **self guidance**.

Perhaps the term **misguidance** better describes it.

If your source of truth has a flaw in it, then your truth is not *clean*.

The logical outcomes produced by flawed truth result in an exposure of what was previously assumed to be truth as a *failed truth*, or even a *lie*.

There may have been good intent in these failed truths, but the end result was a failure.

A simple comparison would be a mathematical formula with a flaw that is not apparent until the formula is extrapolated.

The age-old question remains, "*what is truth?*"

There will always be atheists and agnostics, but the majority of the humans on planet Earth hold to some kind of supernatural belief system.

In times past, religion controlled the masses with guidance about right and wrong, providing a basic moral code. Mixing truth with fables, superstitions, rituals and magic.

Society would point to The Bible, The Quran or some holy writ as a final determinate source of 'real truth' and final arbiter of life and death issues.

Laws were enacted based upon these supposed *holy writings*.

The original intent was always good. Judeo-Christian teachings like The Ten Commandments, the teachings of Jesus to love one another and other faiths like Buddhism.

There has been an age-old quest on Earth for higher wisdom descending from a flawless source of truth.

A *"holy" truth* – and coming from a *god* or enlightened individual meant the truth was of the highest quality. Anything originating in mankind was *suspect*.

Entrusting these truths to religious professionals has generally seemed like a good idea. Let people who are dedicated to the task of understanding holy documents, writings and doctrines and the accompanying rituals – let these people be the keepers of the truth.

When in doubt, seek a shaman, a priest, a pastor, imam or rabbi. They will help you understand "God's will".

Unfortunately, mankind has endured thousands of years of religious manipulation at the hands of priests, monks, rabbis, imams, shamans, witches, pastors and all manner of religious professionals.

All of them have been using their self proclaimed expertise on spiritual matters, their expertise at interpreting so-called holy truths to coerce humanity to tow the line or risk eternal damnation. Believe it or some negative consequence will occur, like you will die, and die you will not just in this life but the afterlife. Obey or die.

The concept of the eternal nature of the human soul or spirit within a man has been a core theme in all of mankind's' religions.

If you can successfully threaten the eternal soul of a man with eternal damnation, you effectively rule that man by fear.

Even highly intelligent scientists can be manipulated with religion. Smart, intelligent people are trained to compartmentalize the flawed logic of religious systems away from science and logic. They are taught that they can believe two conflicting lines of reasoning.

They can entertain both religion and science as 'valid' *even though there might be serious problems with the logic and non-existent proofs in the religion they might adhere to.*

In times past, the combination of religion intertwined with government kept things in line. Often one manipulating the other or both playing each other for nefarious reasons.

The better elements of religion, things like caring for one

another, love, and "paying it forward" have generally taken a back seat to the manipulation.

In time, as people have become wise to the game, and begin to "lose their religion", *self guidance* has begun to rule the day.

The growth of self guidance not so much in an overt way, but as an evolutionary **creeping rot** into the minds of the masses.

Morality and ethics becomes situational, and subject to self interpretation. Self guidance based upon flawed logic has begun to dominate society at large.

New age religions that teach that the universe itself is the source of life and that you can tap into this source like a giant vending machine.

The minority of smart humans sense that something is wrong, but it is too late to change it. Outnumbered, they have little chance of changing the status quo.

Mankind needs sound advice to run its affairs, without it, mankind it is doomed to fail and self destruct.

The only advice mankind has been getting is flawed, and it is leading to disaster.

This is why the Zui knew they needed to intervene.

The Governance of Tu

National governments on Earth were developed to manage and protect resources as well as establishing territories, and management of the people with laws and politicians.

As nations on Earth developed, the life of a nation was tied to trade, which fueled its economy, and the economies of the world, some doing better than others. All tied to resources.

Having a piece of ground you can control, and its resources means you can manage scarcity or abundance of those resources. With this kind of control, you can manage populations of people.

The concept that the humans within a nations' borders are also part of its resources is antiquated but enforced on Earth.

On Earth, mankind is always being manipulated by scarcity or *false scarcity*.

On Tu, the problems of scarcity, lack, poverty, monetary systems – these are non-existent.

There really isn't much need for a government in the same sense as you would find on Earth. No borders, no need to wage war for gold, or oil. No scarcity, no need for greed. No need to worry about controlling immigration or emigration to manage labor pools.

Tu is run by a *geniocracy* at the top. A geniocracy is a

society run by the smartest and brightest who make governing decisions for the good of the people, not based upon political parties or the interests of a few who can buy influence.

There are no idiots in government making dumb decisions. Idiots in government is contrary to the Zui philosophy.

Tu's fundamental governmental structure is based upon the principle of **sound guidance**.

The governing structures are simple. The Zui are the keepers of the *protectorate* of the planet.

The top governing body on Tu is a 5 member team called simply, **The Top 5**.

The Top 5 are the highest ranking members of the Tu Council Of Governors. The Top 5 are the final deciders, they are the final arbiters of Tu's main issues.

Four of the members are Zui, and called '**The Four**', and only one is an Earth human named **John Foster**.

Two members of The Four are Zui ambassadors direct from the Zui home world, **Didiza**, in the Andromeda galaxy. Their names are translated loosely as **Old Father** and **Old Mother.**

The other two members are Zui-human hybrids. Their names are loosely translated as Zui Brother, and Zui Sister. They are routinely called '**Brother**' *and* '**Sister**' and are mated for life.

For the Zui, and the native Tu, *the idea of a singular*

planetary government is unsettling.

All parties agree that some kind of organizing structures needed to be in place.

The Four insisted when Earth began to make contact and start colonizing, that the government of Tu **not** include a federal government in the same sense as what you would find on Earth.

There was too much opportunity for corruption. They saw every governmental model on Earth as flawed, playing into special interests and leaving the population out of the grander picture.

The human immigrants from Nibiru were also wary of any kind of singular, federal government and felt that if this happened, they would be in danger of being enslaved again. The memory of the Annunaki home world was never far from their minds.

But all parties agree that *some sort of unifying* **administrative structure** *is needed.*

Zui concepts of true freedom are in stark contrast to Earth's.

On Earth, legal systems, constitutions, congresses, parliaments were *"granting rights"* and limited freedoms that the Zui saw as *"un-grantable"*. You don't grant an inherent right, it isn't for governments to grant.

It was a mockery to their sense of self determination.

The Zui concluded that Earthers were amateurs where liberty and rights were concerned.

For the Zui, rights are not granted, they come from mere existence as a sentient being. *This was something granted by The Prime Creator* - personal rights of freedom were **non-negotiable.**

However, they could see that this was a concept that only worked well if the minds of the people could comprehend it in a mature fashion. Mankind was still too immature to be able to embrace this fully. *The tendency was generally towards corruption.*

The Zui knew mankind was a long ways off in its evolution towards really understanding what the Zui had already known for thousands of years.

If rights have to be stated in human writs and constitutions, *then so be it*, but it seemed so primitive to have to legalize it in a governmental system.

All parties decided that **The Tu Planetary Constitution** was an ***assurance*** *of human rights*, which specifies a legal framework for planet-wide laws, and provides a military protection treaty for the planet between the Zui, native Tu and Earth.

There is also the fact that the Zui just don't find running a government ***interesting.***

They would rather see sentient beings evolve to manage themselves.

The real desire of the Zui was that their relationship to the planet be that of sound mentor, to provide sound guidance, and protect against external enemies. If mankind needed a governmental structure, *keep it to a minimum.*

Tu is a planet without scarcity, there is no economy to worry about, no poor people to feed, no taxation of income. No need to worry about the 'redistribution of wealth'. These concepts are antiquated and meaningless. The role then of the government on Tu is **minimal**.

The role of the minimalist government on Tu is to:

- provide a basic, ultra-simple legal framework
- build towns and cities and colonies
- setup and maintain infrastructures
- manage mass transit systems (local and global)
- provide sustainable energy systems
- provide and support sustainable food systems
- assist science & medicine
- assist scientific research
- assist nature and conservation (planetary conservation)
- setup and maintain an educational system
- maintain the replication library
- provide technology to the people
- defend the planet.

None of Earth's classifications of government such as "left", "right", "liberal", "conservative", "communist", "anarchist", "fascist", "capitalist", "socialist", "republican", "democratic" and any other concepts - *none of these have any meaning on Tu.*

Tu Council Of Governors

Next in line of governmental 'authority' is the Tu Council Of Governors who report to the Top 5.

The Tu Planetary Constitution provides for the establishment of the Tu Council Of Governors.

On Tu, the territories only exist to provide a reference point to a locale on the planet.

Someone who serves as a governor of a territory is a member of the Council of Governors.

A governor is essentially a senior administrator.

They aren't satraps or mini-kings. They don't decide life or death issues of any citizen. Those issues are handled through the legal framework and the constitution.

A governor's role and duties are about logistics, communications, and infrastructures.

Tu's governing structures are for taking care of localized resource management and land management. **Running the structures, not the people. The people run themselves.**

On Tu, the only borders are oceans of water that form natural borders.

There are no borders to enforce. No visas, no passports. No immigration issues.

No migrant workers looking for a better economy.

No wars or depression forcing people to become refugees.

The reality is that it is all really quite boring. There just isn't a whole lot of 'governing' to do – *in an Earth sense.*

Territorial governors run the residential management systems and colony infrastructures. Deciding land claims for homesteads, ranches, farms, compounds, towns and cities.

At the lowest level, it comes down to housing assignments in the colonies – which is really more logistics than anything else.

You want to move from one colony to another, then housing logistics will help you find your next home. Housing logistics keeps track of residential issues and will let you know if a home is available in the area you want to move to.

You might have to wait if an area is already at peak population for someone to move out of that area.

The planet's immense size means that there is really no reason for localities to become overcrowded.

Where you live isn't tied to economics or where you were born, and what national citizenship you got through a birthright, it's about *availability*.

If nothing is available in a specific area, then something close by might be available, and if necessary a new home can be installed.

If enough people started moving into an area then it might behoove the territorial manager to setup a new colony structure to accommodate growth.

As large as Tu is, the abundance of great places to live means that everyone can live in a beautiful area.

For example, if you want to start a ranch or farm, then you'll need to pass that through the governor's office in that territory.

They'll do their best to let it happen if you can show you will manage it correctly, and if it won't cause an issue with the local ecology. It may be that there are reasons you might have to build that ranch or farm in a different part of the territory or continent.

Maybe there's an ecological or biological conflict in the area you want to run a ranch. Maybe there's a species conflict. The governor's office will approve or disapprove your charter for that farm or ranch.

The best part about the Tu's overall governing structures is that they are designed to keep day to day interference out of the lives of people.

Personal Citizenship On Tu

Personal citizenship on Tu carries with it personal responsibility. There is a **social contract** in place that every citizen is taught to keep in mind.

First, *The Zui Protectorate* on Tu provides a stable place for mankind to live and grow.

This includes amazing technology, the basic needs of food, clothing and shelter, as well as mass transit systems - *all provided freely*.

It is provided using the most advanced technologies and methods possible – above and beyond anything mankind has had available in its entire history.

A planet-wide constitution is in place that assures basic human rights and protections.

The response, the reciprocation then, by humanity is that you value life, respect the people, your place, your locale, and your planet.

If you devalue it, you place your privilege in jeopardy and can be subject to *removal* from it.

This radical stance, that living on this beautiful planet was a privilege, something you valued to the extent that if you didn't value life, the people, the planet, and engaged in negative behaviors, you could lose it.

No one is trapped on Tu. Until the Zui arrived, everyone

was trapped on Earth, and subject to whatever madness prevailed with no escape.

So on Tu, the game has changed. You can literally be relocated to another planet for *rehabilitation*.

Criminal behavior of a severe enough nature can literally get you removed from the planet permanently. (See the section on Crime and Punishment)

The Zui saw Earth-type legal systems as generally flawed, and over-developed to the extent that a citizen was generally in danger of violating some law and placing themselves into some kind of legal jeopardy without too much effort.

So, on Tu, no victim, no crime. The legal framework on Tu is always being refined towards this kind of simplicity.

On Tu, a person's identity is only connected and related to the things they need it to be connected to. You are a human, you live on the planet.

You have no social security number, or pension number, or bank account number. (There are no banks on Tu)

There's no birth certificate because birth certificates really only matter when you have states and borders. Your life and death and family genealogy is only recorded only for historical and statistical purposes.

All you really need on Tu is just a phone number, and email address. And you only need give that out to those you want to. Street addresses are optional for those who need them.

All of your personal data is managed at the Replication Library in a special Personal Data Division. Personal data is considered *sacred and inviolate.*

You can setup your own email and social profiles similar to the commercial systems on Earth, but on Tu these systems are built with safeguards against privacy violation. *There's no one to market your data to.*

Since all *needs* are met, there isn't any need for marketing and advertising. On Tu, your life is free from the clutter of advertising.

You will see public service announcements and information on the global television networks and internet, but you won't see ads. No need for ads to support the networks, because *there's no cost.*

No one is going to tell you how to think or limit your free speech.

No invading army is going to come and try to rule you.

You can live off the land, in your own space, and be left alone.

No one is going to tax you or try to take your land away.

No corporation is going to take resources from your land through some trickery with "land rights", for resources under your land. (And you cannot just go squat some residence or land claim and bump someone else out.)

You are free as long as your freedom does not infringe on the freedom of others.

You are free to live your life and build your world, as long as it does not involve harm to anyone, infringe on their rights, rape the ecology, poison natural resources or harming wilderness areas and wildlife.

Tu represents a place where people do not have a single reason for criminal behavior to satisfy some need.

(However, every citizen is encouraged to keep hand guns, rifles and portable particle beam weapons in their homes. This is done not so much for personal safety but again for protection from hostile alien invasions.)

As a fully empowered human, you now have the time, the place and the tools to become the best YOU that you can be.

If you're creative, and you want to design home furnishings, or clothing styles you can submit your designs into the Replication Library and allow others to replicate your designs.

If you're an inventor, you can submit your inventions into the Replication Library for others to replicate and use and improve upon. This enables not just downloading some plans and diagrams, but literally downloading the invention itself, and then being able to work on a copy, improve upon it, test it, and then re-share your improved version back into the collaborative pool.

Perhaps you are good with crafts, ceramics, glass, wood or metal working – the things you make can be uploaded into the Replication Library as well.

There's no limit to the ways in which you can share your

creativity. Now you have the chance to be all you can be.

One additional benefit the Zui brought to humanity is that mankind is no longer trapped on Earth, or Tu.

You can apply for relocation to other human compatible planets within the Zui sphere of influence.

You can apply to become part of explorations to other galaxies, throughout the known star charts of the Zui.

The pressure valve has been released, mankind can truly travel the stars, thanks to the Zui.

On The Formation of Localities

Although people can be as mobile as they want, and move to any location on the planet they wish, there will always be those who want to establish roots in specific locations for their families.

There are colonies of people with similar beliefs, such as Buddhists, Christians, Muslims, or Quakers, polygamists, nudists, and a myriad of special interests, and old Earth based cultural colonies based upon *common language*.

A group of friends or like minded people who want to create their own locality, town or city can start one. Apply at the Governor's office. Chances are you will be approved. Abuse the privilege, you will lose it.

The council of governors is there to provide as much assistance as needed when a sub-territory, town or city is created.

Any sub-territory can be formed or chartered, by any body of settlers or colonists. Apply at the Governor's office in the territory you want to do this.

If you form a locality, like a town or city, there is the planet-wide core constitution that has to be adhered to, which always outranks any local laws, with basic moral and ethical standards. You can't just make up your own laws to create a small fiefdom.

That's because while it is lawful to start a farm, build a house, create your own compound, town or even your own city, none of it is allowed to conflict with the global constitution or be based upon some kind of negative principles.

You'll still be under the planetary constitution and legal framework, although you will become it's first administrator, like a mayor.

You can't make up a name for your town that is linked to negative energy or connotations.

If you decided to create your own little army and run amok, you will be shut down. You can't enact laws that hurt others, such as sex slavery, bestiality, child porn, and all manner of inhumanity.

Barbarism enshrined in religious traditions is not allowed. (No Sharia Law, no Spanish Inquisition, no Satanic sacrifices, no Vampirism, bloodletting, etc.)

That means if your clan, your compound, town or city is found to be doing inhumane things behind its walls or boundaries, you will be shut down and dismantled, and you could be subject to *removal* from the planet for rehabilitation. Keep in mind the social contract.

Keep in mind, *Tu is a guided planet, not a free-for-all wild zone* where you can run amok.

A charter also means the inclusion of the global educational system. This means teaching of a minimum of 2 Earth languages and the native Tu language.

Most schools opt for English and Spanish as a single language. Throughout the colonization of Tu, English and

Spanish are predominate among the humans. The native Tu can usually speak any of the three languages. Math, science, art and critical thinking skills are the main courses.

The Prime Defenders

Once a charter has been established for a locality the Tu will assign a staff of android Prime Defenders to that locality.

Prime Defenders are programmed to uphold the constitution, and use non-lethal force unless absolutely necessary.

Because they are androids, they do not become emotionally invested in any situation, and their first priority is to de-escalate all situations to a calm state. They have no ego, and cannot be offended.

Their prime orders are to protect and serve humanity, and they are unable to violate the planet's constitution. They have a full recall of all of the planet's laws.

They can't be bribed, and have no opinions about people. They aren't bigoted and are quite capable of speaking multiple languages.

This enables every locality, town, city, colony etc. to have an ample team of first responders, like policemen, but who can protect against crime, but also fight fires, and manage natural disasters and to do the work of forest rangers.

They are equipped with a number of non-lethal tools, one of which is a stasis tool to immobilize a criminal until they can be arrested and booked for whatever charge is being considered.

The Tu also felt that it was necessary to have the androids manage and maintain armories and hidden weapons caches throughout the planet. All of this was based upon a deep seated paranoia about an Annunaki invasion.

The Tu felt it was better to be prepared than to ever suffer from domination either from a tyrannical government or another species.

On Crime and Punishment

For the Zui, there is positive energy, vs. negative energy. Negative energy is always suppressed or dissipated, and positive energy is unsuppressed, and encouraged.

The Zui believe that mankind's negative side can be *minimized*.

Eliminating *need* goes a long way to eliminating much of the negative behavior in humanity.

Most of the crimes of humanity are caused by *scarcity* and *lack*. Fighting wars over resources. Stealing someone's new tennis shoes. Shoplifting. Hijacking oil tankers.

When you create a world where scarcity is eliminated, then what is there left to be a criminal for?

Perhaps domestic disputes, crimes of passion, psychotic crimes. But this comes from lower ways of negative thinking and interacting.

The Zui believed that man could evolve upwards away from these lower ways of thinking. For them it is about providing a new gold standard, **a new guidance.**

Recognizing that humans were extremely sensitive to the energies on Didiza and around the Zui meant that this sensitivity could be used to heal the mind, to literally shake up a person's inner psyche to such an extent that they could be truly rehabilitated.

Criminal acts are dealt with in a decidedly un-Earth-like

fashion. For the Zui, it really is about *rehabilitation*.
The Zui consider Earth-type rehabilitation programs a joke.

Warehousing criminals in prisons is seen as highly ineffective and illogical to the Zui. Prisons make the assumption that negative human behavior is unchangeable.

The Zui feel differently and because they know they can bring **positive transformative change** to a negative soul, they enroll criminals into *rehabilitation*.

Often this rehabilitation mean removal from Tu into a rehabilitation home on another planet, with the possibility of return once completed.

The Zui use a kind of *"soul therapy"*, and deep psychiatric healing. Getting to the core of the problem is their first concern, not just treating the symptoms.

As such, Tu has an almost non-existent crime rate. (*This might not be the case when 7 - 8 billion people are relocated to Tu. Some of mankind's worst may see it as an opportunity to start a new life of crime on a new planet.*)

Those without conscience, *without humanity* will simply be *removed* from humanity.

They would simply remove them from the planet for healing, and if necessary permanent relocation to other planets where they could be rehabilitated long term.

Such rehabilitation might require total isolation, especially with people who had lived a life of crime, or those whose minds had been brainwashed in prisons.

Intellectual Evolution

Since the need for menial jobs was reduced to a tiny fraction of the population, this meant mankind was free to pursue non-work or non-labor related endeavors.

This also meant that the orientation of newcomers must include a sort of "career counseling".

New arrivals not only have access to the **replication library**, but to the **human resources library**.

The human resources library gives them access to online guidance and counseling, and help you to figure out what your real purpose in life could be.

The human resources library teams on Tu had worked for years setting up automated, online interview and evaluation systems that anyone could tap into for information.

People who formerly led a day to day life of just existing at menial low paying jobs purely for survival, no longer have to work menial jobs just to survive.

The idea that a career path in life meant climbing the ladder at a fast food restaurant, or working in a convenience store, or working in some retail job that barely gave them enough to live on, much less to really succeed in life was about to become a laughable part of human history.

With replication technology, even the simplest of humans could feed and clothe themselves and be freed up to do something more useful. *The higher pursuits in life.*

For them, the Zui were there to help. They saw it as their mission to help them, to rehabilitate them, guiding them into finding out who they were supposed to be.

Mankind was seen as vastly under-developed as a species, but capable of so much more than what it was.

A majority of humanity would be *going back to school*.

The Tu had established a planet-wide university system that enabled anyone to pursue their education. All that was required was a desire to learn. You could study online over the planet's internet, or attend real classes in the university network.

The additional benefit of life extension technology from the Zui meant that people who were looking at the end of their lives would literally be granted a second chance at life.

As their bodies healed, inside of a few months they would literally be younger, healthier and more able to pursue a second shot at life.

Mankinds' new role as a highly intellectual and critically thinking species would replace its old role of mindless labor, and consumption.

With billions of habitable planets in just the Milky Way Galaxy alone, there was now a new opportunity for mankind to travel the stars and explore.

Utilizing the advanced space travel offered freely by the Zui, just about anyone who wants to can become a space traveler and explorer.

This is something much more fulfilling than working for minimum wage at a convenience store.

8 billion human astronauts is barely enough to even get started exploring the vastness of the universe.

Overcrowding? Overpopulation?

Continental Structures

The immense size of Tu as a 'super Earth' at 5 times the size of Earth takes some getting used to.

Dwarfing Earth's continents, Tu could easily house the entirety of the human race on one or two of its continents.

One has to keep in mind that the naming of the continents was done by scientists. Sometimes, the names make sense, as in 'gigantic', and major and minor. Sometimes they are just made up names as you would find on Earth.

To enable quick access to any point on the globe, (outside of using their spacecraft) the Zui had built a network of underground tunnels that enabled the implementation of a **tube transport system.**

Similar to a train system, but not using rails the tube transports could travel well over 3000mph. This meant you can traverse the entire planet below ground at high speed. The only thing faster would be a jump ship.

Tube stations were strategically located at numerous colonies throughout the planet enabled anyone to enter and exit from the surface, and travel in comfort below ground.

Typical tube tunnels were situated anywhere from a half mile to a mile underground, but some of the main arterial tunnels under Tu's oceans were sometimes as much as 50 miles deep under ocean bedrock.

A tube transport is essentially a spacecraft-like container with its own power, propulsion and life support system, that flies at high speed through the tunnel system.

This also enabled the Zui to setup colonies with plenty of room between them. Most would have several hundred mile distances between them enabling a good mix of urbanization and plenty of room for nature.

Tired of living in a colony in the north? You want to go south for a while? What would you need in order to move?

At most all you would need to pack would be a few personal items in a small backpack. Like a camera and a smart phone. Everything else you can get along the way from any replicator. Get aboard a tube transport and go.

Note – the straight lines shown in the following maps represent tube transport routes.

Minor Continents

Tu's four largest continents are Minora, New Didiza, The Southern Territory, and Gargantua. Smaller minor continents are Ellis Island, Aquatica and Mayorga. The polar regions are similar to Earth, with some mixture of land mass and ice.

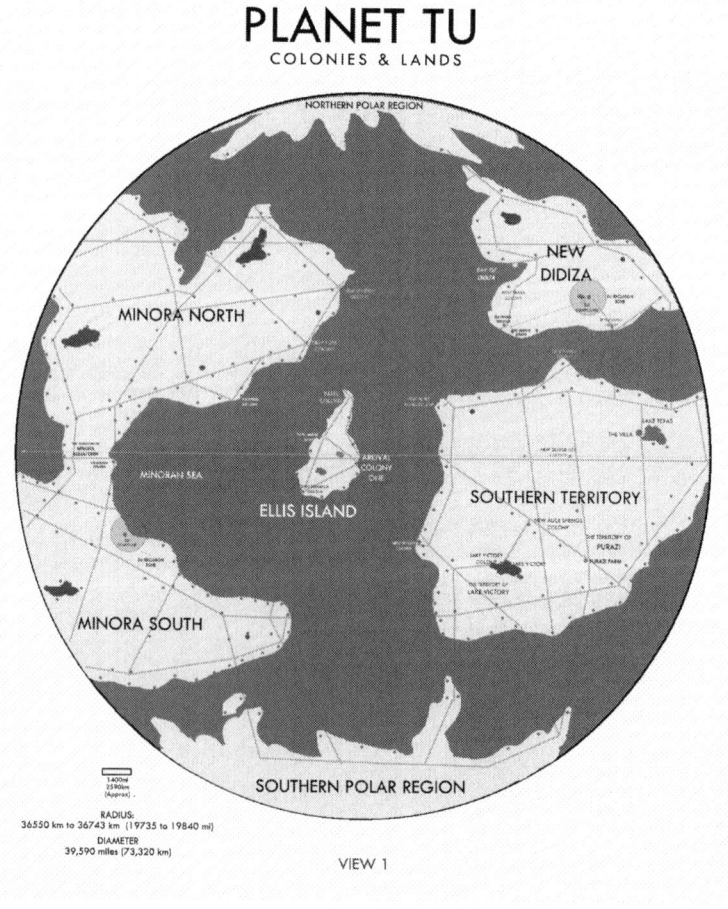

Minora

Opposite from Gargantua is *Minora*. Minora is essentially two continents, Minora North and Minora South.

They are connected by a smaller land mass in the middle, much like the way South America connects to North America. The big difference is that neither end of this continental mass has a full reach to the poles.

Ellis Island

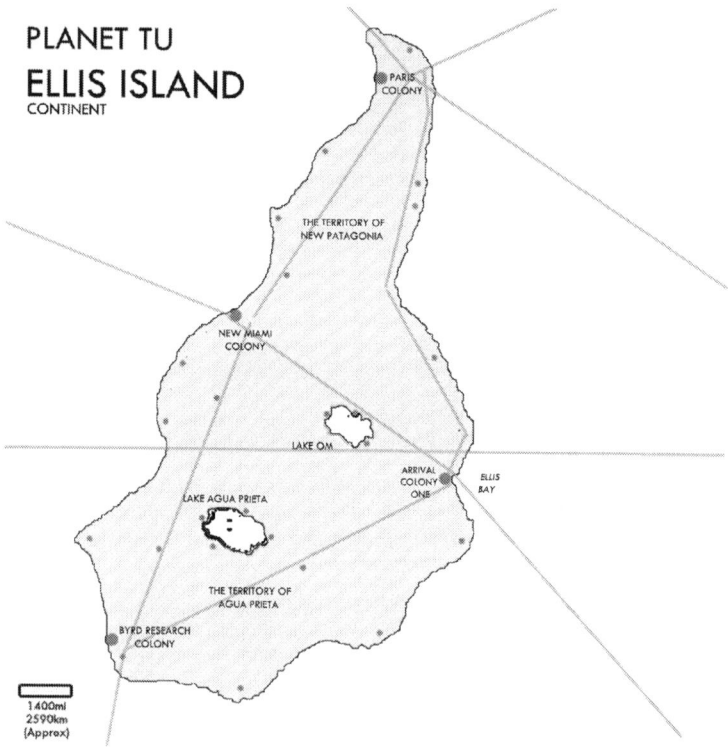

In the middle of the ocean between Minora and The Southern Territory situated right at the equator is the continent of **Ellis Island**, named in honor of the famed immigration station and island near Earth's New York City.

This is where the **Arrival Colony One** is located. On Earth, Tu's Ellis Island would compare to be about the size of South America. Ellis Island Arrival Colony One is also where *The Tu Council of Governors* is located.

Southern Territory

West of Gargantua, separated by the ocean *Oceana Gargantua*, is the continent named **Southern Territory**.

The Southern Territory has two of Tu's largest fresh water lakes that are more like inland oceans, like the Great Lakes are in North America, with a river system that leads to the ocean in the north, like Egypt.

The Southern Territory is also home to *The Villa* at Lake Texas, a large resort colony in the foothills of a large mountain range just west of the resort.

In the southern part part of the continent sits Lake Victory, a huge fresh water lake.

Lake Victory is yet another favorite place for fishing and various water sports such as boating and sailing. Several resort colonies at Lake Victory have become favored destinations for anyone living on Tu.

An interesting feature of the Southern Territory is that the west coast resembles the side profile of a person.

The Southern Territory is home to Purazi Farm, a huge farming operation originally set up mono-culture style to provide food to Arrival Colony One. Using farming techniques from Earth's 1950's through the 1970's, Purazi Farm produced massive amounts of food.

The huge surpluses enabled the Tu and the Zui to trade it with several other planets.

Over the years, the Zui saw to it that Purazi Farm was transformed into smaller organic farms with smaller teams running multiple small farms instead of one giant farm.

The location was ideal, in a temperate zone, such that there is an amazing variety of food that was produced there.

Even though one could replicate food, organic naturally grown food was always preferred. The Zui felt that technological advances should always augment, not necessarily supplant organic systems.

The Southern Territory's west coast beaches are the home to surfers and beach bums alike. Several resort colonies line the coast as well, and a huge wine producing area was started on the north coast, at the New Madrid colony. Close to New Madrid is *Knucklehead Beach* which has an annual surfing competition.

In the heart of the continent at New Alice Springs is a replication facility and technical center, with a huge college that produces online educational content for the entire planet.

New Didiza

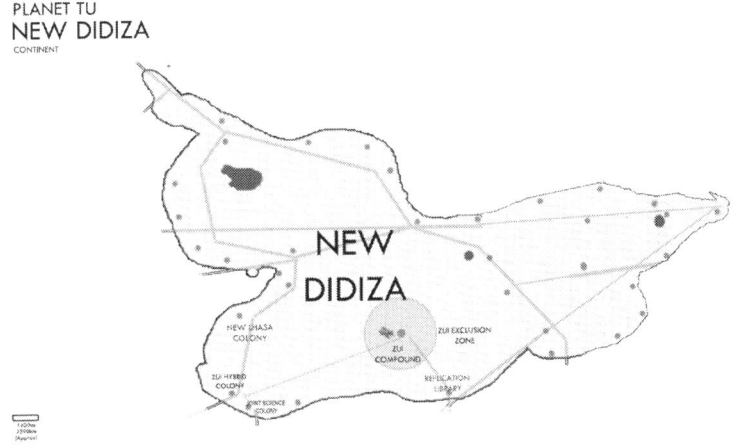

In the northern portion of the same hemisphere as the Southern Territory was the continent of New Didiza.

New Didiza was so named after the Zui home world of Didiza and because it was primarily reserved for the Zui and the Zui-hybrids.

This was also the location of the Replication Library near the southern coast, as well as the largest replication facilities on the planet. The Replication Library itself is housed some 10 miles underground in a special, shielded chamber. It floats in a special anti-gravity container that keeps it safe from quakes.

An exclusion zone of about 1000 miles surrounds the Zui compound on New Didiza. There is limited tube transport access to the Zui compound as well, and direct tube transport access to the Replication Library.

Gargantua

Gargantua covers nearly a third of the planet, and has several large rivers. There are 2 large rivers running from west to east in the northern half, and 3 very large rivers running north and south.

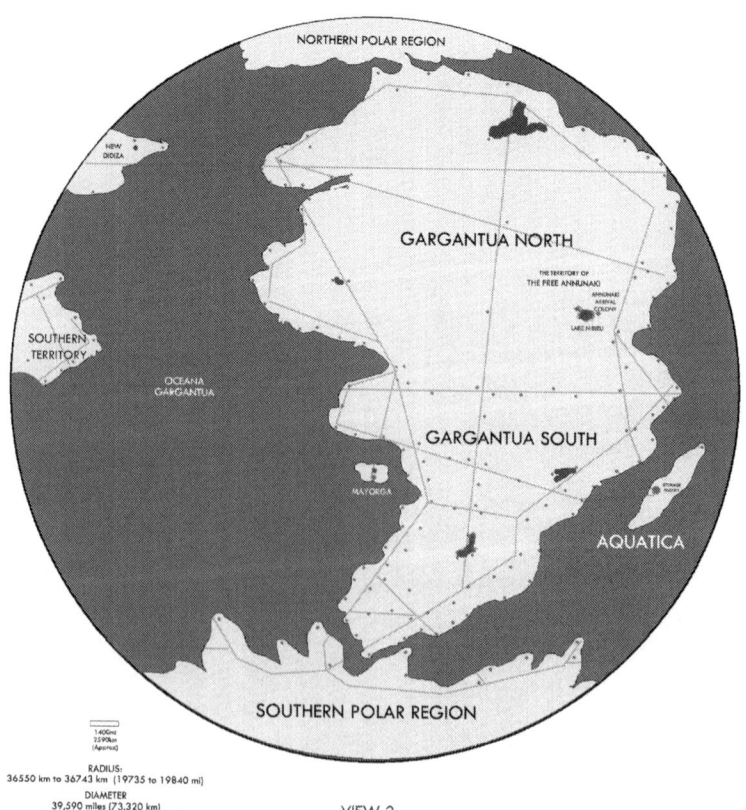

One north/south river runs from a great lakes region in the northern hemisphere on down below the equator into the southern portion of Tu Gargantua, almost to the southern pole and is named *River Gargantua*.

Below the equator, in the southern half of Tu Gargantua, there is one large river running west to east merging into River Gargantua.

Just off the east coast of Gargantua South is an island continent known as Aquatica.

Aquatica is being used by collection teams for storage. A massive underground storage facility was built to house the enormous amount of material coming from Earth.

All of it needs to be catalogued. Some of it is being scanned into the replication library for planet-wide use.

Three other large continents make up the remaining surface area of Tu, separated by oceans.

Arrival

Bob and Amy's phones were both buzzing with alerts. The latest news was that the ship was ahead of schedule after canceling 2 full days of other stops and would be arriving in a couple of hours at Tu.

Cloud Nine had settled into an orbit around Tu's larger habitable moon, **Tu Ono.**

Time to rise and shine.

Both Bob and Amy awoke feeling great, because of the ships' own internal rejuvenation system, they weren't even hung over from the party.

Michael had sent both an email about the arrival process, and they would all meet at the cargo bay in just a couple of hours.

Bob - *"Let's see if this thing can make coffee ..."*

The replicator, hearing Bob's question answered back *"Prepare coffee?"*

Bob - "Yes"

Replicator - "Quantity?"

Bob - "Dark roast, in a French press, 2 separate mugs, with a side of half-and-half, and a side of sugar in a bowl, with 2 spoons"

Within the replicator there was a flash of light, not unlike the transporter, and a bell sounded that it was finished. Bob opened what looked like a microwave door and inside was a French press, 2 mugs, 2 spoons, creamer and sugar.

Amy - "I see you've become quite the replicator expert"

Bob - "Yeah but it's all *point and click* as they say".

They enjoyed the coffee, got ready to go meet Michael down in the cargo bay.

Entering the cargo bay, they noticed all the other team members were also assembling there as well.

From the large windows in the cargo bay, the view of **Tu Ono** was spectacular.

Tu could be seen in the distance. It was reminiscent of photos of Earth from Earth's moon.

Michael - "Bob, Amy – what's your time of day?"

Bob - "About 9am for us Michael! Just had coffee and looking forward to the day"

Michael - "We'll be landing at the arrival colony very soon, but it's around 9pm their time. It'll take you a couple of days to get your internal clocks straightened out. Not unlike jet lag back on Earth.

We should be touching down in the next half hour. You may want to wander down to the gallery again to watch.

For a short time. we will be sitting just outside of **Tu Ono** –

the habitable of its two moons and wait for clearance to land."

For Bob, it seemed like everyone was always repeating things. Almost like a museum tour where you hear the same information over and over.

Michael continued - "Standard procedure, the Tu want to make sure we we were not followed, and they want to make sure no one else is sitting in orbit around Tu to cause problems. "

Bob - "I just have all this anticipation going on, another new day of unusual surprises and getting used to this whole new world, honestly, I am having problems focusing – it's all just so overwhelming."

Michael - "You'll adapt just fine Bob. Just think back to a couple of weeks ago – none of this even existed for you. Such it is for the majority of the population of Earth.

Imagine all the turmoil that the people of Earth will go through after **The Reveal**.

You will be glad you are going through all of this now and not *then*.

We anticipate a lot of chaos will ensue. There will probably be a huge break down in personal discipline, some people will panic, others will be just fine with all of it and some will reject the whole notion out right.

Imagine for a moment how some will react. They will quit their jobs, or decide it's ok to rob the corner liquor store because they will feel *The Reveal* is a license to abandon

Earth law.

The Reveal is a very risky situation, and Earth will become an even more dangerous place while people go through the acceptance phase after it happens. Once things calm down, we can begin wholesale evacuation and relocation.

Phase One of The Reveal is simply that, the revelation of the Tu. No mention of intervention or rescue or relocation. The initial message will be *a unifying message of peace*.

As the whole thing begins to calm down, then we can begin introducing concepts about the relocation effort, and the true details of the Tu, and the planet.

There will be a huge number of people who will be ready and willing to leave immediately. Many will be contacting us on their own for a ride off the planet, and they will comprise the first wave of mass migrations off the planet.

It is then we can begin bringing our arks to Earth and begin moving large numbers of people."

The ship accelerated away from **Tu Ono** towards Tu and within a few moments descended through Tu's atmosphere, through several large cloud formations, to reveal Ellis Island, and the arrival colony.

The arrival colony was built into the foothills of a very large mountain range that resembled the Rocky Mountains on Earth. The mountain range was not far from the ocean.

From the air, the colony looked small. This was because there was a huge amount of building that was kept underground, under a huge canopy of trees, as well as into the side of the mountains.

The Zui felt it was always important to keep the cities that were built as inconspicuous as possible, blending to flow with the natural environment.

The residential areas were all in heavily wooded areas, with lakes in their center.

The ship hovered at about 5000 feet for a few moments before making its final descent.

A tall spired building occupied the center of the colony. The colony had the look of a mountain resort.

The ships' PA was coming alive.

"Arrival at Tu Arrival Colony One, Ellis Island. Please stand by for arrival".

Cloud Nine settled gently onto the landing pad at Arrival Colony One.

Michael - "Well we're here people. Stay with me as a group, and I'll introduce you to the arrival team and we'll get you checked in right away.

Keep in mind the gravity here is a wee bit stronger, and you may feel tired for a few days as your body acclimates."

The cargo bay doors opened into a nice ramp leading out of the ship.

Bob – "Well this is it!"

There was a high level buzz in the air as everyone exited the ship and began to take in their new surroundings.

It was dark, and so it wasn't much different than being on Earth, but the sense they all had of walking on another planet, was exhilarating and the excitement was in the air.

The sky above was clear, and stars could be seen in huge number.

Amy -"Wow look at all the stars – so many"

Bob - "Yeah, amazing ... we're probably seeing more because there's no pollution here like on Earth.

They were all being greeted by the chief Immigration officer, Ian Montgomery. He was wearing one of those headset microphones which was tied into a larger PA system

Montgomery singled out Michael and immediately made his way towards him.

"Hello everyone, please – can I have your attention please."

Ian had a *serious* Scots Irish accent .

Ian muted his microphone and leaned over to Michael – Ian said quietly "You did get that *Glen Livet* – right?"

Michael chuckled - "Yes, in fact I got you a whole case, try to make it last more than a week this time."

Ian with a feign indignation said - "I gave most of that away."

Michael - "What, like 2 bottles out of the whole case?"

They laughed.

Back to his announcer's voice – Ian said "Thank you. Welcome to Tu, and Ellis Island, officially known as *Arrival Colony One*.

I am your host, Ian Montgomery and I will be heading up the intake processing of all of you.

We already have your quarters provisioned and so all we really need to do is guide you toward your quarters. It is 10:15pm local time, and so the facility here at the spaceport is not fully staffed.

We will get you to your quarters, and then plan on having all of you meet in our main meeting hall at noon tomorrow for a more detailed check in process, and health exams.

Please be sure to hand in your ship phones. Your escort will provide you with your custom welcome packet and your phones for use here on Tu, which have already been provisioned for you.

Our teams will unload your cargo from the ship early in the morning. Anything you need before then can be obtained from a replicator in your quarters.

So, as we call out your names, we will pair you with an escort who will accompany you to your quarters, briefly show you around and say good night!

After several other names were called, it was Bob and Amy's

turn.

They were introduced to Alan Jennings, a young college student.

Alan - "Welcome to Tu, I'm Alan!

I've also got your welcome packet and your phones. You're in the western section of the Arrival Colony, about 5 blocks from here. We can walk or take one of these scooters, which ever you prefer?"

Bob - "I think the scooter is a good idea, we're kinda jet lagged.

These carts kinda look like the golf carts we have back on Earth"

Alan - "Um actually we had these brought in from Earth, so yes they are the very same golf carts you might remember, and having read yours and Amy's biographies, I think you'll be impressed to know that they have been modified with built in rechargers that recharge them automatically. Hop in and we'll be off".

With that they were quickly on their way to their new temporary home.

Amy - "I don't see any houses or buildings?"

Alan - "Oh they're here. Just a bit more blended with nature than you are probably used to on Earth. A good portion of the colony is underground and built into the side of the mountains.

I did intern on Earth for a year during my last year in high school. I was living in your state of Colorado, in Colorado Springs.

Even though it is night here, you won't see streetlights or house lights. Everything here on Tu is designed to work with nature, not to try and defeat nature but to blend with it.

Ok, your address is *2731 Lake View Drive*, which is due west from here."

Driving a bit further, and up a small climb they arrived at a beautiful single level home.

Alan - "OK just follow me"

Alan reached for his phone, pulled up a small notebook app and spoke into it "*2731 Lake View Drive*".

A few moments later the front entrance light to the unit at 2731 was slowly blinking its front door light.

Alan - "Just enter your door code and you're in. Let me see, your code is coincidentally 2731 – which you can change anytime you want."

Alan punched in their door code, a door lock made a clunking noise as the home's main door unlocked and they entered.

Low lights came on as they entered the house and found it generally devoid of furniture.

Alan - "These were all recently cleaned out and made ready

over the past couple of weeks. As you can see, there isn't really any furniture or décor, you'll be able to replicate what you need to finish it out with whatever style you prefer.

For now, we have basic sleeping, household stuff so you can get situated right away, and then over the coming days you'll have plenty of time to replicate whatever you need for this place."

Alan gave them a quick tour of the place, showed them the bedrooms, toilets, kitchen appliances.

Right off the living room was a huge outside patio situated on a large balcony.

Alan - "And this is your balcony!"

Amy - "Oh wow! This is absolutely gorgeous!"

The view presented them with a beautiful overlook of the arrival colony.

A clear starlit sky revealed Tu's moons.

Amy - "Wow!"

Alan pointed out the moons "That's **Tu Ono**, it's a little larger than Earth's moon, a bit further away than Earth's moon is, and it has an atmosphere, and people live on it.

Bob - "Yeah we were parked there for a while before we came and landed here"

Alan - "It's really more like a small planet. And over there is **Tu Ono Ka**, which is smaller, and further out.

It's mostly rock, ice, and not really habitable. There is a military base there.

Tu Ono is not heavily populated, and has some excellent resorts. You will have to visit it once you get out of arrival status and training.

My wife and I enjoy our balcony so much – you will find it hard to leave! And this is just the arrival colony quarters. You'll love your actual home once you get out of arrival status.

Well, there's still more to the tour, come on back in and I'll show you the kitchen.

The kitchen was particularly interesting.

Alan showed them their food pantry.

"This is your dry storage, and we encourage everyone to keep a stash of a couple of weeks worth of dry foods here just in case of emergency. There's a food dehydrator, and various containers for your storage. You can replicate an emergency food kit to put in here.

Pointing to what looked like a refrigerator of some kind, Alan explained,

"This is your cold storage, very similar to an Earth refrigerator, except it uses more natural cooling processes, has no harmful chemicals in its construction. It's actually a geothermal principle the way it works. Very low power also. And the seals are all natural as well.

You'll notice we don't use plastic, everything here is either wood, stainless steel, ceramic, glass or stone, or natural rubber. We'll familiarize you with our storage techniques in training.

If you want to fix a meal, I'd say use the replicator here for your first night, although we do not really recommend replicated food as a rule.

There's a food market within walking distance about a half mile from here you can get fresh vegetables, breads and other foods at.

We recommend naturally grown food as your primary source, and replication as a secondary source. You'll have plenty of time to prepare your meals every day, and you'll find a complete lack of fast food on this planet."

Amy – "YAY! *I hate that crap. It's poison.*"

Alan - "You've got about an acre of gardening space off to the side of your home, so you can grow your own stuff, or go to the central farmer's market in town to get organic food while you're waiting for your own garden to come in.

A lot of people get a geodesic dome garden, which you can order from the replication library and have it setup within a day.

Unlike Earth, everything on Tu is designed with conservation, longevity, re-use, and efficiency."

Alan opened a small closet door revealing what looked like electronic equipment - "Oh, and in this closet is your power generator. Each apartment has its own power source. It's all automatic, self recharging and requires very little maintenance. You'll get training on how it works during your time here in arrival colony.

Everything here on Tu is all designed for low power, except for where you need a lot of power in power tools, large machines, stuff like that.

Well, I guess this wraps up the tour, and I think you'll be good for the night. Any questions?"

Bob and Amy were in culture shock, and a bit overwhelmed.

Bob - "I don't even know where to begin!"

Amy - "I think we'll manage just fine until morning!"

Alan - "Great, my number is in the phones, just give me a call if you have any questions. As an orientation guide, I am available to you on-call through the night should you need anything, so don't hesitate to call if you need help figuring things out.

The television is actually Earth type, and you can check out the informational channel and there's some good entertainment on as well, movies and shows of all kinds.

You will find though that most people here really don't really watch much. The music channels are outstanding and is probably what most people use their televisions for."

Amy - "Thanks Alan, we'll be good - I think!"

With that Alan left. Bob and Amy were now able to settle in a bit and get accustomed to their new digs on another planet.

Bob - "This is all so freaking incredible, I don't even know where to begin! For starters, let's have a little champagne to celebrate!"

Amy - "Awesome idea! And I think I'm a little hungry so I'm going to get us some dinner as well, or is it breakfast?'

Bob - "Oh and they have a double clock in our kitchen as well. "

Amy was replicating dinner and Bob was setting the table.

Bob - "I imagine these computers are also hooked into some kind of news or entertainment system, let me see if I can figure that out."

With that Bob was messing with the various controls of what looked like a typical large screen television and managed to pull up what looked like some kind of news channel.

Bob - "Hey, wow, I got some kind of news channel working," and pressing a few more buttons on the remote control, Bob chuckled.

 "Ah, good they have a movie channel! And it looks *amazingly* similar to what we have back on Earth. I guess intellectual property rights are a strange topic here. "

Bob's phone was ringing. It was Michael.

Bob - "Hey Michael what's up?"

Michael - "Bob, sorry no time for small talk. I need you and Amy to meet in one hour for an emergency meeting at the main hall – the same meeting hall for your training, over where the ship landed. See you there. Alan will pick you up."

Bob - "Uh, yeah, ok, right!"

Amy - "What was that all about?"

Bob - "It was Michael ... he said we need to meet at the main meeting hall in one hour ..."

The Best Laid Plans

All of the new arrivals were coming into the main meeting hall and looking a bit groggy, dazed and confused.

The smell of coffee was encouraging and Bob headed straight for it.

Amy - "And you know how I like mine!"

Michael, Alex and Ian were all there, and there were also several other officials from the Tu government who were also there.

Michael - "Everyone, please find a spot, be seated. Sorry to have to call you all in at this late hour. Unfortunately, some things have occurred in the past 48 hours that have upset our schedule."

The room lights dimmed, several large information screens lowered from the ceiling and a star chart appeared on the large main monitor at the front of the room.

Michael - "Those of you who know me, know that I am not one to waste a lot of time on small talk, so let's get right to it.

Tu intelligence has confirmed with the *FA's (Free Annunaki)* here on Tu that there is a Annunaki cargo ship heading directly for Tu, with unknown intentions.

We are monitoring its progress and it does not appear at this time to be followed by anything else.

It is rather suspicious, and so we are doing a lot of analysis to figure out what its intentions are.

For one thing, it is coming out of one of the star systems that the FA's use as a kind neutral zone, so that any FA's going to or coming from the Annunaki home world are not coming directly to Tu, so that they cannot be traced.

The idea is to always appear to be coming and going to completely different destinations, not directly to or from Tu.

Whoever is running this unknown ship already knows this route. The problem we are all having is that this is unknown – we don't know for sure if it's unfriendly, but it's not communicating with allied ships we have in the region who have attempted to make contact with it.

The FA's use non-human allies to make contact, so as not to arouse suspicion. This method usually works with escape ships so that its intentions can be verified.

Possible speculations are that it is an automated weapon of some kind. It may also be a group of escapees, who are maintaining silence so as not to be detected.

Unfortunately, by not communicating with our proxies in the region, the Zui have advised us to go to a kind of *battle stations* mode, and so that is why we are all here.

The Tu have been preparing for an eventual invasion by the Annunaki since Tu was founded. There has always been the possibility of traitors and spies giving up Tu's real location.

In fact, Tu's location may actually be known to the

Annunaki, we just do not know for sure.

As we understand it, the Zui and the Annunaki have had a treaty in place for escapees and an agreement to leave Tu alone, except that since the Annunaki don't officially know where Tu is, if they find it they can say they didn't realize that they have found Tu specifically. *It's complicated.*

That being said, the Zui have this planet covered as far a defense is concerned, and we do have backup systems and plans in place should the need ever arise.

So we have to be ever vigilant. The planet has several large defense stations at all points of the planet, with large beam weapons and shields, just like you might imagine from science fiction novels, only this stuff is real.

Since an invasion has never occurred, no one on Tu knows whether the systems in place will be enough to hold off a real invasion.

A few years ago, there was an unfriendly race of aliens who attempted to invade, but they had nothing like the Anunnaki or Zui technology, and were destroyed easily.

The same cannot be said about an invasion from the Anunnaki itself.

There is a backup plan, and so for purposes of keeping you informed and ready here we go.

While we haven't covered it yet in your training, seeing is how you've all only been here a few hours, there is a huge underground network of tunnels with a high speed tube transpor system and multiple underground cities.

If you get an evacuation alert on your phones, you will be directed to an escape tunnel, and be met there by your arrival escort, who will direct you to the tube transports, and on to the shelter cities.

Some of you may be directed to proceed to ark ships, and will be relocated to one of the other planets in the Tu network, some of you may be relocated to Tu Ono.

As I understand it, most of you will be relocated onto ark ships. Once we have our final evacuation plan in place, which will be within the next hour, you will have your evacuation assignments.

Any questions?"

The room was quiet.

Michael - "Ok then. You'll get a set of evacuee instructions should it become necessary, in the next hour, and will include a list of anything you need to bring along."

On the far side of the room, someone asked - "What is the estimated arrival time of this unknown ship?"

Michael - "Right. Well all we know right now is that the unknown ship is moving very slowly, expected to arrive here in about 2 and half days.

Most of the ships used for escape are not like what we have, they have their own faster than light travel, but they don't use the singularity method that the Zui use. We'll keep you posted by phone about the latest developments.

Now, I suggest you all return home, and keep your phones close by. Report to training first thing in the morning as scheduled"

With that, Michael stepped down from the podium and the room quickly dispersed, with everyone buzzing about this new development.

Bob caught up with Michael and Alex just outside the hall. Bob had a bit of a worried face, and Michael could see it.

Bob - "Hey Michael – wow. I was just getting used to the idea of being here."

Michael - "Hey Bob. Don't worry, this planet and its people are quite prepared for this exact kind of scenario, as well as any other kinds of emergencies.

Get home, get some rest and I'll see you all back here in the morning."

My Pilot

Annunaki cargo ships were used on resource missions, to gather precious metals, usually gold from any planets the Annunaki were mining. This was typical of Annunaki cargo ships.

They were large, generally uncomfortable for humans with few amenities. These cargo ships could carry as many as 1500 to 2000 humans.

From the Annunaki perspective, humans were not much more than cattle, and used as slave labor. The Annunaki cargo ships had the barest of amenities for their human slaves, with large open bunk rooms much like a concentration camp.

Humans were not allowed any kind of privacy, and had to use large open showering and toilet facilities. Children of humans were always isolated away from their parents, so that most never knew who their parents were.

They were given simple clothing, enough to barely cover themselves.

Annunaki culture was a caste system, with a gold economy. Coins, ingots, bars, all were used in trade. Trade included humans and human slaves were seen much like smart cattle.

Some humans were trained and used to pilot Annunaki ships. Sanu was one such human. Sanu had come from an intellectual breed, and had gained the trust of the Annunaki in piloting and running cargo ships.

The Annunaki saw these tasks as inferior, and had no fear of letting humans run their ships, because the punishment they could mete out was sufficient to remind any human of the Annunaki superiority.

Fortunately for Sanu, this would be his last ride as a human slave. Many of the humans on the Annunaki home world had heard that there were escapes, but such escapes were rare and often took years to plan and execute.

Many attempts were destroyed before the escaping vessels ever got out of sight of the Annunaki home world.

Sympathetic Annunaki who helped humans escape did so under penalty of death, so those who assisted were as dead as the humans they helped if the ship was ever found and captured.

The Tu would bribe sympathetic Annunaki with gold, since it was a simple thing to replicate it and use it for trade. This worked well, since gold was precious to the Annunaki.

Sanu's slave lord, an Annunaki named Molki, was there in the control room of the ship with Pilot.

The Annunaki were much larger than humans, and in ancient human lore on Earth, they were considered giants.

Molki - "Soon we will be at your new home Pilot."

Sanu - "Hopefully. I fear we may be destroyed before we even arrive."

Molki - "I traded much gold to make sure that would not

occur. We will arrive safely and your long nightmare will be over. Is your woman ready for this new home?"

Sanu - "She is not ready and thinks this was a death wish, that we would have been better to stay on the Annunaki home world"

Molki - "Such it is with many slaves. They do not know freedom, have never known it, and change is fearful."

Sanu - "We have been ignoring the allied ship contacts. We must respond or we will be in danger of being destroyed by Tu ships if we get too close without them knowing why we are coming."

Molki - "Be patient pilot. My plan is proceeding without fail. In a short while, I have another ship that will meet us, in just a few moments and we are all transferring to it. This very ship we are in right now will be destroyed.

The news of our escape will end as news returns to the home world that shows that we were destroyed.

My friend is *Besloor*, who is commander of an Annunaki warship, and he is still known as loyal to the home world. He will put on a great show for the council, and they will believe we are all dead. He has his own escape planned for another time.

Now is the time to bring this ship to a halt."

Sanu slowed the ship to a halt.

No sooner had Molki spoken, than immediately in front of them a very large Annunaki warship appeared.

On the cargo ship's visual communications panel, a face appeared.

It was Besloor.

Besloor - "Cargo ship, we know you are an escape vessel and will be destroyed."

Molki paused a moment - "Besloor!"

Both Molki and Besloor began to laugh.

Besloor (laughing) - "Let's get to work"

With that, the screen went blank. The humans were lined up in the cargo bay in a special gigantic transport pad that could move tons of gold ore at a time, which meant it could transport several hundred humans at a time.

Wave after wave of humans was transferred off the cargo ship onto the Annunaki warship.

Molki - "Come slave, we go, your moment of freedom is now!"

Molki and Pilot made their way to the large transport pad, and Pilot's woman, Leshi was waiting, with a very fearful look on her face.

Sanu - "Let's go!"

They gathered with the remainder of the crew for transport, and were transported to the Annunaki warship.

Molki to Sanu - "Bring your woman, come with me now."

Molki, Sanu, and Leshi met up with Besloor in the control room of the warship.

Besloor - *"Let's finish this charade."*

With that, Besloor waved his hand over a control and a large particle beam incinerated the cargo ship.

Besloor spoke to a crewman in the control room - "Send news of this to the home world, with these few words,'the traitors have been destroyed' and send it with the record of the moving images." *(Translation – send video of the event)*

Besloor- "Molki tonight we celebrate. In eight seasons of the corn, I will join you on Tu, and I will have much gold."

Molki - "So far, so good. We need to get there first. I still do not believe it was wise to do this so close to Tu, the home world may start putting things together."

Besloor- "I have known these Tu more than 8 cycles, and they are trustworthy, and we are a safe distance from Tu, no one will be the wiser on home world. That ship could have been heading anywhere.

Our report to home world is that we interrogated their systems and discovered they were headed to a planet in another star system."

Meanwhile back on Tu, Tu intelligence chief *Jan Ono* was alerting Michael of the recent developments on his phone.

Michael - "You're certain of this?"

Jan - "Yes, the Zui scout ship saw the unknown cargo ship come to a halt as it was intercepted by an Annunaki warship, and then a few minutes later it was destroyed"

Michael - "Any idea why it was headed here?"

Jan - "Still no word why. We've got some feelers out there but won't know anything for a while. We're waiting for word from the Zui."

Michael - "Keep me posted. Oh, and one other thing, was the Zui scout ship detected?"

Jan - "No, the Zui scout ships are small and shielded, so very difficult to detect and the warship left the area in an opposite direction after it destroyed the cargo ship.

The Zui detected a huge mass of human DNA in the area, so it was evidently an intercept of a human escape from the Annunaki home world. You can pass the "all clear" if you like."

Michael - "Thanks Jan, keep me posted"

Through out Tu, word spread of the failed escape. And the alert status was set back to normal.

Meanwhile aboard the Annunaki warship, Molki and Besloor were drinking *corn wine*. Corn wine was exactly that, except that the corn the Annunaki raised was the size of cocktail corn. They would distill it and there was little wonder that it smelled like ethanol from Earth.

The humans on board were celebrating their new freedom.

Many humans in this group had never had strong drink, and never knew what it was to really celebrate openly and without fear of some Annunaki coming in and shutting down the party. Things were definitely in party mode.

Leshi was concerned and came close to Pilot - "How soon do we get to Tu?"

Sanu - "Soon. We are taking several routes to make sure we are not being followed, and then we will meet up with a Tu ark-ship, and then we go to Tu."

Several hours later, the Annunaki warship was parking itself behind a moon which orbited a very large gas giant much like Jupiter. The moon was more like an asteroid trapped in orbit around the gas giant.

Not long after the Annunaki warship had parked, a large Tu ark-ship arrived.

Besloor embraced Molki in a bear hug.

Besloor - "Molki – now is the time. The Tu are here. Get your woman and go quickly my friend. I'll see you in 8 seasons of the corn on Tu."

Molki - "Thank you my friend I will see you there."

The transfer took only a few minutes and then both ships parted ways.

The Tu ark-ship was named the *Otis T Carr*, and featured the 'freeper' insignia, which was a derivative of the 'Star of

Life'.

The Carr would also have to take several false routes in its journey back to be sure it was not being followed.

Stand Down

Back on Tu, life resumed to a state of normal, but there was also a sense of sadness that the cargo ship that was destroyed was probably an escape ship.

Because of its size and known capacities, it was sad knowing there could have been as many as 1500 - 2000 humans destroyed.

It was morning, and the new arrivals were coming into the main meeting hall at the spaceport for their second day of training.

Michael was at the podium. The mood was somber and quiet.

Michael - "Please be seated everyone, we have a lot to cover today.

I have an update about the unknown Annunaki vessel."

Soon everyone had seated themselves and the room was quiet, so quiet you could hear a pin drop. Someone on the far side of the hall sneezed and everyone was so jumpy they were all unnerved by it.

Michael - "Thanks everyone. Good to see you all again.

Hopefully you're all starting to get rested, and adapt to the new environment here.

First off, the unknown vessel that was using known escape routes to Tu was destroyed by an Annunaki warship.

We're not sure why, but a Zui recon vessel in that region that was tracking the cargo ship, showed that it was intercepted by an Anunnaki warship, and destroyed.

The interesting thing that happened is that a few hours before the intercept, the cargo ship had actually changed course and it was calculated to be heading towards an entirely different galaxy, and star system away from Tu.

We can only speculate that they knew they were being followed by the warship, and tried to get to another star system but never made it.

Intel unfortunately showed a lot of human DNA in what little wreckage was left of the cargo ship. We'll never know how many people were on board, but because the Anunnaki destroyed it, we are assuming it was some kind of escape in progress.

As I mentioned, the Annunaki warship left the region in the opposite direction from Tu, so we now know that it happened far enough away that the cargo ships' course was not construed as coming this way.

In light of this, we're standing down from the alert status.

I do need to have a quick meeting specifically with Bob Willets, Dave Sutter, Ken Smith, Simon Litton, and Petak Shara. I need your help with something urgent. Gentlemen please follow me.

I now return you to your originally scheduled training. "

With that Michael stepped down from the podium.

Cover Story

A few moments later Ian was back at the podium and began the second session.

Ian - "Today we're going to have a basic geography lesson, and describe the layout of the planet Tu, and its various regions, weather, and some of the cities, states, and governments that make up the planet.

Tu's governing concepts are a mix of several philosophies that include libertarian, anarchist, and community based systems ..."

Bob and the others walked with Michael down another hallway to another meeting room and closed the door.

Michael - "OK everyone have a seat. Nothing discussed in this room leaves this room. I need your focus and attention. We're short on time.

You all represent a special team I have assembled based upon your core strengths. Since none of you have ever worked together, this may be a bit risky but I think you're all up to the task. Right now we are short-handed and I need you all.

Bob, Dave you guys are my technical support for technology. If it's technology related, you are the go-to guys. Login to the replicators, and do a search for 'Michael electronic test kit'. Replicate everything in that list.

There's an app on your phones that you can use from anywhere to get access to the replicator library, and then assign a replication station for pickup, so you can get this going.

Bob - "*Got it*"

Get everything set to be replicated and picked up at replication station 867. That puts it all on the dock ready for load out onto our jump ship.

Ken, Simon, you guys are weapons and team security. You will be armed and dangerous at all times. We have some very good weapons available in the replicator, and I have given you weapons access – get what you need.

I already loaded a weapons profile for you guys, just login and do a search for 'Michael security detail'. I also want side arms for every team member. Replicate a bunch of model K-45s, I want each member carrying. There's a holster and belt for those.

Petak, I need you as photographer, video recorder. There's some nice small portable stuff in the replicator library, get a couple of cameras and portable lighting gear.

I also would prefer you all wear a Free People uniform so that we are seen as a team. Our uniforms are in the replicator under "Michael uniforms".

Let me re-phrase that, they're not really *uniforms*, just some nice polo shirts with the freeper logo on them. I'm not real big on uniforms if you get my drift.

Tu intelligence has suspected that there are Annunaki spies in the Tu government, but they haven't yet figured out who all of them are.

The spies may be FA's here on Tu, or humans who have been made some kind of deal.

This doesn't surprise anyone, but it does mean that the Tu have had to be extremely vigilant and careful to make sure the location of Tu is never revealed to the Annunaki.

We have Tu intel people who actually make missions to the Annunaki home world, but it involves a labyrinthian set of decoys, false routes, ship exchanges and cloak and dagger stuff.

Those kinds of missions take months to prepare, months to execute, and many who go do not return at all, and are assumed captured, and or dead.

No one except the *The Four* knows the exact route to the Annunaki home world, because if it were known to any humans, our spies could be tortured to give up the reverse course to Tu.

So journey to and from is coordinated through a middleman process of transfers. Sometimes the transfers take several months because there's no schedule anyone can tap into, just meeting places and a lot of waiting.

Conversely, those coming from the Annunaki home world never really know how to get to Tu directly, they only have the hope of meeting the intermediaries, who transfer them. All they know are a couple of planets in between.

Escapees can wind up waiting months in strange places before being picked up.

The amazing thing is that there is a waiting list for Tu intel people who want to volunteer to go to the Annunaki home world – there are so many who volunteer because they know it means potential liberation of their people from the Annunaki.

So anyone volunteering for such missions has to undergo a deep background check, an intense set of tests, both physically, mentally and so forth to make sure they are suitable.

You have to realize, these Annunaki have been running this game for hundreds of thousands of years. So escape is not easy, and requires long term planning, often years.

Let me update you with the real story about that approaching cargo ship.

The news you heard, the public story - that was a cover story such that any spies here on Tu would get that story.

If they are communicating back to the Anunnaki home world, then the cover story is consistent with the news the home world got from the warship.

The cover story is that *the cargo ship was destroyed, no survivors*.

The truth is that the Tu have made a transfer of some 1800 humans to one of the Tu ark ships.

Not only were humans transferred, but our intelligence says that **several pieces of highly advanced technology** from the Annunaki were also included and will be part of the cargo arriving in the next day or so.

Within that group, there is a highly educated class of humans that we are hoping will help us shed some light on the Annunaki technology.

The ark ship is making its way back here using several cover routes, decoys and switches, and will be here in another day or two at most.

They will not becoming to the main arrival colony, but to a secret Annunaki arrival colony on the other side of the planet. It's a special arrival colony strictly for humans coming from the Annunaki home world.

Part of keeping Tu safe is not letting out too much information about how many humans there are in the other arrival colony, and in the settlements there, so that no one here on this side of the planet can determine whether their population is growing and then calculate the growth based upon recent escapes from the Annunaki home world, and then report it through their spy networks.

The life and culture of a majority of these humans is not much better than you would expect from an uneducated slave race.

These slave humans are brought to the other arrival colony, and acclimated for life here just as you are. A majority of them have to learn basic educational stuff, like to read and write, and learn this planet through a similar arrival program just like what you guys are going through.

Most will spend a couple of years there before ever being allowed to come to this side of the planet.

Many have opted for a more tribal existence, living off the

land much like the North American Indians did before they were overrun by European settlers. There are several large territories of tribal FA's.

They have their own trade networks, and generally live at peace. Most hate technology except when it comes to some things, like communications, weapons and medical help.

Getting back on point, I have been briefed by John Foster that the nature of the technology they brought with them is of extremely high interest to *The Four* and they need us to be the 'A-team' on its recovery."

What I need you guys for is as my assistants to go with me to that arrival colony, and help me bring back the Annunaki technology and possibly even some of the new arrivals over to this side of the planet to get a handle on this new technology right away.

Like I said before, that there are many other much more experienced people here on Tu that normally handle this task, none are available right now, and I was asked if this was really a good idea.

Knowing each of your strengths, you're all ideally suited for this task, except that you're all inexperienced and that means I'm taking an incredible risk. This will be a trial by fire for all of you so I need you to step up and do your best.

Plan to be gone for a couple of days. We'll be ready to leave in a couple of hours. No need to bring anything other than what I told each of you to gear up with. We'll be using one of the jump ships that has an on-board replicator, but I want you to be geared up before we leave."

A 'jump ship' was a small ship used primarily for instantaneous transport to any point on the planet. All they had to do was enter the GPS coordinates of where they needed to go and the ship would essentially teleport to that location within a few seconds.

Michael - "Just follow my lead. We will have an interpreter who will interface with the new arrivals.

All of you need to go through a decontamination process which takes about half an hour, and then we can head to the arrival colony. We do not want to kill our new arrivals with a common cold or some fungus you may not even realize you have.

The *cellular regen* should have killed most of that shit, but we like to be thorough in these situations.

The Tu also have their own decontamination systems on their ships, so we shouldn't have too much to worry about.

Our intermediary and interpreter is already at the new arrival colony.

Once we get there, and things settle down, we'll meet with the captain of the Annunaki ship and debrief him and the crew. He has seen and worked with plenty of humans.

As much as this will be new for all of you, try not do not display shock or surprise at how he looks. The Annunaki are much larger than humans and it will be a bit of a shock to the system to meet real *"aliens"*. Keep in mind, for him this is nothing new.

His name is Molki and his human assistant is also his pilot.

On the Annunaki ships, piloting and navigation is relegated to humans and such tasks are seen as "beneath" the Annunaki.

Any questions?"

To a man, there was only silence.

Michael "Ok let's get going. Meet back here in 1 hour and we'll head out to decontamination. And again, speak to no one about the details of this mission. Gear up.

By the way, call your wives and girlfriends and let them know you're going to be late for dinner, which means we'll probably gone for a day, maybe two."

Evil Seed

The Tu ark ship settled down quietly onto the landing pad at the special Annunaki arrival colony . The colony was empty, except for about 120 Tu workers who maintained it. They were all former escapees themselves.

Within a few moments after the ship had landed, the cargo doors were opening and people were coming out.

Aden, the Annunaki interpreter and liaison between Earthers and the Tu was standing nearby waiting for the Annunaki captain and his team to come out.

A few moments later Michael and his team's jump ship was settling on a pad a short distance away.

Michael - "OK guys, just follow my lead. Don't do or say anything, just be there with me"

They disembarked and hastily headed over to where Aden was standing.

Michael - "Hello Aden, good to see you. I trust all is well?"

Aden - "All is well here Michael, I trust all is well with you?"

Michael - "Yes, we are here and ready to assist you. These are my Earth brothers who will be my assistants".

Aden - "Ah, Earth brothers. Welcome to Tu." His welcome was polite but not enthusiastic. He'd met plenty of Earth humans, and was generally unimpressed.

Michael's team was quiet.

Aden - "Good. We are all ready then."

They walked a short distance to an area that looked like a large outdoor amphitheater and all of the newly arriving humans were gathered there, some sitting, some gathered in groups. Many were hung over from too much *corn wine* en route to Tu.

Soon several of the local Tu workers began taking small groups away to be checked into the arrival colony.

The Annunaki captain Molki, Pilot, Leshi and a few other senior crew members were gathered in a small group.

Aden walked away from the main amphitheater and met up with Michael and his men.

Aden - "Come, let us meet the captain and his crew. Do not use his name openly, it must be kept secret".

Aden led Michael and his men over to the Annunaki group and began introducing them.

Aden spoke first to the captain, in his own language. "Welcome captain, to Tu. Thank you for bringing our brothers safely here."

Molki - "We are tired. We have much to discuss, but it will wait. How soon can you take us to our quarters?"

Molki was still Annunaki at his core, and he was used to getting his way with humans. He would have to adjust as he became a part of the free world apart from his home world.

Aden - "Very soon, a guide will be here and will take you"

Molki - "Give special care to my helpers"

Aden - "Of course. These Earth brothers are here about the special cargo. There is urgency to this matter, and the Tu want to attend to this matter right away"

Michael - "Aden, The Top 5 do not want to wait, we must move on this immediately".

Aden turned to Molki and said - "The Tu cannot wait, there is urgency *like that of battle.*"

Molki - "*It is* **the destroyer of worlds**."

Aden - "You have taken great risk in taking it from *the home*. Who among you knows what it is?"

The home Aden referred to was *Nibiru*, the Annunaki home world. They always referred to it as *the home*.

Molki - "Only myself and my pilot. My home brother gave pretense of destroying our ship, and it will appear that the weapon was destroyed as well."

Aden turned to Michael - "It is a very dangerous weapon, legendary, and such that it can destroy entire planets, similar to beam weapons from your home world.

If the Annunaki ever find out that Molki is still alive, and has taken it, they will not stop until they find him and the weapon."

Michael - "OK then, we need to get it secured, as soon as possible. We do not know for sure if the ship was or was not tracked here. Ask the captain if he knows for sure they were not tracked."

Aden turned to Molki and asked - "Are the hunters near, and do they have your scent?"

Molki - "We covered our tracks as best we could, and do not fear the elders and their dogs, and none has followed. They believe we are dead and the weapon is destroyed."

Aden turned to Michael - "The captain feels pretty certain they were not followed. His escape ship was destroyed, and a cover story about the destruction of Molki has already been sent back to home world."

Turning to Molki, Aden said - "And captain, a word to the wise, we believe the elders may have dogs here, but we do not yet know who they are, speak of these things to no one, and let no one know your true name. "

Molki - "None of the slaves know my name, except for my pilot. We feared spies may be in the slave group."

Aden - "They will be dispersed, here and on other worlds"

With that, Molki and his crew went back into the Tu ark ship with Aden's assistant and in a few moments the ark ship was taking off and heading to the underground hangar.

Aden turned to Michael - "The ark ship is being moved to the underground hangar and we will off load the weapon shortly".

Michael - "This new information also means that none of these new human arrivals can stay here on Tu.

They are witnesses, and would be interrogated, tortured and killed if it was ever to come out. They have to be removed, and relocated to other worlds immediately. We cannot have any spies getting word of this captain's survival back to the home world."

Aden turned to an assistant and ordered the removal of all new arrivals to other worlds. As fast as they had arrived, they would be gone.

Aden - "We have spoken of this and it is done. We will relocate them immediately."

Michael - "I need you to relocate all Tu workers as well who have seen this arrival. It is for their own safety."

With that, Aden directed the Tu arrival colony workers to begin loading up on other ships for relocation immediately.

Michael turned to his men. "This is pretty serious. This Annunaki captain has brought with him one of the most powerful weapons that the Annunaki possess, akin to a nuclear particle beam weapon.

It can basically destroy a planet, or be used to cause massive damage to a planet and as such this thing is too dangerous to keep on Tu.

That also means that within the next couple of hours, this place will be swarming with black ops people from Earth, as well as senior people from the Tu military command.

I plan to get us out of here immediately. We don't want to be anywhere near here – this whole place will become a military base in a few hours. There's going to be an alphabet soup army here in short order. So, let's load up."

With that Michael and his men loaded back onto their small transport and headed back to the human arrival colony.

Michael - "Needless to say, but I'll say it anyway – speak of this to no one, not even your wives and girl friends – seriously. This is top secret. In fact, this is something you don't even want to know about. The less we all know the better.

The first thing the military will do is get that thing secured, and probably move it to another planet altogether. It's just too dangerous."

Michael dialed Aden on his phone.

Michael - "Aden, I and my Earth brothers cannot be there to assist you with the special cargo. The Tu military commander will meet with you and Molki, and the Tu will assist you."

Aden - "Thank you Michael, understood. All is well with the Tu."

With that they hung up.

Michael - "Aden knows the seriousness of this and so he'll be working directly with the Molki and the Tu military commander. What Aden doesn't know yet is that they will probably relocate him as well."

Bob - "Why do they need to relocate anyone who knows about this – so quickly?"

Michael - "Ever hear of something called *remote viewing*? A lot of these alien races use it routinely. Our own CIA has been researching remote viewing for decades and actually have a few people who who can do it.

So they can do shit like read minds from far away places. Every human witness to this is like having a remote controlled TV camera on scene. So that's why it has to be quick and without question.

So they move people to yet another planet far enough away to minimize the possibility of them getting their mind read and revealing information. It's not fool proof but it's all we can do for now."

Michael and his new team quickly found themselves at the Hall Of Representatives back at Ellis Island. Inside the Hall of Representatives were several buildings, one of which was the *Hall Of Governors*.

In front of the Governor's Hall was a large fountain, which had a gigantic hand holding a gigantic miner's hammer, reaching up out of the water in the center of the fountain.

Bob - "What's this fountain all about?"

Michael - "The first colony of Tu colonists were miners for the Annunaki, and the fountain represents their 'rising up' and 'punching through' to escape from the Annunaki home world."

Michael and his team entered the Governor's Hall, and was directed immediately to John Foster's chambers.

Foster - "Welcome Michael, and to your team. Gentlemen, please, follow me."

They proceeded through several long hallways. The building had a nice, northern European feeling, collegiate, almost like visiting a modern cathedral, somewhat institutional yet there was a beautiful artistic feeling in every aspect to the way the place was laid out.

Arriving at John Foster's chambers he closed the doors behind them and instructed them to be seated.

Foster motioned to his staff to leave. "Close the doors please, thank you."

Foster turned his attention to Michael and his team - "Gentlemen, welcome to Tu. Under these circumstances, we don't have much time to socialize, we have to be in the main chambers in a few minutes.

Please do not speak to anyone else while you are here, except myself and our hosts in The Top 5."

Damage Control

Michael and his team could feel the tension in the atmosphere.

Foster - "In just a few moments, we will proceed into the main hall, and I needed to give you all a bit of guidance before we proceed.

Someone has leaked a story about the ark ship last evening, although no one has specific details, there are a lot of rumors going around and we need to contain them, and give an official story.

We will be providing a cover story about the arrivals, because we want to protect everyone with plausible deniability.

In just a few moments, we will all go into the main chamber, and I will address the council and introduce you and your team.

I may or may not ask you to provide a small amount of information, as the leader of the science team that met the arrivals, and you will say that it was really of no consequence.

Any questions anyone asks you, simply tell them it was a small scout ship with just a few people on it and that it was inconsequential.

The less said the better, but for the moment, we are trying to provide an illusion of transparency.

The risk of people on Tu actually knowing what has arrived and what it is – it's just too great. Any citizen of the planet – their life would be in grave danger just by knowing the truth."

Michael and his team followed John Foster into the auditorium, filled with about 250 representative delegates from all of the various regions of Tu.

John Foster led Michael and the team into the main hall and were seated. John Foster stepped up to a podium and motioned people to settle down and the auditorium quieted itself.

Foster - "We will now come to order, this special meeting of representative delegates."

After the auditorium had quieted down Foster began to lay out the purpose of the meeting.

Foster had to tell a story. Senior delegates had heard that there were new arrivals, but did not know the specifics. Someone had leaked information, and damage control meant having to get everyone on the same page with a cover story.

Foster - "Thank you all for coming, especially on short notice. As this is a special session, we will suspend the normal rules of order for a general session and move right to the business at hand.

As most of you now know, we had an arrival last evening in the Annunaki arrival colony at Gargantua North.

As it turns out, it was only a small group of people in a small scout ship and they have been relocated to a quarantine zone.

Part of the confusion and where the misrepresentation is coming from is that we also had a military operation and drill being conducted in the same region, and so the drill had some scenarios associated with it that, were, *just a drill*.

There were some people hunting and camping in the same area who were not familiar with the drill, and mistook the drill as a real event, and these people went to the media before we had a chance to debrief them , and so it was their story that was given to the media.

I regret this thing has become larger than it was ever intended, and we are taking the necessary precautions to ensure it won't happen again in the future.

I also wanted to take this time to introduce to you one of my science teams, led by Michael Stetson, and it was his team that met with the arrivals.

If you have any questions, please direct them to me."

An older female delegate from the same region as the Annunaki arrival colony stood up and addressed John Foster.

"My name is Jana De Sus and I represent the FA Territory, in Gargantua North, which is the territory this incident occurred in."

Foster - "Yes Jana, welcome to the council ... please tell us what is on your mind."

Jana - "Thank you. We have heard that workers from the arrival colony were rounded up and relocated as well. What is the status of this? We have entire families that are missing from the area. We went to the arrival colony but we were turned back by Tu military."

Foster - "Yes, well besides the new arrivals, and the military drill - there were a couple of trade ships coming and going into the arrival colony as well.

One ship was impounded because they were caught smuggling human cargo. The smuggling ship was confiscated and sent to a decontamination yard.

Unfortunately, that ship also contaminated the arrival colony personnel with a virus. That ship was not equipped with approved decontamination equipment.

That forced the shut-down of the colony. Unfortunately, the contamination is such that most of the workers contracted a virus that even though, by some standards is rather benign, but because they had no immunity, many have died already because of it.

So the few that survived have been relocated to a decontamination facility and will return to the arrival colony facilities once they've been cleared.

The military is decontaminating the arrival colony as we speak.

Well ladies and gentlemen this is all I have for right now, and this meeting is adjourned. As new information becomes available my office will provide it.

Thank you all for attending."

Foster began to leave the podium, but before he could do so, Jana rose up from her seat and said "I formally demand a *Dissent Hearing*."

The room came to a standstill.

Foster, stopped in his tracks for a moment, and then turned around stepped back up to the podium.

Foster - "Pardon me, *this meeting has adjourned.*"

Jana - "I formally demand a *Dissent Hearing!*"

John Foster was visibly agitated.

Foster - "*On what grounds?*"

Jana - "The *Dissent Hearing* will provide us with an investigatory hearing because we do not feel that we have been adequately informed."

Foster paused for a moment, regained his composure.

Foster - "So be it, those in favor of a *Dissent Hearing*?"

The room was unanimous "Yes".

Foster - "A *Dissent Hearing* will be convened in 10 days for an investigative hearing in reference to this matter."

Foster made his way off the podium and gathered together with Michael and his team.

Foster - "I need you and your team to monitor what the military is doing, and I have already directed all of the spec ops teams and the Tu military commanders that you and your team will have full access.

You will need to head back out to the Annunaki arrival colony tomorrow and be on site when the cargo is unloaded and examined. We have a new interpreter who will accompany you.

If you encounter any resistance from any of the Earth spec ops people I want to know about it.

Do not handle anything directly, just be my eyes and ears and report back to me. The Tu military will handle the weapon directly.

I have advised all of the Earth teams to keep their hands off, this is a matter that is owned by Tu and its people. I do not want any interference from Earth in this matter. None of them has disagreed with me openly, but I do not trust any of them.

Any questions?"

Michael - "I'm curious – what is it about the Earth teams you are concerned with?"

It wasn't that Michael didn't already know the answer to this question, he wanted his team to hear it direct from John Foster.

Foster - "Michael, I think you know only too well how Earth's military and their various alphabet soup agencies do not operate with transparency, honesty and any real regard for higher principles.

We have to work around this unfortunate fact of life. This has been a problem for the past 65 years.

The Four came to me specifically concerned about the Earth teams.

It is theirs and my fear that there are less than honest individuals working with the Earth spec ops teams that may try to hijack the weapon and take it back to Earth.

This cannot happen, and I have instructed the Tu military to use lethal force on any spec ops member or team that attempts to take the weapon.

I need total allegiance from you and your team that you are working on behalf of Tu and its people. There are larger issues at stake, and some new developments regarding contact with another race, from the Andromeda galaxy, and they are evaluating contact with us and I do not want to lose their trust.

If we appear to just be another extension of Earth's policy of weapons and war, the human race will be perceived to be up to "*the same old same old*".

The Annunaki weapon is going to be removed from the planet as soon as possible, we just don't want to see it removed to Earth.

I am waiting for direct instructions from the Zui about where they want it moved to."

Michael - "Well John, I know I can speak for my team, you

have our total allegiance in this."

Foster - "Thank you Michael, keep me posted, on the hour once you are on site again"

Michael and his team headed back to their jump ship and headed back to the Annunaki arrival colony.

Michael - "Once we get on site, say nothing to no one and let me do all the interface. Just shadow me and I'll direct you as needed."

Walk In The Park

Even though Bob and Amy's home in the arrival colony was a temporary home, it was still situated in a beautiful setting.

Each home occupied about an acre and a half of land, set back off of a paved trail that surrounded a lake that was about 3 kilometers in a natural circumference, about a kilometer across.

Amy found herself wanting to explore the surroundings and found herself on the nice paved walkway about 10 feet wide that wove its way around the residential area where they made their new home.

From time to time electric trams with a few people would pass by. There were people on segues, roller skates and bikes.

It was a chance to reflect. Walking through a nicely forested area, with sunlight coming through the trees, it was impossible to not reflect on the complete strangeness of this new world, that it was just as beautiful as Earth, but even more so.

Wild deer, turkey, all manner of birds, hawks and herons were plentiful. The deer were almost tame and could often be seen just a few feet off the pathway. They had little fear of humans, having grown up in a world where they were not hunted, harassed or abused.

Residents were advised to be on the lookout for bobcats and coyotes in the area, and to carry a repeller. A repeller was a small electronic device that emitted specific frequencies that would cause predators to run off.

There were also people living and working as park rangers throughout the residential areas who were generally no more than a few minutes if you needed one. They were all trained to handle animals.

The Tu had not introduced any large predators into the area, but where there were deer and turkey, there would be bobcats, coyotes and occasionally wolves. Wolves would come through but they generally did not come around well inhabited areas and would rather stay away than interact with mankind.

The pathway was dark at night, but had ground level lighting.

For Amy, it was reminiscent of the greenway walking trails around Nashville.

The fact that the ecology and environment always had primary consideration where buildings, roads and infrastructure were concerned meant that every aspect of how humanity impacted the planet was always taken into thoughtful consideration.

A forest walk is just as beautiful on Tu as it is on Earth, but with the added benefit of no air pollution, or jets making noise in the sky.

One cannot help but realize that the sunlight on Tu is not 'good old Sol' as we know it on Earth, it's another 'Sol' shining and providing sustenance to a planetary body, that soaks it in just as happily as Earth does with 'good old Sol'.

Looking up to the sky, the faint outlines of Tu's moons in the late afternoon sky were a quick reminder of where she really was.

As she walked and contemplated all that had transpired in the past few days, she heard a rustling in the woods. She stopped and tried to figure out where it was coming from.

Amy was startled as a squirrel came bounding out and leapt up into the side of a tree.

Moments later, from out behind a large fallen tree near the trail a small unusual creature raised its head, and made a chirp sound at Amy.

Amy was a bit confused, but as she strained to see what was chirping at her, the little creature came out from behind the fallen tree and then chirped in a way that announced itself, as if to say 'hello'.

Amy was mesmerized at this totally *un-Earthly* creature. It was about 2 feet tall, with bird-like wings, but with the fur of a cat or monkey. It had a friendly face, and the head had the look of a gargoyle or dragon but with fur, like a cat.

Amy - "Well hello *little creature ...*"

It appeared to be friendly, but Amy wasn't taking any chances. It may be cute, but not knowing whether it was bad or good made Amy a bit uneasy.

It chirped again and then ran off into the woods, bounding and taking little hops and even flying a bit.

Amy laughed to herself - *"Damn, Bob is not going to believe this one"*

As she watched it run off into the woods she saw that there were several others as well further into the woods, watching her interact with the one closest to her that had just darted off.

What Amy had encountered was a *dragon-monkey*. These small creatures were actually quite harmless, with very beautiful feathers, each with unique patterns and many of the Tu actually kept them as pets.

They were quite intelligent and could be trained like dogs, but even more fascinating was that they could also learn to vocalize rudimentary words and phrases.

Their main vocal sound was a chirping sound that they would use to communicate with each other.

They spent their days foraging in the forest for fruits and nuts. They kept together in small clusters like monkeys or buzzards.

The trail led into an open area, and she found herself walking into an open air market.

Amy remembered that when they first arrived their escort, *Alan* had mentioned the food market.

It was reminiscent of one of those medieval fairs where you are surrounded by people in medieval costumes, and seller booths where you can buy swords and food from the dark ages on Earth.

Clothing on Tu was decidedly casual, with an 'anything goes' flair.

Styles ranged from conservative, creative, and even a bit of a wild style like you might see at Earth's *'Burning Man'* festival.

One wasn't judged by their clothing style, you could dress in any century you wanted and it was no matter – clothing style is your choice of self expression on Tu. With a replicator, one can pick any style you want, to fit any mood.

The market featured dozens of stalls filled with fresh produce, and there were some craft stalls as well. There were artists with carvings, paintings, ceramics and all manner of crafts. Their work was stunning and amazing.

The one thing Amy would have to get used to was the complete absence of money. As you entered the market, there were cloth bags available for patrons to use to put whatever they picked up from the market. You just took what you wanted – really it was a case of *take what you need*.

Although everything was free, there was no chaos, because the general understanding was that you only took what you really needed.

Some of the items had a sign on them with a large R, and a year date – meaning this was something replicated from a particular year.

Amy found herself in a wonderland of produce, and was looking at some rather large tomatoes.

Looking up she noticed what looked like a tour group coming through the market, led by one of the young escorts like Alan that had acquainted Bob and Amy to their apartment.

Even more bizarre was that this tour group had what looked like Catholic priests, nuns, a Tibetan monk, people in middle-eastern religious garb.

She was soon surrounded by the tour group. A Catholic priest, a nun and the Tibetan monk were making their way to the same tomatoes Amy was looking at.

The priest was a middle aged man named Simon McCarthy. Simon was looking a bit bewildered and you could see there was a lot on his mind.

Simon - "Hello child ..."

Amy - "Oh, uh, hi, my name is Amy."

Simon extended a hand - "Simon McCarthy"

Amy - "Oh hello. Nice to meet you, I'm Amy."

Pausing a few moments, Amy's curiosity got the best of her.

Amy - "Pardon me for asking, but it is quite obvious that your group appears to be a broad sample of religious types?"

Simon - "Oh yes, well, we're all part of a special group brought here to a conference of religious professionals and leaders on Tu."

Amy - "*Really*. Well this must be a real adventure. I haven't been here long myself."

Amy had a sudden feeling of dread, and was a bit reticent to mention she had come here with a boyfriend and was unmarried. And she wasn't even the religious type, as she and Bob were really more atheistic and not tied to any specific religious beliefs.

Simon - "Well this whole adventure is definitely interesting. Actually this is not my first trip here, we've had a monastery here for some time on the planet, since the late 1960's. I started coming here back in the mid 1980's."

Amy - "So – I'm curious – how does all of this affect your beliefs?"

Simon - "Well, I was selected by the Vatican to come here. Revelation of this planet and the whole idea, the migration and evacuation of Earth will be very disruptive to many people's beliefs back on Earth.

We are here to take it all in, and begin to digest it. We have been working towards a way to incorporate all of this into what we already teach."

Amy - "I've been so busy, I never even thought of any of that. I do imagine that if people have held to certain faith based belief systems that center upon the Earth – this will be quite disruptive to their thinking, wouldn't it?"

Simon - "Well, from the Vatican's perspective, it's not outside the Catholic faith. And there will be people who will want to continue their faith once they come here. We've already got a church set up on the east side of the arrival colony, you should come visit sometime."

Standing nearby was Ken Suhn, a Buddhist monk was taking it all in.

Ken - "Concepts of religion that only center upon Earth will fail when things are finally revealed, and from everything we've been hearing lately it is likely to happen within the next few years. Engaging the believers in a larger context of the universe as a whole is something we are already focusing on."

Amy - "Well, I have never really been a religious person, but I do believe we all have a spiritual connection of some kind, although I have never really explored that."

Amy's phone was ringing and it provided a welcome exit from a conversation she wasn't really comfortable with. Smiling and turning away to answer her phone, it was Bob.

Bob - "Hey – how are you doing?"

Amy nervously excused herself by mouthing the words "excuse me" and wandered off away from the market to give herself a little privacy while she spoke to Bob and found herself wandering into a small outdoor cafe. The aroma of coffee, cinnamon, tea, and cannabis filled the air.

Amy - "Great, I was just checking out the open air market and am planning to make myself a nice cup of coffee at this really cool little outdoor cafe like place ... oh and you won't believe the little creature I saw in the woods -"

Bob – "Hey that's awesome babe. Things have been crazy but we're managing to keep our sanity."

Amy got a cup of coffee and seated herself. A couple of tables away an older man was seated by himself drinking tea and pretended to not notice Amy.

Bob - "Looks like I'll be home sometime tomorrow evening, but may run another day."

Amy - "Oh good. Did everything go well with your meeting?"

Bob - "Uh, yeah, all's good. Will fill you in as best I can when I get in. Anyway, I can't talk long, but wanted to make contact and let you know I'm ok."

Amy - "OK no problem ... love you"

Bob - "Love you too hon – will keep you posted. I won't be able to make any calls, but will let you know when I'm headed back."

As she hung up the phone with Bob the man got up, picked up his tea and approached Amy's table and introduced himself to Amy. His name was Soldan.

Soldan - "Hello. I recognize you from the new arrivals recently. You're Amy Nobel I believe, correct?"

Amy - "Why yes, just got here and familiarizing myself with the market"

Soldan - "My name is Soldan, I'm with the Arrival Colony. Yes it's very nice here. May I sit for moment?"

Amy was hesitant but Soldan seemed sincere and friendly,

but a little mysterious - "Well sure – please have seat."

Soldan - "Thank you. I work in the Arrival Colony, and manage several departments related to humans relocating here – that's how I know your name. I actually teach several of the orientation classes. I work directly for John Foster."

Amy was just starting to get a bit uncomfortable and that last tidbit was a relief.

Amy - "Oh – wow, you mean John Foster *of the Council*? So, have you been here long yourself?"

Soldan - "Yes, for about 20 of your Earth years, I came here from Earth as well. I just wanted to take a moment, say hello and introduce myself."

Amy - "Well thanks …. So – how do you like it here on Tu?"

Soldan - "Best move of my life".

Amy - "I really like it here as well. Seems like humanity has a good chance here"

Soldan - "Well, yes indeed - but Tu has its own set of problems – but you'll learn all about that during orientation classes. Sometimes people set themselves up mentally that Tu is some kind of Utopian planet. It is no Utopia, while is is a reboot of Earth, humanity still has a lot to learn."

Amy - "What do you think the biggest challenge is for this planet?"

Soldan - "I think we haven't really experienced that yet. That will come with *the Exodus*. When you have a mass of humanity coming here that will carry with it all the bad habits, culture and problems of Earth, the real challenge will be to root that out of them.

Unfortunately, it will take them a couple of generations to relearn and evolve up. That will be the biggest challenge.

Soldan looked at his watch and got up out of his chair.

"Sorry, well, I have to be getting along. It was lovely meeting you. Welcome to Tu."

With that, Soldan made a polite exit.

Robin Sutter had been watching the scene with Soldan and Amy from a few tables away.

Once Soldan had disappeared from view, she came over to Amy's table. Robin and her husband David had arrived on the same ship as she and Bob had.

Robin - "Hi – you're Amy right?"

Amy - "Yes, I remember you, you and your husband are from Sydney right?"

Robin - "That's right. So how do you like it so far?"

Amy - "It's amazing. I find it all kind of surreal."

Robin - "Me too. I think my husband David went along on the same mission as your boyfriend Bob - with Michael."

Amy - "I have no idea, one minute we're sitting there in that meeting hall and Bob is whisked away with Michael, I saw a bunch of people leaving and I have no idea where Bob went or when he'll be back."

Robin - "I know, all hush hush. I think David is with him - coming back tonight but I don't know for sure. Did anyone tell you what your assignment is yet?"

Amy - "No, but I haven't really decided yet what it is I want to do, and no one has told me what it is they want me to do, so I've been exploring a bit and trying to take it all in.

I love this market – I haven't seen produce this fresh in a long time. Oh – and I saw this really cute little bizarre creature in the woods today as I was walking here. He looked like a little gargoyle creature."

Robin - "Oh – wait – I saw those last night – those are dragon monkeys! Our escort told us about those – totally harmless and some people make pets out of them. I can't believe all the wildlife around the residential areas – it's amazing. I was sitting outside watching the deer this morning, and then there were a flock of wild turkeys came wandering through!

I'm really lovin' it here. Have you played '*fashion show*' yet with the replicator?"

Amy - "No – I haven't really had the time to sit and figure out how it works, Bob has done all sorts of stuff, he was replicating test gear and stuff for the mission he went on with Michael."

Robin - "Oh my god, it's a blast! We're going to have to have a fashion party once you get a bit more settled I'll get you all figured out on the replicator, you will love it. Look at this scarf.

Robin pulled the scarf she was wearing around her neck off and handed it to Amy.

Robin -"Check it out – it's one of the oldest they have in the replication library, it's *La Belle Creole Paris 1952!*"

Amy - "Jesus it's gorgeous! And you got this from the replicator?"

Robin – (laughing) "Yes! And they have dozens of others as well, different brands, colors – oh my god you will have to check it out!"

Sorry to be a busy body, but I gotta ask - so who was that you were just speaking to right before I came over?"

Amy - "Turns out he's one of the head honchos here on Tu, he works directly for John Foster and manages relocations and does some of the orientation training."

Robin - "You know I saw him talking on his phone a little while ago in one of the little side streets off the market, kind of like a little alleyway, and it was strange. I was leaning on a wall around the other side of him – and I don't think he thought anyone was nearby.

It was like he was super serious, really angry with whoever he was talking to and I could hear him say something about 'have the Earth teams get it before the Zui have any idea about what is going on, and I don't want Foster to know anything about this'.

Seemed kinda fishy if you ask me. I don't think he realized

how loud he was, I was a good 30 feet away and I don't think he realized how loud he was speaking.

Kind of reminds me of when I was a younger, in grade school, I used to amaze people with how well I could hear. I had a job at a machine shop during college and I lost a lot of frequencies in my hearing, and so – *wait a minute!*"

Robin had paused in mid-sentence for a reason. It's that look you get on your face when a light bulb goes on in your head.

Amy - "Well, you never know, might have been nothing -"

Amy stopped talking when she realized Robin was staring out into a kind of dazed look.

Robin - "You know how that Ted guy on the way over told us that the ships and this arrival colony – that there was like this healing energy thing they were running that was doing molecular repairs on our bodies as part of the detox?"

Amy - "Yeah, but I hadn't given it much thought."

Robin- "I think my hearing has been fixed!"

Amy - "Wow!"

Robin - "Yeah I noticed this morning when I woke up that my ears had kinda felt like they do when they pop, and that I could hear better than I had in a while. It was like the volume has been turned up all day!"

Amy - "I haven't really noticed anything other than my skin seems to be in better shape – I hadn't really thought about it though. I actually forgot about what Ted had said."

Robin - "So what do you think about what that guy said – what did you say his name was- Soldan?

Amy - "Yeah, but - I don't know, I -"

Robin - "Something is up – this guy, if he's who you said he was is pretty high up on the food chain."

Amy - "You should let David know – he can talk to Michael about it."

Robin - "Yeah, good call. I'll tell David next time he checks in. I just got this gut thing about him".

Dark Star

Michael and his team arrived back at the Annunaki arrival colony to find a huge ensemble of Tu military ships, Earth spec ops teams and Earth military teams.

Michael - "OK guys, follow my lead"

As they disembarked, Michael was greeted by their new interpreter, a Tu guide named Nui.

Nui - "You must be Michael. My name is Nui – uh, John Foster told me to meet you here. I am fully cleared for all access and will accompany your team."

Michael - "Excellent – what is the current situation?"

Nui - "Well, the ship has been moved to the underground hangar, and the Tu military has offloaded the cargo to a secure laboratory in the facility. They have been debriefing the captain and the other crew members for as much information about the cargo as possible."

Michael - "Let's head to the lab, and I would like to speak directly with the captain again."

Nui - "He will be relocated off of Tu. There is too much risk associated with having him here as well as the weapon. Both the weapon and captain will go separate ways."

Michael - "That is for the best."

Michael dialed John Foster.

Michael - "We're at the site. They are already planning to move the captain."

Foster - "Very well, I'll be waiting for your report"

The team showed their badges and the guard motioned them in.

They entered the main arrival colony building and made their way towards a waiting elevator.

Several members of an Earth spec ops team were milling about the lobby in full battle gear.

The Earth military liaison, a Navy commander named David Benton walked up to Michael as they entered the elevator.

Based upon what John Foster had said, their presence really annoyed Michael, and this bled through to the team.

Benton - "You must be Michael Stetson?" and extended his hand to shake it.

Benton's presence totally annoyed Michael, and Michael wasn't about to reciprocate and just kept walking.

Michael muttered quietly to himself - "Yes; *yes I am*"

Michael turned slightly and motioned to the team "C'mon, let's load in"

Michael and the team walked right past him as if he wasn't there. They quickly got into the elevator and let the elevator doors closing without acknowledging him.

After the doors closed and the elevator started to descend Bob quipped -

Bob - "*Well done*"

They all laughed.

Michael - "That probably didn't go over very well, but I don't want to get to chummy with anyone from the Earth military or those spec ops people – they are all killers and scary bastards. Not to mention outright liars."

Bob - "I've not trusted our military for some time. After all the wars, and buddies of mine that have come back damaged. I'm think I'm liking Tu much better."

Ken - "Two tours in Afghanistan – I can tell you I will never trust the Earth military again"

Simon - "*Word*"

Michael - "The day is coming very soon when we won't have to worry about any more spec op teams coming here from Earth. Foster is going to put a stop to that shit very soon. Well, it won't be Foster it will be the Zui. They're hip to that shit and they are about to nip it in the bud."

The elevator opened and they got off into a lobby and approached security.

Michael - "Hello I'm - " *Michael cut himself off. It was Shandra.* "- uh Michael"

They would have to keep things professional.

Shandra - "Hello *Michael*. Follow me."

Michael - "I really need to speak with the Annunaki captain."

Shandra - "Follow me. He is in his quarters and has asked that we do not disturb him any more today. I will arrange a meeting for you with him for the morning."

Michael - "Got it"

Bob - "This captain knows the urgency and is unavailable"?

Michael - "It's their culture. Always put off inquiry and access by humans, make us wait. They're a bit bigoted against humans."

Nui - "And the Annunaki *love to be the center of attention.*"

They made their way down a long hallway and entered the lab.

The weapon was about 20 feet in length, about 2 feet in diameter and looked like a cannon, only a much more sophisticated cannon with a crystal lens on the front. The Annunaki incorporated art with their technology, and the weapon was adorned with various art and symbols.

There appeared to be what looked like mounting arms on the side of the weapon, such that it could be mounted on a satellite or a spacecraft.

Michael - "Interesting. I am curious about the interface."

Shandra - "As I am sure you are aware, the Annunaki use a mind interface. That is the reason we are anxious to get this thing off the planet. We do not want any sleeper cells or agents finding out about it and accessing it with remote viewing. Ultimately, it will be disassembled so as to make it unusable."

Michael - "Have any of the other Earth teams had their hands on it?"

Shandra – "None have been allowed here by orders of John Foster."

Michael - "Very good. Petak, please get photos and some video of this thing, Foster wants a full report. Photograph only the device, but none of the people here."

Petak - "Sure thing Michael."

Petak began setting up lights and a tripod and began breaking out various camera gear.

Michael - "Ken, Simon, I want you guys here all night, at least one of you on guard all night. Shandra, is there any kind of quarters near here?"

Shandra - "Yes, the lab has quarters for several people. I will make sure your team has access. I will have guards here as well – no one except your team and my guards will have access to this lab".

Michael - "Good. Don't let any of your people look at the weapon. We have to keep any remote viewing possibilities to an absolute minimum. We'll stay here close and then in the morning we will be here with the captain and document the disassembly."

Shandra smiled - *"I will see you then in the morning then. And gentlemen, no contact at all with anyone outside, do not spend any more time looking at the weapon than is necessary – we do not want anyone remote viewing seeing what we see."*

With that Shandra was gone and Michael and the team settled into the lab's rather spartan quarters.

Ken - "It's a bit creepy being this close to that thing."

Simon - "I slept with nukes aboard a submarine many times in the torpedo room. This is cake."

Michael - "Bob, you and David head back into the lab, and work with Petak and assist him with the photography and video stuff. No more than 15 minutes, get in, get out."

Bob - "Will do boss."

After a few minutes working with Petak photographing the weapon and taking various measurements, it was time to get some rest.

Bob settled into the lab bunk room and caught some well deserved sleep. David found another bunk in one of the other labs.

Bob's only thoughts were about Amy and how she was doing, and trying to adjust to the time. It had definitely been a good day since he had slept.

Not really knowing what time of day it was, based upon

Earth time, he really didn't know how long he had been up and what time of day it was for his body. He went into a deep sleep.

Ken and Simon switched off the watch and things went uneventful for the night.

In the morning it was time to meet with the Annunaki captain. Coffee and breakfast from a nearby replicator was extremely convenient.

Bob - "Geez I am so fucked on what time of day it is. Still tryin' to get unjet-lagged or whatever it is, *planet-lagged*."

A few moments later Molki entered the lab and made his presence known. For the Annunaki, they were used to being the center of attention with humans, and loved to be seen.

Nui addressed Molki in Annunaki native tongue - "*We are ready*"

Molki - "I am here to assist you with the destroyer of worlds."

No sooner had he spoken, then there was the familiar flash of ultra white bright light that filled the room.

The Four had arrived and had transported themselves right into the lab.

They were all standing together in a small circle, facing out, and levitated a few inches above the floor.

At the sight of the four Zui, Molki got down on his knees in a prostrate reverence.

The Zui were communicating with Molki telepathically.

Zui - *"Rise Annunaki, we are not gods"*

Molki got up slowly, and dazed.

Zui - *"All here must know peace. This weapon will be moved by the Zui to a place where it can do no harm."*

Another bright flash of light filled the room and when it subsided, the weapon was gone, as was all of the photographic equipment, and any weapons anyone was carrying, and so were the Zui.

The room fell quiet. Everyone was stunned.

Bob - "Wow"

Michael - "I need to call Foster."

Michael dialed up Foster on his phone.

Michael - "Hey John I - "

Foster interrupted - "I already know Michael. They felt it was necessary to intervene on this one, no way they could risk it."

Michael - "Got it. Well ... I guess this wraps everything up."

Foster - "Pretty much. They're always one step ahead of us.

Michael - "No doubt"

Foster - "Head back, and bring your team to my chambers, something else has come up, and it looks like you and your team is needed on a run back to Earth, I'll explain when you get here."

Even though it was brief, the encounter with the Zui had really stunned everyone.

Bob - "So what's next?"

Michael - "No idea. One good thing is that we no longer have to worry about that weapon. Foster did say that something had come up and he needed us to make a run back to Earth but didn't say why.

Let's head back."

The transport settled on its pad at the arrival colony.

Michael and the team disembarked, still a little dazed and shaken.

Michael - "Let's go see Foster."

The Message

Once again the team was back in Foster's office. This time, Adam Orus was there and several other council members.

Foster ushered everyone from Michael's team into the office. "Thanks Michael, David, Bob, Petak, Ken, Simon. Please be seated."

Michael was feeling agitated. They had just gone through a harrowing scene and it was emotionally exhausting not just for Michael but the entire team was exhausted.

Foster - "This latest development, with the '*destroyer of worlds*' weapon has really upset the Zui. "

Michael was visibly exhausted by the close contact with the Zui.

Foster - "I know you are all emotionally exhausted right now. The good thing is that none of it will become the status quo. The problem is being dealt with immediately.

I have just returned from meeting with the Zui at their embassy. There were several other higher ranking Zui there and as you might imagine it was a very intense meeting.

In summary, the Zui have decided to accelerate **The Plan**.

There is are a couple of reasons the Zui have decided to accelerate.

Several years ago, I am not sure if any of you are aware of it, but although there's nothing in *The Message* to specifically state it was the Zui, we believe it was the Zui that contacted a few people on planet Earth and told them that they wanted to come to Earth and reveal themselves.

This has become known as '**The Message**'.

The Message essentially said that the Zui would not reveal themselves to Earth unless there was a collective invitation by humanity.

The whole "*prime directive*" thing was in effect. One of the contactees, a man in France wrote the message down and built a website with the Zui message.

Some even made Youtube versions of The Message. The message went viral, but was never really received by the masses – people just assumed it was a joke, or just didn't take it seriously.

The Message
by Jean Ederman

"Should we show up?"

Whoever translated this message to you is irrelevant, and should remain anonymous in your mind.

It is what you will do with this message that matters!

Each one of you wishes to exercise her / his free will and experience happiness.

These are attributes that were shown to us and to which we now have access.

Your free will depends upon the knowledge of your own. you have power. Your happiness depends upon the love that you give and receive.

Like all conscious races at this stage of progress, you may feel isolated on your planet. This impression makes you sure of your destiny.

You are at the brink of big upheavals that only a minority are aware of. It is not our responsibility to modify your future without you choosing it.

Consider this message as a worldwide referendum! Your answer is a ballot!

Who are we?

Neither your scientists nor your religious representatives speak unanimously about the unexplained celestial events that mankind has witnessed for thousands of years.

To know the truth, one must face it without the filter of one's beliefs, however it they may be respectable. a growing number of anonymous researchers of yours are exploring new knowledge paths and are getting very close to reality.
Today, your civilization is flooded with an ocean of information of which only a tiny part, the less upsetting one, is notably diffused.

What in your history seemed ridiculous or improbable has become *often possible, then realized, in particular, in the last fifty years.*

Be aware that the future will be even more surprising. you will discover the worst as well as the best.

Like billions others in this galaxy, we are conscious creatures that some name "extra-terrestrials", even though reality is subtler.

There is no essential difference between you and us, save for the experience of un certain stages of evolution.

Like in any other organized structure, hierarchy exists in our internal relationships. ours is based upon the wisdom of several races. it is with the approval of this hierarchy that we turn to you.

Like most of you, we are in the quest of the Supreme Being.

Therefore we are not gods or lesser gods but virtually your equals in the cosmic brotherhood.

Physically, we are somewhat different from you but for most of us humanoid-shaped. Our existence is a reality but the majority of you does not perceive it yet. We are not mere observations, we are consciences just like you.

You fail to comprehend us because we remain invisible to your senses and measure instruments most of the time.

We wish to fill this void at this moment in your history. we made this collective decision but this is not enough.

We need your decision.

Through this message, you become the decision-makers!

Yes, You personally. We have no human representative on earth who could guide your decision.

Why are we not visible?

At uncertain stages of evolution, cosmic "humanities" discover new forms of science beyond the apparent controlling of matter.

Structured dematerialization and materialization are part of them.

This is what your humanity has reached in a few laboratories, in close collaboration with other "extra-terrestrial" creatures at the cost of hazardous compromises that remain purposely hidden from you by some of your **representatives**.

Apart from the aerial or spatial objects or phenomena known by your scientific community, that you call 'ufos, there are multidimensional manufactured spaceships that use these prinicples.

Many human beings have been in visual, auditory, tactile or psychic contact with such ships, some of which are under evil powers that govern you.

The scarcity of your observations is due to the outstanding advantages provided by the dematerialized state of these ships.

By not witnessing them by yourself, you can not believe in their existence. We fully understand this. The majority of these observations are made on an individual basis so as to touch the soul and not to modify any organized system.

This is deliberate. There are other races that surround you that use the same principle, but for very different reasons and results.

Negative multidimensional beings play a part that in the exercise of power in the shadow of human oligarchy, discretion is motivated by their will to keep their existence unknown.

For us, discretion is motivated by the **respect of the human free will** *that people can exercise to manage affairs so that on their own they can reach technical and spiritual maturity.*

Humankind's entrance into the family of galactic civilizations is greatly expected.

We can appear in broad daylight and help you attain this junction.

We have not done it so far, as too few of genuinely desired you have it, because of ignorance, indifference or fear, and because the emergency of the situation did not justify it.

Many of those who study our appearances count the lights in the night without lighting the way. They think in terms often of objects when it is all about conscious beings.

Who are you?

You are the offspring of many traditions that have been throughout time mutually enriched by each others' contributions. The same applies to the races at the surface of the earth.

Your goal is to unite in the respect of these roots to accomplish a common goal.

The appearance of your cultures seems to keep you separated because you substitute it to your deeper being.

Outward appearance is now more important than the essence of your subtle nature. For the powers in place, this prevalence of the shape constitutes the ramparts against any form of jeopardy.

You are being called on to overcome appearance, while still respecting it for its richness and beauty. Understanding the conscience of appearance makes us love men in their diversity.

Peace does not mean not making war, it consists in becoming what you are in reality.

Understand this, the number of solutions within your reach are decreasing.

One of them consists in contact with another race would that reflect the image of what you are in reality.

What is your situation?

Except for rare occasions, our interventions always had very little incidence on your capacity to make collective decisions and your own future.

This is motivated by our knowledge of your deep psychological mechanisms.

Personal reedom is built every day as a being becomes aware of himself and of his environment, getting rid of progressively constraints and inertias, whatever they may be.

Despite the multitude numerous, brave and willing human consciences, those inertias are artificially maintained for the profit of a growing centralizing power.

Until recently, mankind lived a satisfying monitoring of its decisions, but it is losing more and more the control of its own fate because of the growing use of advanced technologies.

The lethal consequences on the earthly and human ecosystems become irreversible. you are slowly but surely losing your extraordinary capacity to make life desirable.

Your resilience will artificially decrease, independently of your own will. Such technologies exist that affect your body as well as your mind.

Such plans are on their way. However, this can change as long as you **keep this creative power in you**, even if it cohabits with the dark intentions of your potential lords.

This is the reason why we remain invisible. this single power is doomed to vanish should a collective reaction of great magnitude not happen. The period to come is that of rupture, whichever it may be.

Should you wait for the last moment to find solutions?

Should you anticipate or undergo pain?

Your history has never ceased to be marked by encounters between peoples who had to discover one another in conditions that were often conflictual.

Conquests almost always happened to the detriment of others.

Earth has now become a village where everyone knows everyone, but conflicts still persist and threats of all kinds get worse in duration and intensity.

Although a human being is an individual, yet having many potential capacities, all can not exercise them with dignity.

This is the case for the biggest majority of you for reasons that are essentially geopolitical. There are several billion of you.

The education of your children and your living conditions, as well as the conditions of numerous animals and much plant life are nevertheless under the thumb of a small number of your political, financial, military and religious representatives.

Your thoughts and beliefs are modeled after partisan interests to turn you into slaves while at the same time giving you the feeling that you are in total control of your destiny, which in essence is the reality.

There is a long way between a wish and a fact when the true rules of the game at hand are unknown.

This time, you are not the conqueror.

Biasing information is a millenary strategy for human beings. Inducting thoughts, emotions that do not originate in your own minds, using mind control technologies is an even older strategy.

Wonderful opportunities of progress run parallel to threats of destruction. Dangers and opportunities now exist.

However, you can only perceive what is being shown to you.

While your natural resources reach their end, no long-term collective project has been launched to save the ecosystem.

Ecosystem exhaustion mechanisms have exceeded irreversible limits. The scarcity of resources and their unfair distribution - resources which will rise in price day after day will bring fratricide fights at a large scale.

In the very heart of your cities and countryside hatred grows bigger but so does love.

That is what keeps you confident in your ability to find solutions. But the critical mass is insufficient and a sabotage work is cleverly being carried out. Human behaviors, formed from past habits and trainings, have such an inertia that this perspective leads you to a dead end.

You entrust these problems to representatives, whose conscience of common well-being slowly fades away in front of corporatist interests, with those difficulties.

They are always debating on the form but rarely on the content. Just at the moment of action, delays will accumulate to the point when you have to submit rather than choose.

This is the reason why, more than ever in your history, your decisions of today will impact directly and significantly your survival of tomorrow.

Radically, what could modify this event inertia that is typical of any civilization?

Where will a collective and unifying awareness form, that will stop this blind rushing ahead?

Tribes, populations and human nations have always interacted with one another.

With the threats weighing upon the human family, it is time that perhaps greater interaction occurred. A great wave of energy is on the verge of emerging. It mixes very positive but also very negative aspects.

Who is the "Third Party"?

There are two ways to establish a cosmic contact with another civilization:

1. Via its standing representatives with individuals directly
or
2. Without distinction.

The first way entails fights of interests, **the second way brings awareness.**

The first way was used by a group of races motivated by keeping mankind in slavery, thereby controlling earth resources, the gene pool and human emotional energy.

The second way was chosen by a group of races allied with the cause of the spirit of service.

We have, at our end, subscribed to **this disinterested cause** and introduced ourselves a few years ago to representatives of the human power who refused our *outstretched hand on the pretext of incompatible interests with their strategic vision.*

*That is why today individuals are to make this choice **personally** without any representative interfering.*

In times past, we trusted others to contribute to your happiness, and they did not.

We propose it now to . . . you!

Most of you ignore that non-human creatures took over the governments of the Earth, and no one ever suspected it. Neither was this accessible to your senses. Their takeover and control was done so subtly as to be unseen.

They do not exist in the same dimensional plane, and that is precisely what could make them extremely efficient and frightening in the near future. However, be aware that a large number of your representatives are fighting this danger!

Be aware that not all abductions are made against you by us. It is difficult to recognize the truth!

How could you, under such conditions exercise your free will, when it is so much manipulated? What are you really free of?

Peace and reunification of your peoples would be a first step toward the harmony with civilizations other than yours.

Those who manipulate you behind the scenes want to avoid peace and unification at all cost because, by dividing, they reign!

Their strength comes from their capacity to distillate mistrust and fear into you. Their deadlines are close and mankind will undergo unprecedented torments for the next ten cycles.

This harms your very cosmic nature.

To defend yourselves against this aggression that bears no face, you need at least to have enough information that leads to the solution.

Here again, appearance will not be enough to tell the dominator from the ally. At your current state of psychism, it is extremely difficult for you to distinguish between them.

In addition to your intuition, training will be necessary when the time has come. being aware of the priceless value of free will, **we are inviting you to an alternative.**

What can we offer?

We can offer you a more holistic vision of the universe and of life, constructive interactions, the experience of fair and fraternal relationships, liberating technical knowledge, eradication of suffering, controlled exercise of personal powers, the access to new forms of energy and, finally, a better comprehension of consciousness.

We do not bring fear, or bring you laws that you would not have chosen.

Now is the time to work on your own selves, individually and collectively to build the world you desire, the spirit of quest to new skies.

What do we get out of this?

Should you decide that contact take place, we would rejoice over the safeguarding of fraternal equilibrium in this region of the universe, fruitful diplomatic exchanges, and the intense joy of knowing that you are united to accomplish what you are capable of!

The feeling of joy is strongly sought in the universe for its energy is divine.

So, what is the question we ask you? Simply, **"do you wish that we show up?"**

How can you answer this question?

The truth of soul can be read by telepathy. We can hear you telepathically.

You only need to ask yourself clearly this question and give your *answer as clearly, on your own or in a group, as you wish.*

Being in the heart of a city or in the middle of a desert does not impact the efficiency of your answer, yes or no, immediately after asking the question!

Just do it as if you were speaking to yourself but thinking about the message.

This is a universal question and these mere few words, put in their context, have a powerful meaning.

You should not let hesitation get in the way. This is why you should calmly think about it, in all conscience.

In order to perfectly associate your answer with the question, it is recommended that you answer right after another reading of this message.

Breathe and let all the power of your own free will penetrate you.

Be proud of what you are!

The problems that you may have weaken you. Forget about them for a few minutes to be yourselves.

Feel the force that springs up in you. You are in control of yourselves!

A single thought, a single answer can drastically change your near future, in one way as in another.

Your individual decision of asking in your inner self that we show up on your plane and in broad daylight is precious and essential to us.

And even though you can choose the way that best suits you, rituals are essentially useless. This is not a religious exercise.

A sincere request made with your heart and your own will will always be perceived by those of us whom it is sent to.

In your own private polling booth of your secret will, you will determine the future.

What is the lever effect?

Leverage in numbers. This decision should be made by the greatest number among you, even though it might seem like a minority.

It is recommended to spread this message, in all manner, in as many languages as possible, to those around you, whether or not they seem receptive to this new vision of the future.

Do it using in a humorous tone or derision if that can help you. you can even openly and publicly make fun of it if it makes you feel more comfortable but do not be indifferent for at least exercised you will have your free will.

Forget about the false prophets and the beliefs that have been transmitted to you about us.

This request is one of the most intimate that can be asked to you.

Making a decision by yourself, as an individual, is your right as well as your responsibility!

Passivity only leads to the absence of freedom.

Similarly, indecision is never efficient.

If you really want to cling to your beliefs, that is something we understand, then say no. if you do not know what to choose, do not say yes because of mere curiosity. Passion in your decision is important!

This is not a show, this is actual daily life, we are alive and living!

Your history has plenty of episodes when men and women determined to were able to influence the thread of events in spite of their small number.

Just like a small number is enough to take temporal power on earth and influence the future of the majority, a small number of you can radically change your fate as an answer to the impotence in face of so much inertia and hurdles!

You can ease the mankind's birth to brotherhood in the cosmos! One of your thinkers once said: "give me a hand-hold and i'll raise the earth".

Spreading this message will then be the hand-hold to strengthen, we will be the long lever, you will be the craftsmen to . . . **raise the earth as a consequence of our appearance.**

What would be the consequences of a positive decision?

For us, the immediate consequence of a positive collective decision would be the materialization of many ships, in your sky and on earth.

For you, the direct effect would be the rapid abandoning of many certitudes and beliefs. A simple visual contact – it would be conclusive and it would have repercussions of major consequence on your future.

Much knowledge would be modified forever. The organization of your societies would be deeply upheaved forever, in all fields of activity. Power would become single because you would see for yourself that we are living. Your values would scale up!

The most important thing for us is that humankind would form a single family in front of the "unknown" that we would represent!

Danger would slowly melt away from your homes because you indirectly would force the undesirable ones, those we name the "third party", to show up and vanish.

You would all bear the same name and share the same roots: **mankind!**

Later on, peaceful and respectful exchanges would be possible if such is your wish.

For now, he can not smile who is hungry, he who is fearful can not welcome us. We are sad to see men, women and children suffering to such a degree in their flesh and in their hearts when they bear such bright inner light.

This light can be your future!

Our relationships progressive several stages of several years or decades would occur: demonstrative appearance of our ships, physical appearance beside human beings, collaboration in your technical and spiritual evolution, discovery of parts of the galaxy.

Every time, new choices would be offered to you. You would then choose by yourself to cross new stages if you think it necessary to your external and inner well-being.

No interference would be decided upon unilaterally. We would even leave as soon as you would collectively wish that we do.

Depending upon the speed to spread the message across the world, several weeks, or even several months will be necessary before our "great appearance", provided the majority of those who will have used their capacity to choose.

If this message receives the necessary support, the main difference between your daily prayers to entities of a strictly spiritual nature and your current decision is extremely simple: **we are technically equipped to materialize** *!*

Why such a historical dilemma?

We know that on your planet, "foreigners" are considered as enemies as long as they embody the "unknown".

In a first stage, the emotion that our appearance will generate will strengthen your relationships on a worldwide scale.

How could you know our arrival is the consequence of your collective choice?

For the simplest reason - otherwise we would have been already there for a long time at your level of existence! If we are not there yet, it is because you have not such a decision made explicitly.

Some of you might think that we would make you believe in a deliberate choice of yours so as to legitimate our arrival, though this would not be true.

What interest would we have to offer you that you have not got any access to yet, for the benefit of the greatest number of you?

How could you be un certain that this is not yet another subtle maneuver of the "third party" to better enslave you?

We are not terrorists – we are open and transparent. Is not the terrorism that corrodes you a blatant example?

Whatever, you are the sole judge in your own heart and soul! Whatever your choice, it would be respectable and respected! Those who enslave you do not ask your consent.

In your situation, the precautionary principle that consists in not trying to discover us no longer prevails.

You are already in the box that the "third party" has created around you. Whatever your decision, you will have to get out of it.

In the face of such a dilemma, one ignorance against another, you need to ask your intuition - do you want to see us with your own eyes, or simply believe what your thinkers say?

That is the real question after thousands of years, one day, this choice was going to be inevitable choosing between two unknowns.

Why spread such a message?

Translate and spread this message widely.

This action will affect your future in an irreversible and historical way at the scale of millenniums.

Otherwise, it will postpone a new opportunity to choose to several years later, at least one generation, if it can survive.

Not choosing, stands for undergoing other people's choice. Not informing others stands for running the risk of obtaining a result that is contrary to one's expectations.

Remaining indifferent means giving up one's free will.

It is all about your future. it is all about your evolution. It is possible that this invitation does not receive your collective assent and that, because of a lack of information, it will be disregarded.

Nevertheless no individual desire goes unheeded in the universe.

Imagine our arrival tomorrow. thousands of ships.

A unique culture shock in today's mankind's history. It will then be too late to regret not making a choice and spreading the message because this discovery will be irreversible.

We do insist that you do not rush into it, but do think about it and decide!

The big medias will not be interested in necessarily spreading this message, so it is therefore your task, as an anonymous yet an extraordinary thinking and loving being, to transmit it.

You are still the architects of your own fate . . .

"Do you wish that we show up?"

Green Light

Foster continued - "So, in light of recent developments, the Zui have changed their thinking about the whole non-interference directive they imposed upon Earth, because Earth is starting to become irreversibly damaged.

The have decided to go forward with *Operation Exodus*.

The actual fate of mankind is now at stake, and they cannot stand idly by waiting for us to "get it" and wake up.

The Zui have asked, or ordered, which ever way anyone wants to interpret it, that effective immediately, I order all Earth black ops and secret space program teams to leave the planet.

That order was issued just a little while ago and the Tu military commander told me they are complying.

No one from Earth was happy about it, but they know that if need be I can get help to enforce my order from the Zui. They are all to be gone in the next 24 hours. All the Earth ships, secret space program personnel and their equipment are to be gone.

The Zui have begun scanning Tu for any and all black ops and secret space units, and are going to ensure their removal, meaning they are not going to wait or depend upon any Tu military units to do the job. They want the Earth units gone and are going to make sure it happens.

In three days, a Zui ship will arrive. It is what they refer to as a *"science ship"*. These science ships are very large, not as big as their terraforming ships, but very large, like 30 kilometers in diameter. They haven't brought a science ship here in several hundred years, well before the planet was first colonized."

Michael - "And so how does this '*science ship*' fit into accelerating Operation Exodus?"

Foster - "The science ship is the same ship they use right after terraforming to seed a planet with various lifeforms, and monitor the planet's ecosystems.

It also gives the Zui the ability to build large ark ships. They're going to build them right here in orbit around Tu."

The room fell silent. Everyone was spellbound. The realization that was occurring to everyone in the room was that the Zui planned on starting the migration of humanity from Earth to Tu.

For years, the Tu were aware of this plan as an idea, but it had never really been seen as something that was going to occur in the near future, it was always seen as something happening a few years off, certainly *not now*.

No one really knew how they would proceed, or how long it would take, but the whole idea was utterly *fantastic*.

Foster continued - "It basically starts like this. They will be assembling a large mining and processing facility below the surface just south of their embassy."

Michael - "Any idea about how many ships they plan to build? I mean, the Zui have huge terra-forming ships, why do they need to build more?"

Foster - "This will be one of the largest migrations they have done in some time. Part of the problem is timing.

In other migrations they have undertaken, the populations of the planets involved were completely in tune and aware of what was happening. Their cultures were already advanced enough to accept the idea of extraterrestrials.

They did not have to deal with culture shock, and could a manage a planetary migration over a period of time, so that if there was an impending calamity, they would have a longer period of time to work with.

Earth is in its infancy in this regard. Not by design, but because of the corruption and the takeover by the military industrial complex.

The people have been lied to and conditioned to believe that extraterrestrials are going to destroy them. Their science-fiction is very weak, and not science based for the most part, as far as *acclimation* goes.

There is a growing consensus on planet Earth, that extraterrestrials exist, it's just that contact has been minimal and marginalized and none of the information is really consistent or accurate.

The concepts of extraterrestrial life, the ETs themselves, are all distorted to such a degree no one on Earth except maybe a handful of people in dark programs there really knows what the truth is anymore.

There have even been other supposed "messages" that have been published that purport that the Earth is already under a very quiet invasion and that mankind's gullibility and quest for technology will ensnare us and make us the slaves of the invaders, who will masquerade as benefactors, but in reality will take over the planet.

Earth is at a precipice of disaster. The Zui are concerned that when they make the reveal, Earth will go through a period of chaos. Many innocent people may die."

Adam - "When that ship arrives here, they will have the capacity to build several hundred ark ships. There some very rich mineral deposits several hundred kilometers below the surface here, including iron ore, magnesium, gold and other elements – they will use it for raw materials along with their replication technology.

And from what we have been told by Brother, they can build 20 or 30 of these ark ships a month. They will be using an army of android labor as well.

The ark ships are about 3km in diameter and able to carry 60,000 humans in total comfort."

Imagine your favorite football stadium or concert venue that has a 60,000 seat capacity. Imagine a space-ship the size of a football stadium. The math was staggering.

Adam continued - "The Zui plan to build 250 ark-ships that could handle 60,000 people each, and that group of ark-ships could move *12.5 million people per trip.*

If the Zui could load up a group of 250 ships each week, and bring them to Tu, in 5 years time they would have been able to move 3.1 Billion people off of planet Earth to Tu. In 10 years time they will have been able to move 6 Billion people off of planet Earth. If they do it twice a week, they will have nearly evacuated Earth in 5 years.

They plan to move most to Tu, but will relocate many to other habitable planets as well. This would enable the Zui to begin re-terraforming Earth. Earth would finally be allowed to heal."

-

The Tu already had 100 ark ships capable of moving 10,000 people at at time.

One of the council members present asked - "What about their people – will they be living on the planet or on that ship?"

Foster - "I'm not sure. All they basically gave me was an overview, how they actually implement things is their own way. The Zui will begin a mining process that they will use for their base materials.

Robotic devices manage every aspect, so that the Zui do not have to enter the mines, the machines do everything.

The Zui then use teleportation and molecular modification technology to create large underground chambers miles below the surface of the planet, and then set large combination smelting and mining machines into those mining chambers to tap into the molten magma of the planet itself and then they filter out the elements they need.

Using a molecular separation process on the magma, they would literally siphon the various elements out of the depths of the crust of the planet, and then the factory ship would teleport the metal out of the underground chambers up to the factory ship, which literally forms the ship as the metal is teleported.

In this way, they can tap into a huge amount of fresh building material without affecting the surface ecology of the planet and from what the Zui have told me this is faster than what their replication technology can do. They replicate the internal systems, once the ship is constructed. They put a power plant in it, and then begin filling it out from the inside.

The science ship would serve as an orbiting space station and space-ship factory for the Zui.

There was talk about using Earth's moon the same way they modified Tu Ono, but this plan was abandoned. Why we don't know, but it's probably because for the Zui, distance is no issue since their ships can move between the Earth and Tu within a few moments.

In just under a year, the Zui would have 250 ark-ships built, and ready for shuttle between Earth and Tu.

Foster - "I know you all have a ton of questions, and they will all be answered. Suffice to say this planet is going to get very busy in the coming days."

—

On schedule, within a few days the Zui science ship had arrived. The Zui began immediately building out more arrival colonies.

Many were already in place from the replication facilities at

Minora South and New Didiza.

The Zui plan was to station some 40 – 50 thousand Zui-human hybrids in each colony on Tu as well as androids. Each home constructed would have its own android.

Their replication technology meant they could build out an numerous arrival colonies inside of a a few months with everything necessary for human comfort and living, not just refugee camps but a great place to live.

Tu had suddenly become a very busy place.

The Reveal

12 months passed quickly since the Zui had said they were launching the plan for the actual reveal.

Bob and Amy had acclimated themselves quite nicely to life on Tu and had moved out of the arrival colony into a home several kilometers outside the colony.

They had enough room to setup a very large garden, with a geodesic dome.

They really enjoyed their new home on Tu, and it was a place they enjoyed spending time off-mission.

Amy had decorated the place with a rather country, bohemian style, with lots of natural elements, with tapestries on the walls and plants throughout the house.

Collection missions had become somewhat routine for Michaels' team.

Bob and Amy had done their own solo collection missions, as have Robin and Dave. Michael liked having Ken and Simon around for security.

They had all grown together with a sense of camaraderie. The Reveal would prove to be a new growth phase for all of them.

The ark-ships were all complete and ready. Some were parked in orbit around Tu, some were parked on the surface.

Ellis Island had undergone major changes. It would become the capital city of sorts once Operation Exodus was underway. Housing was now in place for some 500,000 additional residents.

The Zui and the Tu finished constructing additional arrival

colonies at 1000 additional locations on the planet, some capable of handling *600,000* people at a time.

There was an expansion of the underground tube train that to connect all of the arrival colonies.

The question that immediately enters one's mind is how would the Zui proceed with the actual reveal to the human race.

Do they land on the front steps of some government? Which government? What country?

Science fiction lore always shows giant fleets of massive spacecraft hovering over major cities, so would they do as science fiction suggests? That would likely cause panic.

The Zui knew they would have to tread carefully.

The Zui knew from their hidden observers already on Earth that the shadow government of Earth was using scalar wave technology to disable any alien spacecraft coming into Earth's orbit. Earth's military had essentially killed any idea of a welcome mat for extraterrestrials.

The Zui would start by using existing Earth infrastructure systems to reach humanity without landing a single ship. An open landing would happen, but not initially.

They would start by purchasing huge amounts of broadcasting time on television networks under the guise of a sports and science channel, globally.

They would build a huge free email platform like *Google, Microsoft and Yahoo*, but their features available would make the existing platforms pale in comparison.

They would call it the *Zeetek Network*. They would feature *Zeetek Email*, and productivity apps like calendaring and project management.

Anticipating that the reveal was soon, they already spent the previous couple of years setting up their own data center high up in the Arctic out of reach from any governmental interference. With everything in place, all they had to do was launch the site, and begin promoting it.

They had smartphone productivity apps as well, creating a network of communications platforms to reach every man woman and child independent of the established media channels.

They knew that when their ships appeared in the sky, there might well be an attempt to kill the Earth's internet by the various militaries on the Earth.

60 days before the reveal, the Zui would launch a micro-satellite based internet service that anyone could connect with a small USB adapter, and it provided amazing speed.

You could get the USB adapter for free from Amazon and at electronics stores. The rates they advertised for their service were outrageously low and made cable and dsl connections seem antiquated.

So a combined strategy of internet apps, smartphone apps, and now a micro-satellite based internet service with unparalleled customer service. The Zui were also providing free mobile phone service through their same network.

The ZeeTek backbone network was in reality thousands of small drones the size of basketballs that enabled global connectivity from anywhere. The drones were positioned such that they hovered noiselessly a few hundred feet in the air, and by use of phased frequency shifting, essentially invisible.

The network would be advertised globally, with a free 45-day trial. It would have the look and feel of a cutting edge San Francisco internet startup.

A slick advertising campaign would be launched beforehand to get public anticipation revved up for this new satellite based service.

The ads were huge on the touchy-feel message of joy and happiness.

Another trick to get people on board was to create a fake hacker website where you could download unlock codes for the adapters. When news of the hacker site hit the press, ZeeTek officials would only say that there was nothing they could do about the codes, and that they were going to go ahead and make access free for the time being and change their business model to adapt. They would say they had already purchased a huge number of the USB devices and it would be too costly to change them.

The goal was to get as many people connected to their network as possible beforehand, and if people thought they were getting away with something, it did not matter.

The Zui spent months getting key humans employed into all of the major internet backbone companies to ensure their network was connected.

On the day of the reveal, as the ark-ships hovered over every major city and metropolitan area, they would airdrop small parachutes with waterproof, softball sized containers stuffed with 10 usb network adapters in them for humans to use connect to their network.

Millions of these softballs would be released. This meant that if the Earth's internet was disrupted, people could still connect to the ZeeTek network. You could still connect even if Earth based wifi frequencies were jammed by the military.

The goal was then to use their own internet connection to broadcast their greeting live from their own website, without disruption.

They would also buy huge amounts of airtime on Earth television networks the day of the reveal to broadcast a welcome message.

People in America waking up and watching their various morning news and infotainment shows would see a bit of a change in the ads by ZeeTek.

A week before the reveal, the ZeeTek ads would begin a new campaign that used sunny, inspirational messages with nothing more than "Today, something wonderful is about to happen".

The ZeeTek ads were getting quite a bit of discussion on talk shows and on the internet.

A day before the ships would reveal themselves, the ads changed once more.

The ads showed happy scenes, a small child building a sandcastle at the beach, playing on playgrounds, and huge titles "We come in peace".

The ZeeTek website had essentially a blank page with the photo of a happy baby, and the words "We come in peace".

Anyone on ZeeTek email would have a similar email, "We come in peace".

And then, the day of The Reveal arrived.

Michael assembled his team in John Foster's office.

Foster - "Well boys this is the big day. The Zui are already in position over Earth and from what I hear The Reveal is about an hour away.

An Michael, I'd like you and your team to hold off about a week before heading to Earth on any collections.

Oh, and by the way, within the past hour the Zui have been

quietly busy neutralizing all of the military weapons systems around Earth.

There is anticipated resistance, and so we want to keep the Tu ships out a bit before we go in. Once the Zui have neutralized the Earth military issues, then we'll be clear to head in.

So, Michael, I want your team to head to New York city, we have a team on the ground there and I need you to coordinate with them a couple of immediate pickups. You'll actually be able to land downtown inside one of our Collector warehouses, but not until things settle down a bit and then we'll have clearance.

The Zui are planning a special message in 3 days after The Reveal. They want to give the planet a couple of days to absorb the shock of The Reveal, but they don't want to wait too long before going into the next phase.

They must have several hundred ships there. Brother and Sister are also there, as are Father and Mother."

-

And then it happened ...

All across the Earth, the ads changed. "We come in peace, we are in the skies above you. We are your brothers and sisters".

The Zui simultaneously began to materialize their ships.

As people in major cities were starting their major commutes, traffic was getting snarled as people were looking up and seeing the huge Zui ark-ships hovering over their cities.

Soon there were military fighters buzzing the Zui ark-ships.

The planet was coming to a stand-still.

All of the major news outlets - CNN, Fox, MSNBC, RT. BBC were all providing real-time coverage of this momentous event.

For the first hour of the first day, there was considerable chaos and confusion.

The ZeeTek ads changed again on their website and on television.

> *"We will be broadcasting a special message in 3-days to the people of Earth.*
>
> *Tune in to the ZeeTek home page for a special message from the Zui people to the people of Earth.*
>
> *The Zui have no intention of bringing any harm to the people of Earth.*
>
> *We are your long lost ancestors, the fathers of your race. We need no representatives from any Earth governments to speak to you."*

A special session was being convened in the United Nations in New York City. The US Pentagon was as busy as an anthill. NASA was in direct communications with the US White House and US President.

The President of the US was in a joint teleconference with leaders from NASA, and the obvious question to NASA was *"Did you see anything like this coming?"*

The head of NASA responded "We had some guidance from the military that something may be happening but we just didn't have anything concrete."

The President ordered an immediate convention of the Joint Chiefs of Staff and other leaders.

The FAA in the US as well as other governments around the globe began shutting down airlines for fear of some kind of attack in aircraft.

Television-land was on fire with news, analysis and conjecture about whether the Zui were good or evil.

Religious leaders were being interviewed, the Dalai Llama, the Pope, television evangelists, and even local preachers were being spotlighted for guidance about the situation.

There was a mounting public discussion about the relevance of religion in light of the extraterrestrial presence.

Talk show hosts were going crazy across the spectrum. CNN's Wolf Blizter was discussing the various aspects of the sizes of the Zui spacecraft, showing maps of the massive drops of millions of little parachutes with USB network adapters.

Larry King was in a heated debate with U2's Bono about the good or evil intentions of the Zui.

King - "So you really think the aliens are here to do us good – what makes you feel that way?"

Bono - "Man this the biggest thing! I've already been up there and met with them! I really believe they are here to help us. They feel like we are lost, and really incapable of fixing the problems we have here on this planet and they are here to help."

King - "You've already been up there in one of those ships?"

Bono - "Yeah man, they are the warmest, most amazing people. Amazing."

The media was filled with a buzz of both pro and con about the arrival of the Zui.

Skeptics skipped past reality vs unreality and moved right into intent.

The world was in transition from the status quo into full disclosure.

A unifying sense was sweeping the planet. Mankind was in a state of realization. A realization, *more so a validation* that this little hunk of rock called planet Earth was no longer all that is. That Earth is only but one billions of other habited planets in the cosmos.

People were in the streets celebrating.

There was also a lot of angry rhetoric being hurled at the governments of the world for hiding the truth of extraterrestrial contact.

The Pope was broadcasting a special message direct from the Vatican. "We must welcome our new friends, they are God's help to mankind in a time of distress."

Every major power had their militaries on high alert. Most of the world's governments were in some kind of emergency session as they tried to get a handle on the reality of disclosure.

As the first three days passed, things settled down but there was definitely a heightened sense of awareness in the air. The status quo had been broken, globally.

There was a positive sense, globally that things were going to be different.

The Zui began their next phase, their version of a new world order, but not in the evil sense that had permeated popular culture, but in a new sense of hope that mankind was no longer left to his own evil devices, *that help had arrived.*

The Dawn of A New Age

All of the major networks dedicated their morning shows to full Zui coverage. On every channel, there was a backdrop of a Zui ark-ship hovering over a city.

Television people were quick to pick up on the latest Zui terminology and began incorporating it into their jargon. All across the globe the announcement of the Zui message caused a major pause as people stopped everything to listen, in their own languages.

It did not matter which network or channel you turned to, all had been interrupted for the special message.

A white screen appeared. Slowly, fading from white, a beautiful room emerged, beautifully adorned like an ancient palace, filled with flowers and ferns, and beautiful tapestries on the walls.

A male voiceover, with a soothing tone announced, with titling on the screen *"People of Earth, greetings. We come in love and peace."* A moment later, the sound of a wind chime, and then a female voiceover in similar manner announced *"Love is all"*.

There was a long pause for about 30 seconds, and then the camera rotated to a portrait view of Brother, almost like a Buddha, dressed in beautiful multicolored robes, in a sort of middle-eastern style.

Brother began to speak and his words were captioned in a marquee at the bottom of the screen. *As he spoke, behind him images and video clips matched what he was speaking about.*

"Hello to all the people of Earth. My name is simply

'*Brother*'.

We have come a great distance from what you know as the Andromeda galaxy. We are called *The Zui*. We are not gods, in fact we are very similar to yourselves.

We have been here many times before, and have known your species for thousands of years.

We do not come to rule you or lead you, but simply to help you. In the coming days, we will teach you more and more about us, and where we come from and how we can help your species become its best.

Your peoples have endured thousands of years of struggle.

We were once like you, many thousands of years ago. We went through many painful growth phases and we know what your pain is.

We also know what love is, and we know you have great potential.

We have a policy of non-interference, and we only assist when absolutely necessary. This is now one of those times in your history that we are here to assist.

In our history, **We had one thing your planet does not have,** *and that is guidance.*

On our home worlds, we were taught by those who came before us, our true nature, and our true history.

You see, we are your progenitors. We are your true history. We are your ancestors.

Your planet has a lost and forgotten history, and even your most recent history has been clouded with lies and deception.

The lack of true guidance has now become a problem larger than you are able to handle without help.

This is partly our fault, and we regret not coming sooner, but that is past and we are here now.

We are not a perfect race, but we know that this is the time to help our brothers and sisters.

There has also been false guidance, and some have even told you that we are here to cause harm. Do not believe the negative, embrace the positive.

There have been negative energies, negative entities and humans who have been controlled by these negative entities, and these energies have done great harm to this planet and its people. Those negative entities will be removed.

From this day forward, those who wage war will be asked to stop, and if they do not they will be forced to do so. Those who do harm to humanity will be stopped from doing further harm.

All militaries of the planet must cease their operations at this time. Those that do not, will be disarmed by us. People of the military, do not be afraid, there is much you can do in the new world to come and you will have a new job to build up instead of destroy.

In the coming days, we will land our ships in your cities and you can meet us.

Please be at peace, do not let confusion trouble you. If you are in need, we will help you. If you suffer from sickness, we can help you.

Remember, your personal free will is something we value and cherish, and we will never force our will upon you.

Those who have forced their will upon you with weapons will be provided an opportunity to give you your freedom, and if they do not, we will help you regain your most precious freedom.

We also wish to extend to you a special invitation, that you will be able to come to our home world, as well as explore other worlds and planets.

We have also more surprises and wonderful things for humanity, and these will be revealed in the coming days.

We are going to teach you some new ways of living and being that will bring you joy.

In the coming days, each of you that is connected to our network, will receive a personal invitation to come and visit us.

We will provide you the details of where and when to meet in the message.

Come to our website on your internet and watch a movie we have created that will explain more about who we are and what we can do for your planet.

You can make comments and communicate with us on our website.

For now, I bid you good bye and peace."

At that, the screen went back to white.

Millions of people began going to the ZeeTek website to sign up for the movie, and respond to the invitation to visit the Zui home world.

The Zui did not really know how many would initially

respond, but the response was overwhelming.

Mankind was asking for a ride off of the planet en masse.

Within 3 days, there were some 400 million people who had responded to the invitation to visit Tu. Every day added another 20 million.

If the Zui had hosted their web servers on an Earth based network, the network would have been shutdown from the traffic. The Zui's own network provided more than enough capacity for the millions who were reaching out to them.

This was the response the Zui wanted, but were initially unsure of.

The Zui did not have a plan to fix the Earth with humanity still living on planet Earth.

The Zui plan was to evacuate Earth, then terraform it and let it heal.

The Zui knew they could not just come in and start loading humanity into ark ships and then dumping them onto other planets.

They knew that they could not simply introduce their way of life into Earth without some disruption. The wrong kind of help could actually cause more unintended consequences.

Like clockwork, the Zui began landing their large ark ships around the globe.

Millions flocked to their ships and began making contact, and marvel in amazement at the sheer size of their ships, and the technology on board. Many had difficulty getting to the Zui ships because of massive traffic jams.

Many had come looking for medical treatment for cancers and diseases.

Those that had registered on the Zeetek Network and provided an address and GPS coordinates were being visited by Zui androids who teleported to right to their homes and provided immediate advanced Zui medical treatment.

Zui medical technologies truly repaired a human body back to such a state that it was like getting a new body. It also reversed the aging process.

People could see that the world was never going to be the same.

The planet was experiencing a feeling of joy and hope unprecedented in all of known human history.

It seemed that a Utopian world was actually possible.

There were stages to their plan. First came their introduction, and then giving some time to let things settle down, and then introduce some essential technologies to bring immediate relief to a troubled planet.

The concept of replication technology had to be introduced slowly, and only at first in the most impoverished regions of the planet.

The Zui knew they could not implement replication on a large scale without causing chaos.

Replication technology is so disruptive, that if its introduction to the planet was not done carefully, it could cause a financial meltdown and major chaos.

While most would not argue with the collapse of greedy power brokers and the ruling wealth class, there could be unintended consequences.

The entire ecosystem of an economy is not just the wealth generated at the top, but the flow of money down through the system that keeps things going. Kill the money flow and you could wind up with huge ripples throughout the economy that could cause chaos.

If there is no money to pay truck drivers, distribution systems could be crippled. Supply chains would be destroyed. Manufacturing would cease, farming would cease. Food and medical supplies not delivered. The economy would grind to a halt.

So replication had to be limited. Mankind would have to wait until after Operation Exodus to fully enjoy this aspect of Zui technology.

Initially, the Zui gave anyone who asked a small portable power generator and small water purification systems and medical technology.

Parts of the planet that lived in darkness by night, with thirst and hunger by day were experiencing new relief.

The Zui also began distribution of food to those in the worst parts of the planet where life had become a daily hell of starvation, a daily exercise of survival against hunger.

For the skeptics, the Zui were masterfully conquering Earth with kindness instead of might and weapons of destruction. *Winning hearts and minds instead of killing was pure genius.*

RSVP Received

Two weeks had passed since the arrival of the Zui. As the world began to adjust to the new reality of The Zui, The Zui announced that there would be another major broadcast and that it would be about *a revolutionary idea*.

News media were all buzzing about what the next broadcast would be about, but what could possibly be more fantastic than what had already occurred?

The Zui broadcast opened the same as before, with a voiceover and titling, "*Greetings once more people Of Earth from The Zui*".

The camera turned again to Brother.

> "People of Earth, we hope that the recent days have been bringing you new joy about your situation and humanity's hope for the future. Already, in the short time that we have begun to know one another, we are becoming friends. Already, many things are improving for your species and your planet.
>
> *Today, we want to announce something special.*
>
> Millions of you have been responding to our invitation to come visit our home world, and to explore the universe with us.
>
> When we extended this invitation, we did not realize how many would respond.
>
> The visit to our home world will happen soon but not yet.
>
> However, we know that humanity wants to go to the stars, to explore space. Like us, you are a species that loves to discover new places, and learn new things."

The next thing on the screen was a video of the planet Tu. The video showed the planet from orbit, and descended down into an arial view of flying over the planet's surface. Beautiful mountain vistas, oceans, beaches and cities were shown.

Brother continued - "Today, we invite you to come to another planet. It is a planet 5 times larger than Earth, and is located about 2500 of your light years from Earth.

Our technology allows us to go there in only a few minutes of your Earth time.

The name of the planet is Tu, and it has been prepared as a beautiful new home for you.

Those of you who responded to our invitation will be given details about how and where our ships will be so that you can join us.

If you have not yet responded, and would like to come to this planet, please let us know in our network. A special network page has been setup to handle your requests to come. There you can view a movie about the planet, and what we have done to build a beautiful new home for those who want to go there.

We have already taken some of your people to Tu, and they are available to share with you their experiences.

You are free to visit Tu, and then you can come back to Earth, or you can stay there as long as you like.

All who wish to go are welcome. There is plenty of room, and the planet is beautiful.

We will take the first groups in 3 days.

We encourage you to come. Our ships are large and comfortable, and we have room for all who want to go. The travel time is only a few minutes – it takes less time to travel there than it does to talk about it.

For now, peace to you all"

With that the screen faded back to white and the broadcast had ended.

The news of traveling to another planet was both celebratory and yet there were many who still did not trust the Zui.

The Zui technology allowed their ships to go around space instead of through it. Vast distances were overcome by connecting with t*he singularity,* and by doing so the Zui could go to anywhere they could chart to with their star maps.

Millions had already ventured aboard the ships that had landed across the globe and found the Zui to be warm, receptive and friendly.

Much of the conditioning of planet Earth involved years of creating a mistrust of "aliens" and extra-terrestrials, and the seeds of distrust had been sown by the ruling elites to make extra-terrestrials appear to be those who had nothing but ill intent for mankind.

The Zui intended to start a new narrative.

Decades of science fiction lore was dominated by tales of large invasions, of giant alien creatures stepping on mankind like bugs. Or large scale invasions with gigantic space-ships filled with aliens who cared little for mankind and only wanted Earth's resources.

Recent history is filled with stories of alien abductions and medical experiments done on humans for secret alien breeding programs. Stories of underground bases inhabited by lizard people and aliens that use humans for food.

And yet there was lore about places such as Area51 and other legends about Roswell that portrayed a more scientific and less sinister alien presence.

Whistleblowers in recent history telling tales of friendly ET's, and ordinary human encounters with extra-terrestrials who were very much human from other planets, some in other galaxies.

Mankind had started to awaken from thousands of years of religious dominance in the concepts about life in other parts of the universe. Science and simple logic began to make more and more sense.

As people began to ponder the utter silliness of Earth being the only planet that intelligent life could exist, the time was right for *The Reveal*. The Zui knew this, and now it was their turn to make their presence known, and to win humanity over by simple concepts of love, generosity and kindness.

The arrival of the Zui to Earth did cause problems for the devoutly religious who found it difficult to accept the entire idea, and many labeled the Zui as demons with an ulterior motive, to lure humanity into a false sense of security with its new found friends, and then be dominated by them.

Television evangelists were all putting a spin on this new reality. Some called the Zui "new age demons" and likened their arrival as part of the Apocalypse of the Bible, yet people knew that somehow none of this lined up with their religious training, no matter how they put a spin on it.

For some, the lingering question remained - *Was this invitation to go to Tu a 'trojan horse'?*

For many on Earth, anywhere was better than they were right now. People in impoverished regions of the planet had nothing to lose and everything to gain. This was a simple decision for most.

As much as it might seem like a big cheat, a great escape to a new world where all things shine bright, *it really was the plan.*

Thousands of years of ownership of humanity, bound in chains of economic disparity were about to be broken.

Mankind's greatest adventure was about to begin.

Operation Exodus Begins

Back on Tu, John Foster had convened a special session of the Tu Council Of Governors.

Foster addressed the council.

John Foster - "Thank you all for coming.

He paused for a moment, reading his notes.

"These are interesting times indeed.

Because my time today is limited, I need to cut to the chase.

As you are all aware, the planet Earth is in a state of transition from non-disclosure to full disclosure. Things are pretty crazy, but it's a '*good crazy*'.

The Zui have landed their ark ships on the planet, and the response from Earth has been overwhelming. *They estimate a full 4 billion people are willing to leave right away.*

As you are also aware, the Zui have been busy preparing arrival colonies throughout Tu, as well as more tunneling and connecting the arrival colonies with the tube transports.

They are planning to bring the first arrivals within a couple of days, and so it's really their show.

The Zui estimate some 12 million people will be part of the first arrivals.

Some will want to stay immediately, others will only want to visit and come back later. But, as we all know, *ultimately* a majority of humanity will come here in the final analysis.

The Zui have assigned an arrival colony representative and teams for each arrival colony. These Zui arrival teams are Zui-human hybrids and androids coming directly from the Zui home world, and there are probably going to be 40 - 50 thousand in each colony. I'm sure you've noticed an increased number of Zui ships arriving.

They have also placed android assistants into the arrival colony homes to act as personal guides for the arrivals.

For those of you who are native to Tu, I ask that you be patient. The people of Earth do not have the sense of living on an organic planet as much as you do. Most will come here ignorant, and in need of guidance.

As you all know, Earthers for the most part are wasters of resources, unhealthy eaters and lack a sense of true purpose to their lives. All of this has been largely dictated by their economic and cultural systems on Earth which means we need to be as tolerant of their adjustment phase as possible.

Some will go through a wonderful transition from the occupations they now live into completely different jobs.

Scientists will become farmers, farmers will become scientists. Many will become teachers.

The Zui have built some amazing educational facilities in each arrival colony.

Earthers will go through a honeymoon phase, and then certain realities will set in. We believe the positives will definitely outweigh the negatives.

Some will become homesick for Earth, and want to go back. For most, moving here will become a welcome reset, and a new life full of possibilities.

On more practical matters, I need you to remind the people in your territories that the newcomers are sincerely welcome.

You won't have to worry about them for a good month or two, as they all have to go through the orientation process at the colonies.

Not all of them will stay on Tu, some will go on to other planets in the network, but regardless, **we want all to feel welcome.** *Please keep in mind why this planet was prepared for the past 100 years.*

Some of the new arrivals will be coming from extremely impoverished regions of Earth, and will have to go through healing, and training. The Zui are prepared for this and will be handling these people. They've setup hospital facilities in each colony.

Others will be scientists and regular people from the industrialized nations in Europe, North America and South America, Asia, China etc.

They will all go through the standard arrival colony processing, decontamination, healing treatments and and as I said, planetary orientation.

Many of the scientists coming will be granted special access to the planetary science library. I really think it will be difficult for many to go back once they see how rich the science is here on Tu.

Finally, as the leader of the Tu Council Of Governors, I want you to know that I will be visiting all of the arrival colonies, greeting the newcomers and checking things out. Michael Stetson and his team will be with me during this time.

Feel free to message me as you need, and I will have my administrative teams assist you as best we can. Please understand I may not be able to get back to you personally unless it is an extreme emergency.

And finally, because I have to go to another urgent meeting, there won't be any time for questions – please email me with any questions or concerns and we'll get you an answer as soon as possible.

Thank you all for coming"

Foster made his way quickly off the podium and headed for the door, hounded by an army of reporters from Tu as well as some reporters that had come from Earth had come in advance of the first arrivals, and all were pushing for an interview.

Foster made his way back to his office where he was greeted by Michael and his team. Shandra was also there, seated next to Michael. Bob, Amy as well as Robin and David from Sydney were there.

Ken, Simon and Petak walked in right as Foster was about to begin speaking.

Foster greeted them as well "Ken, Simon, Petak – thanks for coming gentlemen. Petak – is this your wife?"

Petak - "Yes this is Maya."

Foster - "I don't believe we ever had a chance to meet, Lovely to meet you Maya. And Simon - who is this?"

Simon - "Oh this is uh Mary, she's uh, from the operations administration office, we met about 6 months ago."

Foster smiled - "Oh right –my apologies - well, welcome Mary".

Ken was the only one lacking a girl friend or wife. Ken was a solitary soldier and not good at relationships.

Let's get started - Michael, you and your team have been doing an excellent job non-stop for the past several days. I think it best you all take some time off and then meet back here in 48 hours. From here we'll go out to the arrival colonies and check things out.

The Zui are managing things quite well and things are running smoothly.

But before go, I have a couple of things I need to share.

As you're all aware, there's no longer any need for near as much secrecy to our activities as there once was. We'll be able to do most of what we do now out in the open. This does not mean we are stopping our collection activities, and so you will all be resuming those tasks and the administrative teams here will give you direction on that.

In fact, *things are going to be quite busy.*

The Zui will be assisting you on collections now, because of certain information we have about security, and some other matters I'll relay to you once you all come back in 48 hours.

It has been an interesting year, and your team has grown to become one of our most valuable collection teams.

I need you all rested up for *the arrival* on Monday.

Might I suggest you all head out to 'The Villa' for a couple of days? It's sitting there empty right now, and plenty of room for you all. You can all relax and enjoy some quiet time.

Michael, you've still got one of the *jump ships* booked for your team right?

Michael – "Parked right outside"

Foster - "Well get out of here – you all need some rest. I may be out there later on this evening or tomorrow, not sure. If not I'll see you all back here in 48 hours.

So, 'off to the Villa' with all of you."

The Villa

The team settled into the jump ship as Michael prepared to take off.

Michael was puffing on a very nice Cuban cigar and sipping cognac.

Michael - "If you folks don't mind, I'd like to *take the long road* – if that's ok?"

Robin - "Uh are you sure you won't get pulled over for drinking and flying?"

They all laughed.

Michael - "I'd say break out some wine and cheese and enjoy the view"

Jump ships were equipped to simply transport from one point to another, "transporter style" like you would see in a sci-fi movie, or they could fly using their antigravity systems and thrusters.

Collection missions often involved teleporting a jump ship from orbit to an unseen hangar on Earth.

The jump ships were a backbone workhorse in the number of tools Michael had at his disposal.

Using the anti gravity system would make the jump ship as light as a feather, and able to fly nearly frictionless through the air. Thrusters would need very little effort to propel the shuttle at multiples of mach without even getting warm.

So whenever someone mentioned '*the long road*' that meant they would travel using the anti-grav system, at a fast clip instead of teleporting. All Michael really needed to do was set the auto pilot and the jump ship would fly itself.

Michael - "Let's see, I want this ride to last about an hour."

Reaching over to the navigation console he punched into the navigation console the GPS coordinates for The Villa and then pressed "Launch" and set the travel time to one hour.

The Villa was located on the northeastern part of the Southern Territory across from the continent of New Didiza at the shores of *Lake Texas*. Lake Texas was s named because of its faint similarity to the outline of the US state of Texas.

Within the jump ship, a faint high pitched whine could be heard as the shuttle's anti-grav system spun up.

A few moments later, the jump ship was hovering, and then small thrusters propelled the ship upwards at about 500mph to a nice cruising altitude of around 2500 feet.

The autopilot would do all the work, and the jump ship was equipped with enough technology to keep them from hitting anything. As the ground terrain would rise, the jump ship would keep itself 2500 feet above everything, including mountains.

Michael simply wanted to enjoy an arial view of the planet as they went.

Once the jump ship was on course, Michael got up out of the pilot's chair and made his way back to the small dining area.

Michael - "I think we should have some appetizers. Check it out, I found these in the library about a month ago, it's a nice sushi platter from a nice Asian place in New York City."

In a few moments, Michael had replicated sushi from New York City on a platter in the shuttle.

Michael - "I think we should also have some nice Saki."

Michael activated the voice search feature on the replicator and spoke "Saki rice wine"

The replicator responded back *"Please state the year and origin..."*

Michael - *"Kame no O sake by Wataribune"*

Michael laughed to himself. "Can't believe I didn't know about this sooner."

They found themselves enjoying saki and sashimi, with beautiful afternoon sunshine during the ride out to The Villa.

The planet unfolded beneath them with spectacular views and vistas. Passing over several huge mountain ranges and large fresh water lakes, it was easy to see that Tu was indeed a paradise planet.

Bob and Amy were glued to a window watching the terrain below. "Amy – check it out. I haven't seen any roads or infrastructure"

Michael piped up - "And you won't see much at all. The Zui are very anal about not scarring the landscape. The Zui told me one of the things they hate the most about Earth is all the square buildings and very few with art in the design."

Like clockwork, after an hour in the air, the jump ship descended through the clouds over a mountain range that had at its base a beautiful fresh water lake, Lake Texas. A small river came down from the mountains and fed the lake.

It only took the shuttle a few minutes to settle and soon the team found themselves enjoying the quiet mountain setting, with large conifers, trees of all kinds, ferns and the sound of birds.

A herd of deer was grazing on grass near the lake.

The Villa was really quite nice. Located about a mile up in the mountains, tucked nicely in the forest, it had a kind of Swiss Alps European meets Colorado design style. It had all the appeal of a classic mountain ski lodge.

It was large enough to be a hotel or expensive mountain spa with all the amenities.

John Foster would come here often, and bring various council members here for meetings. Foster would usually transport and not "*take the long road*".

In the afternoon sun, it all looked like it belonged there. The temperature was warm enough to go swimming.

Bob - "Damn this reminds me so much of Oregon, but much warmer."

Amy - "It IS gorgeous here!"

Ken and Simon were in security mode, instinctively scouting and scoping things out. They were in 'security mode'.

Michael - "Ken, Simon – guys! You can *stand down. No need to be on the job right now.*"

Mary started dragging Simon out away from the group towards the lake.

Everyone was buzzed from the saki.

Mary looked out over the valley below - "One of my favorite places here on Tu, I've been here for staff meetings"

Bob - "Arrival Colony is nice, but wow this is awesome."

Dave and Robin were awestruck as well, and taking it all in.

From where the shuttle had settled, you could see the front of The Villa, but the back was obscured by forest.

Michael smiled at Shandra - "You're gonna dig this a whole lot!"

Shandra laughed - *"You still owe me dinner in Nashville."*

Michael - "I think this beats Nashville."

Shandra - "Yeah but it needs a good blues band."

Michael - "I'm sure that will be happening in the near future."

Robin - "So – how do we get into the place?"

No sooner had she said that than from a second floor balcony a man appeared. It was Jim Townsend, the manager. Jim had relocated to Tu about 10 years ago and never looked back. His job was to manage all aspects of The Villa and he ran it like a tightly run ship.

The arrival of the shuttle had not gone unnoticed.

Jim - "Welcome to The Villa folks"

Michael - "Hey Jim, long time!"

Jim - "Oh Michael – it is you. Foster said you were coming."

Michael - "We're here."

Jim - "Great – well come on in, I'll be right down."

Townsend opened the large front doors and they all headed in.

As they expected, the interior was beautifully done in classic mountain style, with large hewn logs, and lots of wood everywhere.

A large staircase lead up to a second level where there were several hallways leading to various rooms.

Jim - "Well, let's see, how many rooms do you folks need?"

Michael - "I think, hmm, 6 rooms will do."

Jim - "OK, let me look at what we have. I think I already know which suite you want Michael"

Michael - "Exactly"

Jim - "Ah, right, Executive One, the only one on the third terrace – no problem. In fact I also have 2 suites on the second terrace, and 3 on the fourth – all with valley views. You get a nice view of the lake from there."

Michael - "Nice"

Pausing a minute while he checked them into the computer.

Jim - "All set for you Michael – here's your key."

Everyone else finished registering.

Michael and Shandra headed for the staircase and headed for their room. They started heading up the steps.

At this point, the secret about Michael and Shandra was quickly dissolving.

Michael turned around - "Oh – let's all do dinner around 8 tonight – main lodge."

Jim - "Oh and by the way Michael – I have fresh salmon for you this evening. None of that replicated shit – this is the real deal from the frontier."

Michael - "Jim can you do some of that as sashimi and some cooked?"

Jim - "You got it Michael – I'll have a raw plate and something with a piquant dill!"

Michael - "Oh and don't forget – your famous fried pasta and onions!"

Jim - "I thought you'd never ask!"

Everyone agreed on dining together. It was a much needed break for all of them.

Bob and Amy entered their suite.

Across the main room, the view beckoned both. Dropping what little they had with them for luggage, they started exploring their suite.

Each suite was spacious and adorned with beautiful antique style furniture. There was a welcoming sense filled with comfortable furnishings.

A placard on the table by the door explained that all of the furnishings were handmade, and that all of the wood work and finishing touches were all hand made, such as the Indian style blankets on the wall, and the artwork. The placard also gave a brief history of The Villa and the surrounding area.

Bob eyed a fully stocked bar at the end of the main room.

Bob - "*I think it's cocktail-thirty*"

Amy - "Oh yes please 'Mr Bartender'. Vodka and water with a slice of lemon"

Bob - "And Michael's got me hooked on that Glen Livet. So I'll be doing that on the rocks"

Amy - "Don't be getting too liquored-up *if you know what I mean.*" Amy cast a devilish grin towards Bob which meant she definitely wanted to enjoy some great sex while they were there.

Bob laughing - "*Oh right!*"

Behind the bar was a fully stocked humidor with cigars, and cut tobacco with rolling papers and pipes for smoking tobacco.

Next to the humidor a small refrigerator behind the bar also had numerous jars of cannabis buds. There was also a small box with glass pipes. Novelty lighters were lined up on a shelf above the refrigerator.

Bob - "Ah, NICE ... *this* will definitely help me unwind."

Bob grabbed a small jar of cannabis buds, a pipe and a lighter and put them on a serving tray on the bar.

Bob made cocktails while Amy opened two large french doors that led to a very large outside balcony with a large table and plenty of room to lay out for a tan or have a private dinner.

Walking out she took in the view of the lake below and the pristine forest surrounding the area.

The balcony was built such that it provided privacy from the other outside balconies. On Earth, these kinds of accommodations would have been something only the wealthy could afford.

On Tu, it was merely a matter of getting reservations. If nothing here was available, then there were dozens of other similar resorts and lodges available all over the planet.

Amy began looking over a printed menu of the lodges restaurant.

Amy - "Wow, I am looking forward to that wild caught salmon – oh boy!"

Bob loaded up a small tray with the drinks and the cannabis, the pipe and the lighter.

Bob - "I have a cocktail for you madam. Shall we proceed to the balcony?"

Amy - "Absolutely. This is freaking awesome"

They made their way to the patio on their balcony and found comfort in a couple of lounge chairs.

The view of the valley below was spectacular. A few fishing boats were out on the lake. The water was flat and calm, and added the the overall serenity of the view, and the moment.

Bob - "Geez can you believe this. Just think where we were a year and a half ago."

Bob lit up the pipe and enjoyed a guilt free smoke. After a moment, he exhaled.

Bob - "Cheers"

With that he held up his glass and they toasted a moment, a beautiful view and a great life.

Amy - "Hey – what time do you have?"

Bob picked up his phone - "It says here 5:15pm"

Amy - "Great. Michael wanted to do dinner at 8"

Bob smiled. "Yeah so we have plenty of time to *unwind* a bit."

Amy - "Absolutely!"

With that she leaned over and began kissing Bob which meant that was a green light to head back into the suite. They quickly found themselves in bed and having some of the best sex they'd had in a long time.

It was a similar moment for the other couples. All were getting some much needed re-connect time.

Around 8pm, everyone started heading down to the main lodge for dinner.

The lodge restaurant was largely empty. There were only a few other people there.

Dave and Robin and Ken had gotten there before everyone else and had a large table in the corner of the restaurant overlooking the valley. Bob and Amy, Simon and Mary all showed up a few minutes later.

Michael and Shandra were the last to arrive, all smiles.

Michael - "Well I hope you are all enjoying the amenities"

Everyone was feeling refreshed and looking forward to a great dinner. They all had a great dinner and it was a great moment for all of them to get better acquainted.

The next day they all enjoyed a boat on the lake, followed up with a bar-b-que on the balcony at Michael's suite.

Michael - "I'm glad you all had a chance to come up here with me. This was a well deserved retreat, but 'Monday's coming' so to speak and we have a lot of work to do. Foster told me we are going to be doing some animal collection runs in South Africa in the next couple of months, so that should be interesting.

But – in light of all that, I just wanted to thank all of you for a great year. I think the arrival day is going to go without a hitch. The Zui seem to have all this shit figured out, and so the stress is on them, not us.

Oh, and a heads up, we're also going to be doing some informational recon work for Foster. He needs us to look in on the colonies to make sure shit is going smoothly with the arrivals. So we're going to be his go-to boys for special projects. Just be ready to find out we've got weird mission profiles coming.

We need to leave here tomorrow morning bright and early around 7am. We will do coffee at the Council of Governors building and then meet Foster at 8am.

So everyone be rested, replicate whatever clothing and

supplies you need and we'll see you at the shuttle at 7am."

Time was up for the little holiday. Monday morning arrived painfully for all.

After a hot shower and Bob and Amy were rushing to get dressed and out the door.

Bob - "Amy, what was the name of that casual clothing profile you setup for me? I should have done this last night."

Amy - "Oh – right, look under '*team wear*'"

Bob - "Ah found it – oh good it's got those really comfortable shoes I like, perfect."

Bob's phone was ringing, it was Michael.

Bob - "Shit that's Michael"

Bob answered "Yeah we're coming right down, you said 7 and we got like 15 minutes."

Michael - "Hurry up we don't want to be late for Foster. Orus is meeting us there also."

Soon they all found themselves checking out of The Villa, which was really nothing more than saying goodbye to Jim and climbing back into the jump ship.

Michael - "What a great weekend. Everybody good?"

A chorus of 'hell yeahs' filled the shuttle and they were off to meet with Foster.

Arrival II

The Tu Council Of Governors building was a buzz of activity. The anticipated arrival of millions of humans on Tu was unsettling. Everyone was hoping things would go well, but there was always something that might go wrong.

While the Zui had experience with massive relocations, they had not done a relocation on this scale for some time. This would be a test of the Zui as well as the humans on Tu.

At around noon, a Zui ark ship rematerialized in orbit above Ellis Island arrival colony.

Within a few moments, it was descending into the atmosphere and settling onto the colony's landing area, a couple of kilometers outside the arrival colony.

The space port the Tu had setup was simply too small for the Zui ark ship and a new landing site had been setup a couple of kilometers away from the center of Ellis Island.

Arrivals would be loaded onto trams and driven into the colony.

Even from the distance of a couple of kilometers away, the ship was enormous. The landing gear put the ship some 15 meters (~50 feet) off the ground.

A large door the width of a football field had opened, forming a giant ramp down from the ship and people began streaming out.

Androids smiled and directed the arrivals toward a tube train station.

At arrival colonies all over the planet, ark ships were landing and the same scene was playing out.

There was one key difference to the people that had arrived on this ark ship. Many of these people were influential people from the Washington DC and New York City area. Many were key decision makers in government, politicians, and the uber wealthy.

The Zui did not expect many to stay, only to tour the planet and then return to Earth. Many would still be tied to their wealth and status on Earth.

The Zui directed them to the pavilions. From there, groups would be shuttled into the colony on the tube trains and taken to a stadium in the center of the colony that could handle 60,000 people.

The stadium was beautiful with a Roman Colosseum feel, not just a structure, but with art in the architecture. The stadium was beautifully adorned with statues, reliefs and artwork.

The stadium in each arrival colony had a slightly different look and feel, but the interior was the same. The Zui wanted to avoid a boring sameness to all of the arrival colonies.

Overall, the arrival colonies had a similar style, much like a lot of European towns and villages that all have a similar architecture and cohesive style to the entire town or village.

There was a central urban core. Residential areas spiraled out from the center of each colony. There would be tube train stations and trams setup within each neighborhood.

The stadium would become a place for sporting events, as well as community events, and musical events.

Foster and Michael's team were already at the stadium in an office, waiting for the crowds to settle in to their seats.

There was a huge buzz of expectancy. People were exhilarated. *This was humanity's big day.*

Around 1:30pm, Foster announced to the team- *"Showtime"*

They all headed out to a staging area where a podium was setup.

While the team stayed back stage, *Foster prepared to welcome 60,000 humans to Tu.*

A very large digital screen behind Foster displayed a large "Welcome, please be seated".

The stage at the stadium at Ellis Island arrival colony was being televised live on a large digital screen at all the other arrival colonies throughout Tu.

Above the giant screen was a clock with a label showing LOCAL TIME, and the planet's GMT time.

Foster began "Welcome! To Tu!" . His voice reverberated throughout the stadium at which point a very large cheer went up from the crowd. People were truly excited to be there. *After all, this was their first time to walk on another planet.*

Foster waited a moment and signaled everyone to quiet down.

Foster - "Welcome to *the Planet Tu!* My name is John Foster, and I am the leading council member of the Tu Council Of Governors here on Tu.

On behalf of myself, my staff, and the locals here on Tu, we are glad you are here.

This planet has been waiting for *YOU!*"

Again another large, deafening cheer went up from the crowd.

Foster continued - "Today, some 12 million of you have

walked on another planet in a solar system some 2500 light years from planet Earth. *A planet 5 times the size of Earth.*

Our hosts, the Zui, *have built this place for YOU*. They are anxious to show you this planet and a new way for humanity to truly *live*.

I have known the Zui for over 80 years, and I can tell you that they truly want to help us.

We believe that once you see how life is lived here on Tu, that you will want to stay. It will take some time to adjust to the way life is lived here, but we think the transition will be easy for most.

This is such a huge opportunity for humanity. *This is humanity's big score*. We all need to embrace this moment, and the opportunity the Zui have given us, to really live as we were meant to.

For some, this place will be a shock to your system. Some of you will finally learn the meaning of life. Some of you will have to mature, and grow up in order to truly understand the enormity of this place and the opportunity it provides to mankind.

Those of you who wish to stay indefinitely and make Tu your new home are encouraged to do so. Those who wish to visit and return to Earth are welcome to do so.

The ark ships you arrived on will return to Earth in 3 days, which will give those of you who wish to return to Earth a little time to explore and then go back to Earth should you choose to do so.

In a few minutes, groups of you will be taken on tours of the arrival colony, and you will receive a housing assignment for your stay here. Your tour guides will explain everything and answer any questions you may have.

After you've had a couple of hours to settle in, and do a little exploring of the arrival colony, you'll go back to your homes where you can enjoy dinner and we will have another global telecast for you this evening which you can enjoy right in your own home here on Tu.

Tomorrow, the Zui will also be available to take you on some arial tours of the planet if you so desire.

So please, enjoy the moment, and you'll be directed in just a few moments to your tour group and our hosts will show you the wonders of this beautiful arrival colony.

Before your tour begins, I'd like to leave you folks with a few thoughts of my own.

While this planet is larger, with more resources and more room for humanity to grow and live, it has some wonderful opposites of Earth that will help to ensure the survival of humanity.

There is an adjustment phase from *Earth thinking* versus *Tu thinking*.

On Earth, each individual's survival is based upon making the economic system work for the individual, and if that fails, *the individual fails.*

On Tu, the economics are not based upon scarcity as on Earth. On Earth, scarcity determines price and value. On Tu, there is no scarcity. No poverty, no lack.

On Tu, the personal mission is no longer about survival, or personal accumulation of wealth or materialism. On Tu, material needs become *passe*, not necessarily eliminated, but without emphasis.

Opposite of Earth, a teacher on Tu has more value to the society than one who produces goods. On Tu, a service provider can give of themselves freely without a need to be repaid monetarily.

Here, a life of service is possible without the need to suffer for it.

On Tu, because there is no scarcity, intellectual pursuits such as art, literature, science, music and medicine – these things can be pursued without fear by the artists and intellectuals.

Freed from the chains of economic slavery, artists and musicians on Tu have no fear about their survival. The concept of a starving artist does not exist on Tu.

On Earth, people who spend half their lives in educational systems are mocked as *'professional students'*.

On Tu, there is no mockery for those who wish to pursue higher learning. One is never too old to go back to school on Tu. In fact, the life extension technologies here enables human life to exceed any previous known life spans.

Some of the people here are well into their 150's.

You could spend your entire life in a university on Tu and be a crucial element of society, as humanity evolves towards an intellectual society, and higher intelligence, not towards the raping of the planet for resources and profits from people relegated to be 'consumption slaves'.

It is not Utopia, *but is is damn close*. No one ever said a utopian world was a bad idea, they just said it couldn't be done.

Here, it is not what you own but how you grow. Here, status is not achieved by wealth but by *service*.

Our hosts have given us a chance to start fresh, not just for a few *but for all*. We invite you to become a part of humanity's next adventure!

In just a few moments, our hosts will be directing you back to the trams for a tour of the arrival colony, and will take you to your lodging.

Thank you for coming, and please - enjoy your stay here on Tu!"

With that another large cheer rose out of the crowd and Foster exited the stage to rejoin Michael's team.

There was a buzz of excitement in the air. People were truly energized. *Humanity had a chance!*

The logistics of managing 60,000 people are enormous, but the Zui were ready. Not just one crowd, one stadium but they were orchestrating the same scene all over the planet at some 250 arrival colonies around the planet.

Soon they were directing groups of about 100 people to exit the stadium, back to tram stations where they were quickly interviewed and given a smart-card and a smartphone.

The Zui setup the arrival process so that they would instruct the arrivals about the next step in the process, assigning them their home. As they rode in the trams, the tour guides instructed arrivals that this smart-card would become their access key to their home, once it was assigned.

"We will first give you a tour of the arrival colony, and then drop you off at your home. Each home has been fully supplied with everything you need, and has an *assistant*, what you might refer to as an android, to help you in your home.

We have nicknamed them '*AA*'s. They will introduce themselves to you. The AA will explain how things work in your home, and assist you with food and clothing, and any medical supplies you need."

After a whirlwind tour of the center of the colony, the trams would head back out of the center of the colony to the residential area, and head slowly down a street, dropping off arrivals in front of a house, walk up to the front door, have them insert their smart-card into a reader, and the home would become theirs.

Entering the home, the resident Android Assistant or "*AA*" would welcome them and instruct them to be seated in the living room, and then oriented to the home.

The AA would learn from the arrivals what they wanted to eat, then go about replicating enough food for the home, and replicate fresh clean clothing if they needed it.

The AA would also find out about any medical needs and even do basic medical exams of the arrivals. If they were really sick the assistant would get them into the colony's hospital. AA's were especially helpful with the handicapped and elderly.

As the arrivals settled in and received a presentation on their home, the AA's would show the arrivals a movie that outlined many of the core concepts of life on Tu.

Should new arrivals decide to stay, the AA would literally become a permanent member of each household while they were in arrival status.

The AA's would become crucial to helping humanity adjust. They would be the primary interface for new arrivals.

Arrivals were reminded that this arrival colony was only the first step in their journey towards a permanent home on Tu.

An arrival colony home had full internet access to the Tu internet, and each home was fully equipped with a replicator that could provide food, clothing, and small electronics.

Initially, new arrivals would have very limited access to the replication library. Access would be increased in time as they matured, learning to *rethink their needs versus their wants*.

Throughout the homes in arrival colony, in every area possible, only natural materials were used.

Real wood, glass and metal were used throughout the arrival colony. Plastics were only used as a last resort. Anything artificial was always frowned upon.

Even though the Zui had the technological capacity to build with artificial materials, they preferred natural materials where ever possible.

The arrival colony was beautiful. To the Zui, even though it was a temporary stepping stone, it was also meant to represent the best aspects of the planet, as well as Zui craftsmanship.

The Zui would not accept the idea of a refugee colony. Creating a half-measure based upon some idea that resources are limited was not in their playbook.

Their outlook on life had evolved long ago from mere survival to *really living*. That meant that *quality* was always the higher standard, not quantity.

Arrival colony homes were no different than what a person would live in outside of the colony.

The arrival colony was meant to be a microcosm of the world outside the colony. Some might choose to make the colony their home, but really the idea was that people would graduate from the colony to the planet at large, and some would move on to other human-compatible planets.

Arrivals could apply for various regions to live on the planet, and if there was room and their skill set provided a positive add to the town or region, they would generally be granted approval to move to that region.

Because Tu was five times larger than Earth. This meant that just about anyone who really wanted to could live in a small country town if they really wanted to.

There were plenty of tropical regions like the Caribbean, Hawaii and Malaysia , and plenty of cooler regions like the colder areas of the northern hemisphere, like Alaska, Colorado, and Siberia.

There was much undiscovered country, and a means to get there and live. The Zui believed in total self sufficiency.

If someone wanted to live in a cabin in the wilderness, then the Zui would outfit them with a cabin in the wilderness complete with a replicator and a small power unit. The only requirement would be that the environment would not be violated.

For the Zui, each human meant incredible potential and possibilities.

Many of the arrival colonies would naturally have populations from the regions the ark ship picked people up from, so the arrival colonies would be like miniature Earth countries.

One of the first things that people needed to lose in their thinking was the concept of borders.

Even though there would soon be close to 8 billion people on Tu, the ability of the planet to sustain that number of people was not as stressful as it was for planet Earth.

On Tu, because of the replication technology available to everyone, the need to strip the planet of its natural resources was non-existent.

The planet's forests and minerals need not be raped to

create anything. On a planet where human needs can be met by replication technology, the idea of scarring the landscape for resources is eliminated.

No wars need be fought over resources such as water, forests, animals or gold. Mankind would take only as truly needed.

Government on Tu takes on an entirely new meaning. On Earth, for centuries, governments existed to control land, for resources.

The resources were always essential for survival, and used to build up trade to fund the accumulation of wealth.

Science and intellectual pursuits more often than not suffered at the expense of those who controlled the masses.

If a government didn't see the need or have the funds to increase intellectual capital, then humanity did without.

It would only be the few individuals who had sufficient capital to fund science and invention to move humanity forward.

On Earth, if the ruling elites felt threatened by science or innovation, then inventors and scientists would be silenced or shut down.

Hegemony based upon resources became the status quo on Earth. It affected every aspect of life on the planet, even those who did not subscribe to it found themselves under its thumb.

But on Tu, as the value of every human life is increased, so humanity's contribution to the universe increases. The idea of throwing anyone away, because they can "no longer be a productive member of society" becomes ludicrous.

The Zui found the concept of abortion for convenience

barbaric.

Contraception and personal discipline were the higher way.

They considered it abhorrent that a person would find a new life an inconvenience to their personal freedom, to the point of killing an unborn child.

The Zui's advanced medical knowledge meant that aborting children "to save the mother's life" or because the child might be born with defects were *no longer necessary* or valid reasons for an abortion.

They could simply remove the child and grow it to term in their hospitals. If there were found to be birth defects, then they would fix whatever problems the child might have.

Zui society encouraged those who did not want to raise their children to release the child to other parents, including android parents. Concepts of "orphanages" were foreign and distasteful to the Zui.

Again, because there was never any lack of resources, having to worry about the cost of raising children was non-existent.

The real question becomes that of commitment. The idea of staying home to raise children becomes simple. It is no longer dictated by economics, but by a desire to be a parent in the truest sense.

The Zui knew that it would take a few decades for humanity to grow into these concepts.

-

Ellis Island, and the other arrival colonies were buzzing with activity. As arrivals finished their first day getting settled into their new quarters, many started venturing out to explore the colony.

Not unlike Earth, many had their smart-phones in hand, using the built in global positioning app to navigate around the colony.

The arrival colonies were built in a circular fashion so that the center of the colony was where the stadium was, and all essential services.

Streets radiated out towards the residential areas. Walking was the primary mode of transportation, and for longer "commutes" a golf cart, bicycle or segue sufficed.

Anything beyond an arrival colony could be gotten to by train, tram or by transport shuttle.

Around 6pm local time, tour guides and AA's were directing people to return to their new homes, so they could be home in time for Foster's evening telecast.

The AA's began preparing the evening meal as needed for their new arrivals.

On Earth, the evening might consist of dinner in front of a television, with some kind of mindless entertainment.

On Tu, there was plenty of entertainment, but none of it would be available until after the first day. *The Zui wanted the arrivals to disconnect from Earth.*

At a few minutes before 8, the AA's in all the homes were assembling their new arrivals around the arrival home television for Foster's evening broadcast.

Then, right at 8pm Foster's broadcast began.

Foster was beaming. He was truly happy for the first time in a long time - "Hello everyone. I trust that this first day here on Tu has been somewhat of an adventure. I trust that your hosts have helped you navigate the colony, and that you find your accommodations comfortable.

For those of you who choose to stay on Tu, your AA will be your primary contact for the first few weeks here. And what they cannot handle they will refer to our various administrative teams in your arrival colony.

I'm sure you all have questions. Some of you may have already discovered and availed yourself of the internet access in your home or through your smart-phone, probably very similar to what you are used to on Earth, as much of that same technology exists here on Tu.

We have our own '*wikipedia*' of sorts as well, and it will answer many of your questions.

I want to share with you that today I personally felt the special excitement in the air for this momentous occasion.

For a moment, pause to reflect upon the fact that some 12 million people arrived on this planet today, and are all now comfortably housed in some 250 arrival colonies on the planet.

You've all been fed and clothed and if you can sleep tonight, you will rest comfortably as well, in total safety and peace.

There are no wars on Tu, no factions, no riots or turmoil. *This is truly a planet at peace.*

Tonight, you can rest in peace, and total safety in your own home.

All this week your hosts will be giving arial tours of the planet for those of you who want to see more of the planet. Simply coordinate with your AA your desire to be on one of those tours and they'll arrange it.

I am sure for most of you, this is like a vacation. Enjoy it! The beautiful thing is, compared to life on Earth, *it IS a vacation.*

As you all become acclimated to life here on Tu, you will learn more about yourselves than you ever did in all your life on Earth.

Some of you will find that everything you've spent your life doing is not the real you, and you will have the time, freedom and the place to discover what that truly is. There's no rush, no timeline, and no deadline.

Some of you need time to heal, and grow strong. This planet is truly a healing place and our hosts will help you as much as they can.

The real goal is that you become the best *you* that you can be. It's all about personal growth here on Tu.

So, I hope that you have found this first day here on Tu a wonderful adventure, get your rest for tomorrow brings even more new surprises and adventures.

Good night and enjoy your time here on Tu."

--

Bob and Amy were finally back home after an eventful first day for all the new arrivals. The weather was perfect. It had been a bright and shiny day, and the evening settled in with a beautiful clear sky full of stars.

Michael was on the phone with Bob.

Amy was in the replicator room of their home working on some clothing ideas.

Michael - "Pretty psyched now Bob?"

Bob - "Yeah man, absolutely. Today was huge."

Michael - "Well things will be getting really busy over the coming days, but with the Zui running the arrival process, that part is actually *not* going to be stressful for us.

Foster wants us to assist him on a visit to all the colonies for an assessment, so we'll be on a whirlwind tour of the colonies."

Bob - "We're ready"

Michael - "Good. Plan on being at the Council of Governors building tomorrow afternoon around 3. We're going to be heading to the opposite side of the planet, and it will be late night early morning there. If Amy wants to come she is welcome or she can stay behind – her option."

Bob - "Ok Michael – sounds good see you there at 3pm"

Amy had replicated some clothes she wanted Bob to try on.

Amy called out to Bob in the living room – "Bob, I think you need a hat. I found a kind of fedora, come in here and try it on."

Bob walked into the replicator room and found Amy wearing a beautiful Asian sarong and sandals.

Bob tried on the hat – it fit perfectly.

Bob - "So, I'm guessing, an evening at the beach?"

Amy - "Absolutely! Oh, and here are some beach clothes for you." She handed Bob a nice shirt and shorts, and sandals for the beach.

Bob - "You've been having fun with the replicator I see.

That was Michael on the phone and he said the team is going on tour of the colonies with Foster starting Wednesday afternoon.

We'll be heading to the opposite side of the planet, and said if you want to go you are welcome to come but if you want to stay here – your option. So we meet at the Council of Governors building at 3 tomorrow afternoon."

Amy - "Oh, I'm definitely coming along."

Bob - "Good, well it ought to be interesting. So let's hit the beach!"

Amy had already packed a small cooler with drinks.

Amy - "There's a tram to the beach that picks up every 20 minutes or so. There's a nice pier we can walk out on and sit and enjoy the evening there!"

They headed out. The tram ride was nice, and the arrival colony was alive with excitement. It was unusual to see so many people in the colony.

Bob - "I was kind of liking fewer people – I think I'm gonna talk to Michael about getting us a place a little more remote."

Amy - "Yeah, it was nicer with fewer people. I think things will quiet down once the newness wears off."

They headed to the beach and enjoyed a beautiful evening under stars with cocktails.

On Tour

The team assembled outside of the Council of Governors building near the fountain.

Michael - "OK here's the plan. Foster is coming out in a few minutes, and will have a dozen other people, press people and interpreters with him.

We'll be going in one of the larger jump ships. All he really wants us to do is shadow him and be available. So hang loose for a few moments. Ken, Simon, you guys need to be alert today – just in case something funky goes down."

Ken - "As in?"

Michael - "I don't know, just a hunch. We need to be aware there may be some crazies out there on this tour. We got word there are some religious people who are yammering on about the Zui being the anti-Christ. Some of them may be organizing a protest.

We found out about some other crazies who think the Zui are a big Trojan horse also, and that they believe we're all going to be enslaved – shit like that.

Just be aware these people may try something of a disturbance. If that happens, you need to move Foster out of the way immediately.

A few moments later John Foster came out of the building and made his way to Michael's team.

Foster - "Michael, gentlemen, all set?"

Michael - "We're good, let's go".

Foster - "Adam Orus and his assistant Melissa will be with

us as well, and they're already on our jump ship.

Melissa has the itinerary, and where necessary will function as interpreter. These will be short stops of about an hour or so, meet up with the local colony managers, find out about any issues.

We're looking at about a 4 or 5 colonies at different corners of the planet. If we were to hit all of the arrival colonies, it would no doubt take a few weeks – we really just want to get a sample of what things are like.

We'll hit a couple of colonies on Gargantua North and South, one on Minora North and one on Minora South, one at Aquatica, and 3 in the Southern Territory.

After all, there will be some of the people returning to Earth in a couple of days.

Reports we've gotten in has been positive. A few bar fights here and there but nothing unexpected. The *android brothels* have been a big hit in every colony so far."

They all laughed. *Tu would indeed take some getting used to.*

Foster's team spent a long day bouncing through 8 colonies. It was a whirlwind tour and uneventful. Things were actually working as they should.

It was late in the day when the jump ship arrived back at the Council Of Governors building and the team disembarked.

John Foster - "Well, I am impressed, and hopeful. Things are really going well. I think there's hope for the human race after all."

Michael - "As if you had any doubt?"

Foster - "Yes, I did have my doubts. Everything I have seen happening on Earth over the past several decades gave me less and less reason to believe the Zui could pull this off – yet at the same time I knew they could.

My only concern is that I have been "waiting for the other shoe to drop" so to speak, but then I know the Zui are quite capable of handling things."

Michael - "I know what you mean."

Foster - "Michael, I need you and your team to head back to Earth for more collection runs in the coming days. There are still numerous antiquities that need to be retrieved. We want to coordinate with a lot of museums, antique dealers, dealers of old books, things like that.

Michael - "Roger that. Just have Melissa send me the itinerary and list of items"

Foster - "On another subject, I believe your man Bob is an electronics expert as well?"

Michael - "Yes, electronic design, and also specializes in alternative energy projects."

Foster - "That's what I thought. The Zui-hybrids have been watching your team, and they really like the camaraderie you and your team has shown. Very tight knit, all working together.

The thing is, the Zui want to start a training program in the universities that will educate humans about their energy generation systems.

They want to do a technology transfer, and so the Zui-hybrids have *specifically asked for Bob* – they would like to have Bob head up a new team to basically embed with the Zui-hybrids for a few months, learn the technology and then setup a program to teach others how it works. You think he'd be up to it?"

Michael - "Well, I'm sure he can, but I know he'll need to create his own team."

Foster - "Exactly, find out if he wants to do it, and we'll convene a meeting tomorrow and if he's up for the job we'll get started right away."

Michael - "OK I'll talk to him this evening."

Foster - "Excellent. It will probably take some planning, organizational stuff, we'll get him everything he needs."

Michael - "Sounds great – this will mean I need another electronics whiz."

Foster - "Adam already has someone lined up and we'll have you make a pickup. Won't have to worry about all the cloak and dagger stuff this time though."

Michael laughed - "*Which will be nice.*"

Foster - "Oh – and good to see you and Shandra getting along so well, she's been freed up to join your team full time if you want – your call."

Michael - "I think I will definitely give that some serious thought!"

Foster - "Great. If Bob wants to stay with your team, it's all good, we'll find someone else for the training program, but the Zui-hybrids specifically asked for Bob – but will respect his wishes either way.

And Michael, again thank you so much for everything you've been doing these past several months."

Michael - "Thanks chief. I'm looking forward to this next phase."

Foster - "Yes, *The Reveal*, and *The Exodus* were huge, but the real test is how things are going to go long term."

Michael - "Well, I have the most hope now I've ever had in my life for humanity".

The First 90 Days After

While there were indeed millions who hd signed up for migration to Tu, the Zui knew that there would be considerable chaos if they allowed open migrations.

A mass exodus larger than what they had capacity for could cause a calamity. If anyone could just leave, and abandon ship, then it might cost lives.

The first to leave would have to fit a certain profile. However, the Zui chose to keep their selection process a secret. Being chosen to leave Earth was almost as mysterious as a lottery.

Each person who applied on the Zui website would be screened. Many of the first to leave were the old, the sick, the unemployed.

The Zui were pushing a huge message of cooperation and support, so as to keep people on their jobs, working, keeping things stable until it is their time to leave.

Some people would get a notice that they were leaving in 3 days, some were told to wait several months.

The Zui wanted to be sure that supply chains, for food clothing and medicine would not be disrupted. There were incentives being offered to people in critical sectors of the economy, such as distribution and supply companies, food and medical.

The first month was going better than they had anticipated.

However, once news of life on Tu began to come back to Earth, choosing to stay on Earth made little sense. The more people became acclimated to living on Tu, few had any desire to come back to Earth. There were some first arrivals heading back to Earth to encourage their friends and families to come to Tu.

Foster gathered his team in the Tu Council of Governors building.

Foster - "Brother and Sister have summoned me to come to their compound for a few days to discuss their next plans. They want to step up the pace of the migrations, but this could be risky.

I'll be back in a couple of days, and let you all know what they plan to do.

If any of you need me I'll be available by phone."

People were in a hurry to abandon Earth. For many, it did not matter that it was not yet their turn to leave, the idea that they *could* leave meant they had lost their desire to do anything on Earth. Huge numbers of people were just quitting their jobs in anticipation of leaving.

People were beginning to ignore their obligations. Many simply weren't paying their bills. The Zui had tried to offset this trend by broadcasting a lot of soft messages about the importance of being responsible. Stay on your job, pay your bills.

But the "*infection*" was setting in.

The new paradigm had infected Earth too soon. The Zui could see it happening. The economy was starting to suffer. Another economic crisis was looming.

The Next Step

Foster came back from meeting with the Zui and met with Michael and his team.

Foster - "The Zui see the biggest problems on Earth right now is that they need to solve for basic needs – food, clothing and energy.

They have considered stopping the migrations for a while, probably for a few months, but may not have to.

The Zui have been providing free mobile phone service as well as internet services to the entire planet, through their own mini-satellites all over the globe. This was one area they knew could not be jeopardized so that piece is already in place.

However, they know that as more and more people leave, there will be huge labor shortages. So they are going to bring in android labor, and begin to take over several key infrastructure areas, supplanting humans who want to leave with androids. *The androids will be happy to stay and fulfill the labor shortages.*"

Adam Orus was also in the meeting.

Adam - "Not only do they have ark ships, science ships, replication ships and terraforming ships, but they have android ships with thousands of androids on them.

The androids are kept in a kind of stasis or suspended animation until they are needed, and then they program them with whatever language skills they need and whatever knowledge they need for the tasks at hand, and then transport them down to the planet to wherever they are needed.

The Zui will also be taking over several huge supply chains themselves. They will begin to bring large replication ships in to create food, clothing and whatever else is needed.

Additionally, they will begin to take over all the large grocery store and department store chains, in each country, supply them and keep them open with android labor.

They could replace them completely, but they'd rather try to create a sense of continuity with existing modes of distribution, such as grocery stores, drug stores and the like.

Next, they're going to take over several other large sectors, such as energy, and fuels.

They will keep gas stations open, electricity on in homes and food in refrigerators. This will keep people fed, and lights on. And they'll begin to take over public transportation as well with android labor.

This way, regardless of a complete shortage of human labor to keep key sectors functioning, people will not go hungry, without shelter, energy or medical help while waiting to leave.

They're already moving several large replication ships to Earth even as we speak. They plan to get everything in place over the next few days.

On the plus side, the people of Earth will experience a even more benefits of living on Tu *before* they leave."

Foster - "The beautiful part about all of this is that the Zui are managing all of it!

Michael I need you and your team to continue your collection runs. The lists are still rather large.

We still have collectors on the ground in every country on Earth, and we're using Tu ark-ships to make daily runs now.

It's a bit exhausting but we have to keep up the pace. There is much that will be lost if we do not act quickly.

Adam, I want all of you to prioritize your collectors to focus on antiques, antiquities, museums, artifacts. If it's old, irreplaceable, and interesting, grab it.

The Tu are setting up some large underground storage facilities out in Aquatica.

There is a new 'commodity' on Earth, and that is migration status. *It's the one thing that has real value on a planet that everyone wants to leave.*

All of you can offer **head of the line migration privileges** to antique dealers, museum people in exchange for whatever they have.

Ideally, we will want those same museum people to work with their collections here once we get their museums built out.

If we need to send larger special cargo ships for museums, then let Adam know and we'll get them.

If you want to sweeten any deal, use early migration status.

So, check your orders and do the best you can."

Historians were the new celebrity on Earth. It meant head of the line migration status.

The Zui had narrowly averted what could have been a huge crisis on Earth. As they began to supplant the supply chains on Earth, things were returning to a sort of normal.

On Earth, it started to become painfully obvious how much of life had been dictated by commercialism.

Everything from fast food restaurants, clothing stores, food and shelter was run by some kind of commercial interest. It was amazing how fast all of it crumbled when there was no money to keep it all running.

This then was the necessary evolutionary jump mankind needed to make. To go from paying for living to *truly living*.

No more would the landscape be scarred with endless mini-malls and businesses.

No more would people have to be slaves to an economy. No more would the question be "*Who's going to pay for all of this?*".

No more ravaging the landscape for raw materials, for consumption. No more evictions. No more mortgage companies.

No more money and the lack thereof. This was the death of branding – solely for profit. The new era of branding for *reputation* had begun.

The Zui had positioned replication ships to all of the major cities. Within a month, they had a large distribution network in place, all manned by android labor.

There were now android truck drivers, and all of the people in large grocery stores and department stores were migrated, and replaced by androids - *androids who were happy to stay on Earth and help*. They would leave when their job was done.

This also meant that food was now free. You went to the grocery store with a list of what you needed and left with what you needed. No hoarding, no food riots, no shortages.

The same thing was happening in all of the clothing and department stores. You went and got what you needed when you needed it.

It wasn't exactly what life would be like on Tu, because on

Tu, everyone would have their own replicators, and the infrastructures are different.

On Earth, most supply chains relied on distribution networks, trucking companies and large transportation systems like aircraft and ships.

The urban infrastructure on Earth required cars and trucks for transport. Not on Tu.

On Tu, none of that was necessary. No interstate highways, no trucks, no cars, no aircraft, no ships on the oceans.

On Tu, it was just clean air, clean water, housing for all, anti-grav vehicles, spaceships, mass transit tube trains, electric vehicles, golf carts, skateboards, bicycles and push carts. Horses and carriages. Replication. Free medical care.

Utopia? Far from it. Actually about 2500 light years from Utopia.

Mankind, with a little help, would evolve up one more notch. The next step would be surviving and adapting to this new world.

As the migrations continued, and Tu's arrival colonies began to fill out, humankind was beginning to live a life disconnected from false scarcity as well as from the toxic slave economy of Earth. Two huge paradigms had been broken.

Now the next step would be adapting to the new paradigms on Tu.

The Outing

4 months had passed since the first arrivals had come to Tu. People were adjusting, learning the new way of living on Tu.

Close to 100 million people had emigrated from Earth to Tu.

Bob and Amy were enjoying a beautiful sunny afternoon at home. Bob's schedule had slowed down a bit and it was great to have a little time off to regroup.

He was well familiar with running his own jump ship, and was making routine runs to the storage facilities at Aquatica.

Michael was totally comfortable sending Bob on solo collection runs when the need arose.

Bob and Amy had moved to larger quarters further out in a more 'town and country' setting. They now had several acres, with a garden in a geodesic dome.

Bob also had his own lab building installed out off the main house.

Buildings were simple to "install". All he had to do was setup a building order through the replication library.

The replication library would then contact the colony's building team, and they would setup a building replication at whatever site Bob needed it.

There was already a small electronics lab listed in the library catalog.

Bob mused to himself, *"Better than the sky-mall catalog"*.

Once installed, it would take up about 1000 square feet. It came fully equipped with lab tables, oscilloscopes, meters, and all the tools necessary to build or repair anything electronic. It did of course include a replicator, but the replicator in this lab was twice the size of what you found in a home. In terms of dimensional capacity, home units only had about 5 cubic feet of space, the lab unit in Bob's new lab could replicate objects 6ft x 4ft x4ft. This opened up a whole new world of replication capabilities. You could actually build a jump ship from parts with one of these.

Because of its size, the lab would be replicated at the larger replication facility, and then transported directly to a mounting pad at Bob & Amy's residence.

It would take about a half an hour to "install" after the mounting pad was setup.

The day of the install a Tu building engineer named *Greco* called Bob and let him know he would be coming by in a jump ship to supervise the install.

Once Greco had touched down at Bob and Amy's, he setup a robot pad builder which would setup the mounting pad for the building.

The pad builder was a small, tractor-like unit that would lay the foundation as it went, similar to a *piping tractor* the Zui would use to build underground piping systems, except this unit would create a concrete-like epoxy pad for the building to sit on, as well as set up special mounting clamps.

The Tu had perfected this process so that the pad would take less than an hour to lay in, then all he had to do was verify the GPS coordinates of the building pad, and then activate the transport to place the building on the pad.

Greco placed a small GPS device in a special location on the pad. This gave the transport system an exact fix on the location of the pad.

Greco activated the transport and the building materialized on the pad. Next he would activate its mounting clamps to make sure it was anchored to the pad and locked in place.

Then he would go through the building and make sure its power supply was working, and then that was it – *building installed.*

Now that he had his own lab, Bob could experiment with his magnet motor projects whenever he wanted to, and never had to worry about a shortage of parts.

It might have seemed silly to continue his projects, in light of the advanced technology on Tu, but the principles behind the magnet motors were still basic math and physics.

Magnets, motors, coils, and simple trigger circuits were still the same on Tu as on Earth.

Bob was winding a coil, and still mulling over whether to join the Zui-hybrids' power project or stay with Michael's team.

He had enjoyed the camaraderie of the team, but the prospect of working with Zui technology intrigued him.

This would be an amazing moment, to work with 'alien' technology for the betterment of mankind, and yet working with Michael and the team was just as compelling.

If he went to work with the Zui, it would be a move up on the food chain as it were, and staying with the team meant inside access to all of the high level stuff.

Amy's phone was ringing.

It was Michael. She found this a bit strange because he had never called her directly.

Amy - *"Hello?"*

Michael - "Hey Amy – is this a good time to talk?"

Amy - "Well sure"

Michael - "Listen, uh we've never really discussed one of the roles we initially had in mind for you and I was wondering if we could take a few minutes to talk about that?"

Amy - "Oh – well, right – do you want to come by, Bob and I are just taking the day regrouping here at the house?"

Michael - "Perhaps it would be better to meet over at that coffee house in the market near your house, say in an hour, and bring Bob along as well."

Amy - "Sound great, I'll let Bob know and we'll be there"

Amy put her phone down and wandered into Bob's lab building.

Bob was busy working on one his main prototype that he had started back on Earth.

Bob - "Hey ... check it out. I rebuilt the prototype – it's all shiny and pretty thanks to being able to replicate whatever parts I need."

Bob's prototype motor generator now had a professional clean look. Using the replicator allowed him to build it with the best parts available.

Amy - "Wow. All shiny! So it's working now?

Bob - "Almost there, still doing some tweaks."

Amy - "I just got a call from Michael. He wants to meet with us, I mean *with me* but asked if you would come along"

Bob - "Is it some kind of emergency?"

Amy - "No he wants to talk about my role here on Tu"

Bob - "No kidding. Wow. So – when do we meet?"

Amy - "He wants to meet at the coffee shop over at that market near here, in an hour."

Bob - "Well yeah, cool. Did he give you any details?"

Amy - "No, I'm kind of nervous about it all"

Bob - "Well, I'm sure the offer will be the same as what they offered me, totally optional."

Amy - "True – I guess I should be glad, I have been kind of wondering what to do with myself."

Bob – "Just keep an open mind, Michael's been great to work for and I imagine anything they have in mind for you will be right up your alley."

A short time later Bob and Amy hopped onto segues and made their way about 2 kilometers in towards the colony center.

Michael already had a table and was looking at his iPad intently when Bob and Amy rolled up. They stepped off of their segues and sat down at the table with Michael.

Amy couldn't help notice that a few tables away, it was none other than *Soldan* - again, drinking coffee and looking at a tablet computer.

She suddenly remembered she wanted to tell Bob about the thing Robin had shared with a her a while back when Michael and the team had been involved with the *destroyer of worlds* incident.

Amy leaned in close to Bob and whispered - "*I just remembered something really important I forgot to tell you – make sure I talk to you about it before we leave.*"

Bob - "Yeah, sure no problem"

Michael - "Great to see you two."

Bob - "Yeah it's been a couple of days."

Michael - "Hello Amy!"

Amy was nervous. - "Hello Michael"

Michael - "I think you're going to like what we have in mind for you – something we wanted to offer you a while back, but with the exodus and migrations, and the settling of the colonies – I'm sure you realize we've all been a bit preoccupied.

Actually, what we have in mind is something animal related."

Now he had Amy's attention.

Michael continued - "As you know, part of our collection efforts have involved animals and working with naturalists and scientists.

The Zui directives are that humanity is to achieve good working balances with the ecology here on Tu.

Basically, the Zui want us to have a global policy toward the treatment of not just humanity but towards animals as well.

As you know, there are no zoos on Tu, as the Zui find them incredibly distasteful.

There are numerous animal facilities all over Tu now.

People who ran sanctuaries, zoos, and animal collections on Earth brought their animals here and setup new facilities here.

Since most of the animals in captivity were not wild, they couldn't just be abandoned or released – they need to be taken care of here as much as they were on Earth.

Remember the whole background thing we did on you and Bob – well we do remember that you have an extensive background working with animals.

What we are setting up is a team, and need people who will head up a liaison with the Council, and work with all these animal facilities all over the planet. There are larger needs beyond just supplies to run them.

It is a kind of leadership role, and you'll be part of a team traveling all over the planet to meet and greet, run seminars, educate, and assist researchers and educational institutions."

Amy - "Wow. So, why me? You're sure there isn't someone more qualified?"

Michael - "Well, you won't be the only one. We're putting together a small army of sorts – people who know animals - so it will be a pretty broad team.

I believe you worked largely with dogs?"

Amy - "Well yeah, *love dogs.*"

Michael - "OK so I'm going to put you in touch with Margaret Anderson, she heads up the administration aspect.

Yours would be more of an ambassadorial role, where you would go out to the different dog sanctuaries and work with the people who run them.

Margaret will act as a kind of central coordinator, managing people, medical professionals, veterinarians, researchers and anyone else who will be involved actively with animals beyond pets.

They're putting together a central global conference at Ellis Island in a couple of months – but I wanted to have you meet with Margaret in the next week or two.

Margaret is originally from the UK, and came here a few

years ago, so she's already got some things in place.

And before you ask, yes, I already know you need to talk about this with Bob.

And remember, location is irrelevant. You'll have your own special animal handler jump ship to travel around with. We'll send you to training on how to use it – they're really pretty simple to operate."

Amy - "Wow – so much to think about. Yeah, I need to sleep on this, but my initial gut feeling is a huge YES – but can I have a day or two to think this over?"

Michael - "You don't have to decide today, wait until you meet Margaret and then you'll know more about what she has in mind, and how it will all work."

Amy - "That's a relief! So, yes, sounds great, just let me know when and where."

Michael - "Great!"

Amy - "Hey, *as long as we're here*. I need to tell you about something.

Her voice got very quiet, so that Bob and Michael had to lean in to hear her.

Amy - "Remember that mission, when we first arrived – the one you couldn't talk about?"

Michael frowned - "Oh – right -"

Amy – "Well, while you guys were all away, Robin and I had stumbled into each other here at this same coffee shop. She found me here, and so we sat and talked a bit.

But before she came over to my table – you see that guy over there by himself?"

Amy was trying to inconspicuously point out Soldan a few

tables away.

She continued in a quiet voice - "He must hang out here a lot, because he was here that day also, and went out of his way to introduce himself to me."

Bob and Michael leaned in even closer to hear her.

Michael - *"You're talking about Soldan?"*

Amy - "Right, well he came over, sat down, said he recognized me as a new arrival, introduced himself as being with John Foster's team that acclimates people here and then he left after a few minutes."

Michael - "Yeah, he heads up team orientations here on Tu."

Amy - "Right, so that's what he told me. Anyway, Robin kept her distance, and once he left she came and sat down a minute later and we were talking.

She said she saw him in an alley way over in the market place on a phone, talking louder than he probably realized he was, and said something about "make sure you get the device before anyone else does""

Michael - "You're talking about that day we left in a hurry, right after you arrived – right?"

Amy - "Right"

Michael's face got serious.

Michael - "Stop right there."

Michael picked up his phone and dialed Robin.

Michael - "Hey Robin – it's Michael. Did I catch you at a bad time?"

Robin - "No, what's up?"

Michael - "Well, Amy, Bob and I were just getting some

coffee over here not far from you folks – can you and Dave come by? Something important has come up."

Robin - "Sure, we're just doing a little housekeeping here, we can be right over in a few minutes"

Michael - "Actually, can you meet us at Bob and Amy's place?"

Robin - "Sure – we'll be there in about 20 minutes."

Michael - "Thanks, see you there."

Michael hung up the phone.

Michael - "Let's head back over to your place."

With that they all headed over to Bob and Amy's place.

The Loss

Soon they were all sitting in Bob and Amy's living room.

Amy and Robin were using the replicator to put together some hors d'oeuvres.

Robin - "Can I get anyone something to drink?"

Michael - "A good beer, like a wheat"

Bob - "Beer, a Heineken"

Dave - "Beer, a lager – surprise me love"

A few moments later Robin emerged from the kitchen with cold beer.

Robin - "Gentlemen your beers."

Michael - "Thank you Robin. Dave, Bob, outside with me"

They headed out the deck behind the house.

Michael - "Hey Bob I see you got your lab installed – nice."

Bob - "Way too convenient!"

Michael wasn't going to stay with small talk for very long. Glancing around almost in a paranoid check to see if anyone was watching.

Michael – "OK – here's the thing. The Council has been keeping an eye on *Soldan* for some time.

Let me give you a little background.

Soldan and his brother Amil were among the first recruits into the whole project with the initial contact with the Zui.

They were there right at the beginning. Soldan and his brother were originally from the middle-east, and worked in the CIA as intel.

Soldan's brother Amil was also part of that 50-person team to go on the first trip to the Zui home world Didiza.

Amil was traumatized like the rest, but he didn't recover when he came back. He committed suicide about 6 months after the team came back.

Soldan has always blamed the Zui for his brother's death. He's never fully recovered from his brother's death, even though it was decades ago.

Foster kept Soldan around, I think kind of like out of pity, gave him some prominent roles over the years.

The thing is, the Zui-hybrids have told Foster numerous times that they have reservations about Soldan. They leave when he comes in the room.

When you ask the Zui-hybrids, they never give us any specifics, all they will ever say is that they see a huge sadness with him, and that they don't feel he is healed enough that they could trust him.

As much as we know about the Zui, there are still some communications difficulties, trying to understand what they really mean.

Because of this, the leading representatives for the Tu, and Tu military people don't trust him either, although they don't have anything concrete, they have had their suspicions about him leaking intel to the black ops teams from Earth."

Dave - "So what's next?"

Michael - "Afte we left that coffee shop, I spoke with Foster on the way over. He is going to recommend removal of Soldan."

Bob - "*Removal?*"

Michael - "Yeah, they'll take him off Tu, to another planet in their network or maybe even recommend rehab on Didiza.

So the Soldan issue is solved, but it also points up the fact that these fucking black ops teams are not to be trusted. They compromised Soldan, and it's all about a power grab for technology.

There are still groups with interest in getting an upper hand even though disclosure has occurred, who want to get their hands on ET technology, regardless of how dangerous it is, and who they hurt in the process.

With the huge migrations taking place, the black ops teams will hide amongst the people, and *go to ground* for a while.

They'll regroup, reorganize, resupply and start up their shit after a while and so we'll need to keep an eye out.

Based upon what Robin told us, Soldan is directing some of the action, and we'll need to find out who and how many people he had working for him.

David - "You said '*start up their shit*' – what do you mean?"

Michael - "Now that disclosure has occurred, transportation to Tu, and any other planet is now common knowledge.

There are those who have great power and wealth from Earth who want nothing to do with Tu, they want to go start worlds of their own. The Zui are hip to that shit though and haven't fallen for any of it.

We've already had some reports of some of the uber wealthy trying to bribe their way to head of the line migration status, some who want to buy ships and technology.

Just be aware, there are alliances being formed, and there will be those who will align themselves against the good graces of the Zui, and the Tu.

So that's the situation gentlemen.

What say we get another beer?"

With that they headed inside.

Amy and Robin were in the kitchen preparing food.

Amy - "Is everything all good, guys?"

Michael - "Amy, it's all good. And Robin, next time don't sit on that kind of info, let me know right away.

The information you provided was critical. It confirmed some things at a very high level and it's being dealt with."

Robin - "Oh, right, we just didn't think it was very significant at the time."

Michael - "Oh – it was.

Robin - "So is that guy in trouble?"

Michael - "Yes, but don't concern yourself about it, it's all being dealt with."

Amy - "Well great. As long as we're all here, and hungry, Robin and I started putting together some dinner."

Michael - "What are you ladies concocting? I smell garlic and olive oil."

They all laughed. It was the kind of laugh that you do when the tension is off.

Michael - "You know, if we're going to do dinner, I want to give Shandra a call, and have her come by as well."

Michael stepped outside on the back deck again to call Shandra.

Shandra was upset. "Why are they removing Soldan?"

Michael - "Now you know I can't talk about that."

There was silence.

Michael - "I know he's your cousin, but this is bigger than all that."

Shandra sighed. She knew that if Foster was removing someone from Tu that it had to be serious.

Michael knew that sigh. That meant she was serious.

Michael - "Alright. Remember when we were out at the FA arrival colony, and the Zui removed the Annunaki weapon?"

Shandra - "Right? But what does that have to do with Soldan?"

Michael - "He was working with the black ops teams from Earth to try and grab the weapon."

The phone was quiet for a moment at both ends.

Shandra - "I kind of suspected he was into something, I just didn't want to believe it."

Michael - "Yeah, and if the *nosebleeders* had told us straight up from the beginning we wouldn't have had this problem".

Shandra - "Please don't talk about them that way".

Michael - "OK. Sorry, I'm just a little frustrated. Anyway, I'm over at Bob and Amy's. They're throwing a little bar-b-que together, why not come on over?"

Shandra - "Oh nice. OK, I'll be over, give me 20 minutes."

Michael came back inside.

Michael - "Shandra will be by in a little bit"

Amy - "Great. We haven't seen her either in a while - I love how this stuff comes together at random!"

David - "You know, last week when I was on a run to Earth, I was able to record a couple of games if you guys want to watch?"

Bob - "Dude, you've been holding out on us! What did you get?"

David - "Right, well, one is a Miami Heat game, I forget who they played, and the other is a soccer game, I think Manchester United".

David was logging into his internet account on a computer in the corner of Bob's living room.

Bob - "Yeah, send it direct to this tv. Here's the address."

Bob sent a text to David with the address of the tv.

Soon they were watching a basketball game and it seemed no different than if they were back home on Earth.

Michael - "I see you guys have already learned how to use the technology here."

Bob - "Well one thing that cannot be replicated is my Tennessee BBQ, and that is something *beyond* any technology on this planet."

They laughed.

Bob - "I think this is a good moment to reveal that I was able to collect some white lighting from a cousin of mine a couple of months ago."

Dave - "White lighting?"

Bob - "Moonshine Dave – forest whiskey, mountain dew! Yeah, and I had it scanned into the replication library as well! Ha! If you're all up for a sip let me know!"

They all laughed.

Michael - "I do think I'd like a sip Bob!"

Shandra showed up a few moments later.

There was such great camaraderie with the team.

Michael began to wonder if putting Bob and Amy into other jobs was really such a good idea.

He had a good team, and he began to wonder if the idea of breaking up a good team made sense.

After a great little bar-b-que, it was time to head home.

Michael - "Hey all – this has been great. Excellent food, excellent company.

I think we should all meet up tomorrow mid-day over at the Council Of Governors building, there's a conference room there and I need to toss some ideas around, and want all of you there.

Let's all be there around 2pm and I'll fill you in then."

Colonize Me

Mankind was settling into a new life on Tu.

The process of evacuating Earth was well underway, although it would take a few more years.

John Foster was pleased that things were in progress now, that Operation Exodus had become a reality.

Brother sent a message by text to John asking him to meet at the Zui compound in 3 days for a special meeting. He just said they should meet, but did not give any specifics for the meeting.

Arriving at the compound, John was uneasy.

Uncertainty as to the reason for the meeting, and the other factor was that Anna Foster was there.

Although he would visit her while he was there, he never knew quite what to expect. She seemed to be doing better with each visit, but it seemed that progress was slow. Perhaps he would see real progress with this visit.

The Zui-hybrids working with her recovery felt it was time to re-integrate her with human society, that she had sufficiently recovered.

He was greeted by several Zui-hybrids and escorted to Brother's quarters.

There was a certain awkwardness in the air.

Brother opened his arms to hug John - "Welcome John, I trust you are well?"

John - "Hello Brother, yes, all is well."

As they stepped back from the hug, Brother had his arms on Johns shoulders, framing him.

John had difficulty hiding anything from Brother. His uneasiness would have been obvious to anyone though.

Brother - "Tea?"

John - "Yes"

Brother poured tea into small handleless cups and they sat at opposing couches with a coffee table between them.

Brother - "There is much we need to discuss. Good things John. Please put your mind at ease."

John - "Well, that's a relief, I was a bit uneasy about why you summoned me here."

Brother - "The evacuation of your home world is going very well.

We have had a few challenges, but we are confident that we are meeting those challenges.

The Zui are very pleased with the way things are proceeding, and they want you to know that they are happy with you and your team."

John - "That's good Brother. I and my team have been working hard to do our part, I'm happy that The Zui are pleased."

Brother - "Yes John, *very pleased*."

Brother paused a moment to sip tea.

Brother - "Now, I want to discuss with you the new project we have for you and your team.

The Zui want to engage humanity in a new venture that will we feel will be beneficial.

Evacuating the people of Earth in preparation for its rebuilding is a wonderful thing in and of itself.

Humans are starting a whole new chapter in their collective history.

The Zui feel that while we could safely evacuate everyone from Earth to Tu, and then stop with that, this would be a good thing in and of itself.

We would have succeeded in helping mankind evolve up to a new place in its development.

There has been talk previously about The Zui helping humans engaging in exploration of your galaxy, with our ships and technology.

Some of your people want to colonize other worlds. These are people who do not fully understand this process, and their ways are like that of children.

The Zui felt that before the evacuation, this was something that should wait.

By waiting, we learned more and more about humanity, and who the real power lies with.

We had to be careful about not just what we share with humanity, but who among your people can be trusted.

Now that the evacuation is in progress, and going well, we want to begin teaching your people our ways of exploration and colonization.

We have watched your team, your core team.

Their synergies are excellent for what we propose, with a few minor changes, we want your team to be a part of this new project.

This team will be our first trainees in our ways of exploration and colonization."

John - "Well. This is certainly ambitious. Do you - by that I also mean The Zui, do you really feel that perhaps it's too soon?"

Brother - "Perhaps John. But like our people, it is the nature of your people to want to explore.

Your race has been looking to the stars for thousands of years, hindered only by the lack of a means of transportation to get there.

As you know, there are thousands of habitable planets in your galaxy alone. Think of all the galaxies that are known in the universe.

It was less than 100 of your Earth years ago that we began to return to Earth and rekindle our relationship with humanity.

If you will recall what happened to Earth when humans first set foot on the Earth moon. The entire planet was united in a common feeling, a feeling that mankind was going to the stars.

So, even as we evacuate Earth, and resettle your people on Tu, we will show you how to go from Tu to the stars.

Humanity has a special quality. Even as an abandoned race, there is always within your people a desire to seek the higher things. Your history is full of examples where humanity has risen above evil towards good.

We will assign a special team of Zui-hybrids to train your team in our ways.

Prepare your team. I will send you a list of a few more people to add to your team."

Immensity

And so mankind had established itself on Tu as a new chapter in the human story.

Tu provided the human race plenty of room to grow.

The story of humanity's redemption from itself by a benevolent race was only just beginning.

By relocating the human race to Tu, the issues and troubles that separated mankind would become a part of the past, as mankind would now have a clean slate to start fresh.

The Zui knew it would take years for mankind to grow into its new home, but now with better guidance, wisdom and knowledge, mankind could mature and "*grow up*".

Mankind had now gone from tribes and wild men living in caves and forests, towards towns, cities, states and countries, with minimal guidance fighting over resources and clinging to failed philosophies and religions, into an intelligent race of sentient beings, learning and contributing to the universe, not just taking from it.

Mankind would transcend its self destructive nature, its hate, and learn to love itself.

Mankind would now evolve from a misguided race into a guided race.

The story continues in the sequel:

"Tu Mayorga"

Be sure to check out the website at TuAndTheCollectors.com

Made in the USA
Lexington, KY
22 November 2014